A RECKLESS CHARACTER
AND OTHER STORIES

Muzio first played several melancholy airs

From a drawing by Stanley M. Arthurs

THE NOVELS AND STORIES OF
IVÁN TURGÉNIEFF

A RECKLESS CHARACTER
AND OTHER STORIES

TRANSLATED FROM THE RUSSIAN BY
ISABEL F. HAPGOOD

Short Story Index Reprint Series

BOOKS FOR LIBRARIES PRESS
FREEPORT, NEW YORK

First Published 1904
Reprinted 1971

118515

INTERNATIONAL STANDARD BOOK NUMBER:
0-8369-4066-0

LIBRARY OF CONGRESS CATALOG CARD NUMBER:
78-178465

PRINTED IN THE UNITED STATES OF AMERICA
BY
NEW WORLD BOOK MANUFACTURING CO., INC.
HALLANDALE, FLORIDA 33009

PREFACE

For three years after the violent reception of "Fathers and Children" Turgénieff published nothing, as has already been said. But during those three years events occurred in his personal life which reconciled him with literature and proved to him that the cultured public—the European, and, in particular, the Russian—fully comprehended and was able to appreciate his merits.

In 1878, at the meeting of the Literary Congress, during the Paris Exposition, the representatives of all European literature unanimously, and by acclamation, elected him the president of one of the sections of the Congress. In 1879, during a visit to London, he received from the University of Oxford the honorary degree of LL.D., because he had displayed in his works (especially in the "Memoirs of a Sportsman") a thorough knowledge of the manners and customs of the common people.

At the end of February, 1879, Turgénieff went to Russia for the purpose—as he himself jestingly remarked—of "making peace with the Russian public," and, in particular, with the

Russian youth. The rapturous reception which was given to the great romance-writer, completely unexpected as it was by him, proved to him to what a degree Russian society sympathised with its beloved author. At a reception in Moscow, where he appeared on the platform before the Russian public for the first time in twelve years, he took part in a session of the Society of Lovers of Russian Literature; then he appeared in St. Petersburg, where he read at several literary evenings, chiefly from his " Memoirs of a Sportsman." He also enjoyed a whole series of triumphant ovations, in which young people took a particularly lively part. All this was like the celebration of his thirty-fifth literary anniversary, which should have occurred in 1878, and served as a proof that all former misunderstandings between the Russian public and a writer who had consecrated his labours to current topics of interest had been relegated to oblivion.

Turgénieff's triumph evoked violent irritation in that section of the press which had zealously hounded him ever since he had ceased to publish his writings in the *Russian Messenger,* and an opportunity to cast a shadow upon his literary activity speedily presented itself. In October, 1879, a small sketch, entitled " En Cellule, Impressions d'un Nihiliste," appeared in the *Temps* of Paris, accompanied by a letter from Turgénieff to the *Temps.* In this letter Turgénieff

PREFACE

said that, while he did not, in the least, share the author's convictions, he nevertheless assumed that this simple and sincere recital might serve as a proof how little preliminary, solitary confinement could be justified from the point of view of rational legislation. This letter gave rise to a vicious attack upon Turgénieff himself, and even to his being directly accused of " disgracing his grey hair " and of " turning somersaults " before the Nihilists, " for the sake of winning popularity and having fun with them."

Turgénieff replied publicly to this attack in a long letter, which may be called a remarkable page from his autobiography. The letter winds up with the words which Turgénieff had a full right to utter: " The public," he says, " knows the author of this attack, . . . and I venture to add that it knows me also."

The Russian public speedily demonstrated that it did know and value Turgénieff, in spite of all calumnies. In Moscow, during the famous " Púshkin Days " (June 6–8, O. S., 1880), such honours and ovations fell to the lot of the famous romance-writer as completely threw into the shade all the honours which had been paid to him in both capitals a year previously. The Moscow University in a solemn session, on the day when Púshkin's monument was unveiled, elected him an honorary member of its body, thus, as it were, uniting the names of the two great representatives of Russian literature in the past and the present. (Turgénieff was also an honorary member of Kíeff University, and a corresponding member of the Imperial Academy of Sciences.)

There can be no doubt that these were the best days of his life. He himself acknowledged the fact by selecting for his reading, at a literary evening, the poems: "Once more in the Fatherland," and "The last cloud of the storm has dispersed."

His visit to Russia in 1880 was his last. His health grew worse and worse, and for months together no news of him reached Russia. During this period "The Song of Love Triumphant," "Old Portraits," and "A Reckless Character" appeared in the journal *Order* of 1881. His malady, which puzzled even the most celebrated Paris physicians, developed gradually but without a halt, and caused him suffering which he was able to endure solely thanks to his athletic constitution and to narcotics, to which he was compelled to resort more and more frequently for relief. But he did not lose his spirits and continued to work as his strength permitted. Thus, in the summer of 1882 he wrote "Clara Mílitch," which he intended, at first, to call "After Death"; but he changed the title for fear he should be accused of being a spiritualist. He also prepared for publication his "Poems in Prose," already written at intervals. The latter appeared in the

PREFACE

European Messenger for December, 1882, and " Clara Mílitch " in the same journal in January, 1883. Later on, he revised all his works, and dictated various fragments of his " Memoirs." He died on August 22, O. S. (September 3, N. S.), 1883.

The post-mortem examination showed that his malady had been one of the spine, which had completely destroyed three vertebræ. His brain was found to weigh two thousand grammes. His body was taken to Paris from Bougival, where he had chiefly resided during his last years, and his funeral was held in the Russian church there. Memorial services were held in almost every town in Russia; and not only Russia but all the civilised world displayed grief, acknowledging Turgénieff's death as a heavy loss to all literature. The German critics even compared him to Goethe. Shortly before his death he said that he would like to be buried in the Monastery of the Assumption, at Svyatigórsk, at the feet of Púshkin, whom he always called his " Master." But he considered himself unworthy of that honour, and ordered that his body be interred in the Volkhóff Cemetery, at St. Petersburg, by the side of his friend, the critic, Byelínsky. As there was no room there, he was buried near the chief church (cathedral) in that cemetery, near the entrance, on the left, on September 27, O. S., 1883.

Concerning the stories " A Reckless Charac-

PREFACE

ter" and "Old Portraits" the Russian critics have, practically, nothing to say. Of "The Dream" it is said that it is a representative of those artistic, semi-fantastic little tales in which the mystical romanticism of Turgénieff's nature outwardly expressed itself from time to time.

"Father Alexyéi's Story" represents (as has already been said, in the Preface to Volume XV) the conflict of the natural with the supernatural. It is one of the less known of the author's writings; but, says one critic, "it may be called one of the most profound examples of artistic perspicacity and inspiration. But justice demands the statement that doubts more frequently reigned in Turgénieff's soul during the last period of his life than did faith, and this fact undermined his mighty genius. Yet the poet's lofty heart yearned toward faith, panted with thirst for it. He was more of a sceptic than an enthusiast,—more of a Hamlet than a Don Quixote, as he himself would have expressed it; but his heart was more inclined toward Don Quixote."

"The Song of Love Triumphant" deals with the marvellous in the direction of magnetism. Turgénieff's talent was a musical talent, so to speak; and music evokes indefinite but good, agreeable, radiant sensations. Thus he had positively no rivals in his power of communicating musical emotions, as we have seen in "The Singers "; in the description of Lemm's playing (" A Nobleman's Nest "); and of the violin-playing in " The Song of Love Triumphant," which is, in its line, a masterpiece.

The " Poems in Prose " constitute a wonderfully-lyrical series of memoranda, filled with profound thought and illumined by genuine feeling, chiefly sad, and sometimes inconsolably desolate. " Nature " expresses the idea of Nature's hostility to all things, and her devastating power over our personality. A man beholds Nature in the very inmost sanctuary of her creative power, and questions her concerning man. Her answer is cheerless and discouraging to the last degree.

Quite another idea is conveyed by " The Sparrow." It is the same, replete with faith and encouraging to man, with which the author concluded his famous speech on " Hamlet and Don Quixote ": " All shall pass away, all shall vanish, —the loftiest dignity, power, all-embracing genius,—all shall crumble into dust.

> The vast earthly whole
> Like smoke disperseth. . . .

But good deeds do not disperse into smoke; they are more lasting than the most radiant beauty. ' All things shall pass away,' saith the Apostle; ' human love alone abideth.' "

The hidden religious ideal of Turgénieff's poc-

PREFACE

try is expressed in this thought, as it was in the character of Liza ("A Nobleman's Nest"), and also in the concluding words—marvellous in the profundity of their view of the universe—of "Father Alexyéi's Story," and of the great romance, "Fathers and Children."

IN concluding this series of prefaces to my translation, I wish to say a few words concerning my method. Many foreign critics, more or less competent through knowledge of the language, history, and institutions of Russia, have expressed their opinions on the great author's works. What the foreign public has never previously been told is the views held by his own countrymen, critics and readers. Obviously, this is precisely what is most valuable for the thoughtful foreign reader and the student. Accordingly, I have compiled these prefaces from five or six different volumes—criticisms of Russian literature in general, the biography prefixed to the Collected Works, a couple of volumes composed entirely of a reprint of the criticisms, by Russian critics, in different Russian journals (of various dates), preceded by a critical study of all the works, Turgénieff's "Literary Memoirs," and a volume of letters to his friends.

The constant use of quotation-marks in such a compilation and condensation would have been both cumbrous and confusing. Therefore I take

PREFACE

this opportunity to warn the reader that in the whole sixteen prefaces one page, at the utmost, would cover all the original remarks from myself. I trust that the strictly Russian point of view thus furnished, together with the explanatory notes, with which readers are now equipped for the first time, will result in a fuller and more judicious appreciation than ever of Russia's great writer. I. F. H.

CONTENTS

A RECKLESS CHARACTER

(1881)

A RECKLESS CHARACTER[1]

I

THERE were eight of us in the room, and we were discussing contemporary matters and persons.

"I do not understand these gentlemen!" remarked A.—"They are fellows of a reckless sort. . . . Really, desperate. . . . There has never been anything of the kind before."

"Yes, there has," put in P., a grey-haired old man, who had been born about the twenties of the present century;—"there were reckless men in days gone by also. Some one said of the poet Yázykoff, that he had enthusiasm which was not directed to anything, an objectless enthusiasm; and it was much the same with those people—their recklessness was without an object. But see here, if you will permit me, I will narrate to you the story of my grandnephew, Mísha Pólteff. It may serve as a sample of the recklessness of those days."

[1] See foot-note to "Old Portraits," in this volume.—TRANSLATOR.

3

A RECKLESS CHARACTER

HE made his appearance in God's daylight in the year 1828, I remember, on his father's ancestral estate, in one of the most remote nooks of a remote government of the steppes. I still preserve a distinct recollection of Mísha's father, Andréi Nikoláevitch Pólteff. He was a genuine, old-fashioned landed proprietor, a pious inhabitant of the steppes, sufficiently well educated,—according to the standards of that epoch,—rather crack-brained, if the truth must be told, and subject, in addition, to epileptic fits. . . . That also is an old-fashioned malady. . . . However, Andréi Nikoláevitch's attacks were quiet, and they generally terminated in a sleep and in a fit of melancholy.—He was kind of heart, courteous in manner, not devoid of some pomposity: I have always pictured to myself the Tzar Mikhaíl Feódorovitch as just that sort of a man.

Andréi Nikoláevitch's whole life flowed past in the punctual discharge of all the rites established since time immemorial, in strict conformity with all the customs of ancient-orthodox, Holy-Russian life. He rose and went to bed, he ate and went to the bath, he waxed merry or wrathful (he did both the one and the other rarely, it is true), he even smoked his pipe, he even played cards (two great innovations!), not as suited his fancy, not after his own fashion, but in accordance with the rule and tradition handed down from his ancestors, in proper and dignified style.

A RECKLESS CHARACTER

He himself was tall of stature, of noble mien and brawny; he had a quiet and rather hoarse voice, as is frequently the case with virtuous Russians; he was neat about his linen and his clothing, wore white neckerchiefs and long-skirted coats of snuff-brown hue, but his noble blood made itself manifest notwithstanding; no one would have taken him for a priest's son or a merchant! Andréi Nikoláevitch always knew, in all possible circumstances and encounters, precisely how he ought to act and exactly what expressions he must employ; he knew when he ought to take medicine, and what medicine to take, which symptoms he should heed and which might be disregarded . . . . in a word, he knew everything that it was proper to do. . . . It was as though he said: "Everything has been foreseen and decreed by the old men—the only thing is not to devise anything of your own. . . . And the chief thing of all is, don't go even as far as the threshold without God's blessing!"—I am bound to admit that deadly tedium reigned in his house, in those low-ceiled, warm, dark rooms which so often resounded from the chanting of vigils and prayer-services,[1] with an odour of incense and fasting-viands,[2] which almost never left them!

[1] The Vigil-service (consisting of Vespers and Matins, or Compline and Matins) may be celebrated in unconsecrated buildings, and the devout not infrequently have it, as well as prayer-services, at home.—TRANSLATOR.

[2] Meaning the odour of the oil which must be used in preparing food, instead of butter, during the numerous fasts.—TRANSLATOR.

A RECKLESS CHARACTER

Andréi Nikoláevitch had married, when he was no longer in his first youth, a poor young noblewoman of the neighbourhood, a very nervous and sickly person, who had been reared in one of the government institutes for gentlewomen. She played far from badly on the piano; she spoke French in boarding-school fashion; she was given to enthusiasm, and still more addicted to melancholy, and even to tears. . . . In a word, she was of an uneasy character. As she considered that her life had been ruined, she could not love her husband, who, " as a matter of course," did not understand her; but she respected, she tolerated him; and as she was a thoroughly honest and perfectly cold being, she never once so much as thought of any other "object." Moreover, she was constantly engrossed by anxieties: in the first place, over her really feeble health; in the second place, over the health of her husband, whose fits always inspired her with something akin to superstitious terror; and, in conclusion, over her only son, Mísha, whom she reared herself with great zeal. Andréi Nikoláevitch did not prevent his wife's busying herself with Mísha—but on one condition: she was never, under any circumstances, to depart from the limits, which had been defined once for all, wherein everything in his house must revolve! Thus, for example: during the Christmas holidays and Vasíly's evening

6

preceding the New Year, Mísha was not only permitted to dress up in costume along with the other "lads,"—doing so was even imposed upon him as an obligation.[1] . . . On the other hand, God forbid that he should do it at any other time! And so forth, and so forth.

II

I REMEMBER this Mísha at the age of thirteen. He was a very comely lad with rosy little cheeks and soft little lips (and altogether he was soft and plump), with somewhat prominent, humid eyes; carefully brushed and coifed—a regular little girl!—There was only one thing about him which displeased me: he laughed rarely; but when he did laugh his teeth, which were large, white, and pointed like those of a wild animal, displayed themselves unpleasantly; his very laugh had a sharp and even fierce—almost brutal—ring to it; and evil flashes darted athwart his eyes. His mother always boasted of his being so obedient and polite, and that he was not fond of consorting with naughty boys, but always was more inclined to feminine society.

" He is his mother's son, an effeminate fellow,"

[1] The custom of thus dressing up as bears, clowns, and so forth, and visiting all the houses in the neighbourhood, is still kept up in rustic localities. St. Vasíly's (Basil's) day falls on January 1.— TRANSLATOR.

his father, Andréi Nikoláevitch, was wont to say of him:—"but, on the other hand, he likes to go to God's church. . . . And that delights me."

Only one old neighbour, a former commissary of the rural police, once said in my presence concerning Mísha:—"Good gracious! he will turn out a rebel." And I remember that that word greatly surprised me at the time. The former commissary of police, it is true, had a habit of descrying rebels everywhere.

Just this sort of exemplary youth did Mísha remain until the age of eighteen,—until the death of his parents, whom he lost on almost one and the same day. As I resided constantly in Moscow, I heard nothing about my young relative. Some one who came to town from his government did, it is true, inform mé that Mísha had sold his ancestral estate for a song; but this bit of news seemed to me altogether too incredible!—And lo! suddenly, one autumn morning, into the courtyard of my house dashes a calash drawn by a pair of splendid trotters, with a monstrous coachman on the box; and in the calash, wrapped in a cloak of military cut with a two-arshín [1] beaver collar, and a fatigue-cap over one ear—*à la diable m'emporte*—sits Mísha!

On catching sight of me (I was standing at the drawing-room window and staring in amazement at the equipage which had dashed in), he

[1] An arshín is twenty-eight inches.—TRANSLATOR.

8

burst into his sharp laugh, and jauntily shaking
the lapels of his cloak, he sprang out of the calash
and ran into the house.

"Mísha! Mikhaíl Andréevitch!" I was beginning . . . "is it you?"

"Call me 'thou' and 'Mísha,'" he interrupted
me.—"'T is I . . . 't is I, in person. . . . I have
come to Moscow . . . . to take a look at people . . . . and to show myself. So I have
dropped in on you.—What do you think of my
trotters? . . . Hey?" Again he laughed loudly.

Although seven years had elapsed since I had
seen Mísha for the last time, yet I recognised him
on the instant.—His face remained thoroughly
youthful and as comely as of yore; his moustache had not even sprouted; but under his eyes
on his cheeks a puffiness had made its appearance, and an odour of liquor proceeded from his
mouth.

"And hast thou been long in Moscow?" I inquired.—"I supposed that thou wert off there in
the country, managing thy estate. . . ."

"Eh! I immediately got rid of the village!—
As soon as my parents died,—may the kingdom
of heaven be theirs,"—(Mísha crossed himself
with sincerity, without the slightest hypocrisy) —
"I instantly, without the slightest delay . . .
ein, zwei, drei! Ha-ha! I let it go cheap, the
rascally thing! Such a scoundrel turned up.—
Well, never mind! At all events, I shall live at

my ease—and amuse others.—But why do you
stare at me so?—Do you really think that I ought
to have spun the affair out indefinitely? . . . My
dear relative, can't I have a drink?"

Mísha talked with frightful rapidity, hurriedly
and at the same time as though half asleep.

"Good mercy, Mísha!"—I shouted: "Have
the fear of God before thine eyes! How dreadful is thine aspect, in what a condition thou art!
And thou wishest another drink! And to sell
such a fine estate for a song! . . ."

"I always fear God and remember him," he
caught me up.—"And he's good—God, I mean.
. . . He'll forgive! And I also am good. . . .
I have never injured any one in my life as yet.
And a drink is good also; and as for hurting . . . .
it won't hurt anybody, either. And as for my
looks, they are all right. . . . If thou wishest,
uncle, I'll walk a line on the floor. Or shall I
dance a bit?"

"Akh, please drop that!—What occasion is
there for dancing? Thou hadst better sit down."

"I don't mind sitting down. . . . But why
don't you say something about my greys? Just
look at them, they're regular lions! I'm hiring
them for the time being, but I shall certainly
buy them together with the coachman. It is
incomparably cheaper to own one's horses. And
I did have the money, but I dropped it last
night at faro.—Never mind, I'll retrieve my for-

tunes to-morrow. Uncle . . . . how about that drink?"

I still could not collect myself.—"Good gracious! Mísha, how old art thou? Thou shouldst not be occupying thyself with horses, or with gambling . . . thou shouldst enter the university or the service."

Mísha first roared with laughter again, then he emitted a prolonged whistle.

"Well, uncle, I see that thou art in a melancholy frame of mind just now. I'll call another time.—But see here: just look in at Sokólniki[1] some evening. I have pitched my tent there. The Gipsies sing. . . Well, well! One can hardly restrain himself! And on the tent there is a pennant, and on the pennant is written in bi-i-ig letters: 'The Band of Poltéva[2] Gipsies.' The pennant undulates like a serpent; the letters are gilded; any one can easily read them. The entertainment is whatever any one likes! . . . They refuse nothing. It has kicked up a dust all over Moscow . . . my respects . . . Well? Will you come? I've got a Gipsy there —a regular asp! Black as my boot, fierce as a dog, and eyes . . . regular coals of fire! One can't possibly make out whether she is kissing or biting. . . . Will you come, uncle? . . . Well, farewell for the present!"

[1] A park for popular resort in the suburbs of Moscow.—TRANSLATOR.

[2] Incorrectly written for Poltáva.—TRANSLATOR.

A RECKLESS CHARACTER

And abruptly embracing me and kissing me with a smack on my shoulder, Mísha darted out into the court to his calash, waving his cap over his head, and uttering a yell; the monstrous coachman [1] bestowed upon him an oblique glance across his beard, the trotters dashed forward, and all disappeared!

On the following day, sinful man that I am, I did go to Sokólniki, and actually did see the tent with the pennant and the inscription. The tent-flaps were raised; an uproar, crashing, squealing, proceeded thence. A crowd of people thronged around it. On the ground, on an outspread rug, sat the Gipsy men and Gipsy women, singing, and thumping tambourines; and in the middle of them, with a guitar in his hands, clad in a red-silk shirt and full trousers of velvet, Mísha was gyrating like a whirligig.—"Gentlemen! Respected sirs! Pray enter! The performance is about to begin! Free!"—he was shouting in a cracked voice. — "Hey there! Champagne! Bang! In the forehead! On the ceiling! Akh, thou rascal, Paul de Kock!"—Luckily, he did not catch sight of me, and I hastily beat a retreat.

I shall not dilate, gentlemen, on my amazement at the sight of such a change. And, as a matter of fact, how could that peaceable, modest lad suddenly turn into a tipsy good-for-no-

---

[1] The fatter the coachman, the more stylish he is. If he is not fat naturally, he adds cushions under his coat.—TRANSLATOR.

thing? Was it possible that all this had been concealed within him since his childhood, and had
immediately come to the surface as soon as the
weight of parental authority had been removed
from him?—And that he had kicked up a dust in
Moscow, as he had expressed it, there could be
no possible doubt, either. I had seen rakes in my
day; but here something frantic, some frenzy of
self-extermination, some sort of recklessness, had
made itself manifest!

III

THIS diversion lasted for two months. . . And
lo! again I am standing at the window of the
drawing-room and looking out into the courtyard. . . . Suddenly—what is this? . . . Through
the gate with quiet step enters a novice. . . . His
conical cap is pulled down on his brow, his hair is
combed smoothly and flows from under it to right
and left . . . . he wears a long cassock and a
leather girdle. . . . Can it be Mísha? It is!

I go out on the steps to meet him. . . . "What
is the meaning of this masquerade?" I ask.

"It is not a masquerade, uncle," Mísha answers me, with a deep sigh;—"but as I have
squandered all my property to the last kopék,
and as a mighty repentance has seized upon me,
I have made up my mind to betake myself to

the Tróitzko-Sérgieva Lávra,[1] to pray away my
sins. For what asylum is now left to me? . . .
And so I have come to bid you farewell, uncle,
like the Prodigal Son. . . ."

I gazed intently at Mísha. His face was the
same as ever, fresh and rosy (by the way, it never
changed to the very end), and his eyes were
humid and caressing and languishing, and his
hands were small and white. . . . But he reeked
of liquor.

"Very well!" I said at last: "It is a good
move if there is no other issue. But why dost
thou smell of liquor?"

"Old habit," replied Mísha, and suddenly
burst out laughing, but immediately caught himself up, and making a straight, low, monastic
obeisance, he added:—"Will not you contribute
something for the journey? For I am going to
the monastery on foot. . . ."

"When?"

"To-day . . . . at once."

"Why art thou in such a hurry?"

"Uncle! my motto has always been 'Hurry!
Hurry!'"

"But what is thy motto now?"

"It is the same now. . . . Only '*Hurry*—to
good!'"

---

[1] That is, to the Trinity monastery of the first class founded by
St. Sergius in 1340. It is situated about forty miles from Moscow,
and is the most famous monastery in the country next to the Cata-
combs Monastery at Kíeff.—TRANSLATOR.

A RECKLESS CHARACTER

So Mísha went away, leaving me to meditate over the mutability of human destinies.

But he speedily reminded me of his existence. A couple of months after his visit I received a letter from him,—the first of those letters with which he afterward favoured me. And note this peculiarity: I have rarely beheld a neater, more legible handwriting than was possessed by this unmethodical man. The style of his letters also was very regular, and slightly florid. The invariable appeals for assistance alternated with promises of amendment, with honourable words and with oaths. . . . All this appeared to be— and perhaps was—sincere. Mísha's signature at the end of his letters was always accompanied by peculiar flourishes, lines and dots, and he used a great many exclamation-points. In that first letter Mísha informed me of a new " turn in his fortune." (Later on he called these turns " dives " . . . . and he dived frequently.) He had gone off to the Caucasus to serve the Tzar and fatherland " with his breast," in the capacity of a yunker. And although a certain benevolent aunt had commiserated his poverty-stricken condition and had sent him an insignificant sum, nevertheless he asked me to help him to equip himself. I complied with his request, and for a period of two years thereafter I heard nothing about him. I must confess that I entertained strong doubts as to his having gone to the Caucasus.

A RECKLESS CHARACTER

But it turned out that he really had gone thither, had entered the T * * * regiment as yunker, through influence, and had served in it those two years. Whole legends were fabricated there about him. One of the officers in his regiment communicated them to me.

IV

I LEARNED a great deal which I had not expected from him. I was not surprised, of course, that he had proved to be a poor, even a downright worthless military man and soldier; but what I had not expected was, that he had displayed no special bravery; that in battle he wore a dejected and languid aspect, as though he were partly bored, partly daunted. All discipline oppressed him, inspired him with sadness; he was audacious to recklessness when it was a question of himself personally; there was no wager too crazy for him to accept; but do evil to others, kill, fight, he could not, perhaps because he had a good heart,—and perhaps because his " cotton-wool " education (as he expressed it) had enervated him. He was ready to exterminate himself in any sort of way at any time. . . . But others—no. " The devil only can make him out," his comrades said of him:—" he 's puny, a rag—and what a reckless fellow he is—a regular dare-devil! "—I happened afterward to ask Mísha what evil spirit prompted him, made him indulge in drinking-bouts, risk his life, and so forth. He always had one answer: "Spleen."

"But why hast thou spleen?"

"Just because I have, good gracious! One comes to himself, recovers his senses, and begins to meditate about poverty, about injustice, about Russia. . . . Well, and that settles it! Immediately one feels such spleen that he is ready to send a bullet into his forehead! One goes on a carouse instinctively."

"But why hast thou mixed up Russia with this?"

"What else could I do? Nothing!—That's why I am afraid to think."

"All that—that spleen—comes of thy idleness."

"But I don't know how to do anything, uncle! My dear relative! Here now, if it were a question of taking and staking my life on a card,—losing my all and shooting myself, bang! in the neck!—I can do that!—Here now, tell me what to do, what to risk my life for.—I 'll. do it this very minute! . . . ."

"But do thou simply live. . . . Why risk thy life?"

"I can't!—You will tell me that I behave recklessly. What else can I do? . . . One begins to think—and, O Lord, what comes into his head! 'T is only the Germans who think! . . ."

A RECKLESS CHARACTER

What was the use of arguing with him? He was a reckless man—and that is all there is to say!

I will repeat to you two or three of the Caucasian legends to which I have alluded. One day, in the company of the officers, Mísha began to brag of a Circassian sabre which he had obtained in barter.—"A genuine Persian blade!"—The officers expressed doubt as to whether it were really genuine. Mísha began to dispute.—"See here," he exclaimed at last,—"they say that the finest judge of Circassian sabres is one-eyed Abdulka. I will go to him and ask."—The officers were dumbfounded.

"What Abdulka? The one who lives in the mountains? The one who is not at peace with us? Abdul-Khan?"

"The very man."

"But he will take thee for a scout, he will place thee in the bug-house,—or he will cut off thy head with that same sabre. And how wilt thou make thy way to him? They will seize thee immediately."

"But I will go to him, nevertheless."

"We bet that thou wilt not go!"

"I take your bet!"

And Mísha instantly saddled his horse and rode off to Abdulka. He was gone for three days. All were convinced that he had come to some dreadful end. And behold! he came back, somewhat tipsy, and with a sabre, only not the one which he had carried away with him, but another. They began to question him.

"It's all right," said he. "Abdulka is a kind man. At first he really did order fetters to be riveted on my legs, and was even preparing to impale me on a stake. But I explained to him why I had come. 'Do not expect any ransom from me,' said I. 'I have n't a farthing to my name—and I have no relatives.'—Abdulka was amazed; he stared at me with his solitary eye.— 'Well,' says he, 'thou art the chief of heroes, Russian! Am I to believe thee?'—'Believe me,' said I; 'I never lie' (and Mísha really never did lie).—Abdulka looked at me again.— 'And dost thou know how to drink wine?'— 'I do,' said I; 'as much as thou wilt give, so much will I drink.'—Again Abdulka was astonished, and mentioned Allah. And then he ordered his daughter, or some pretty maiden, whoever she was,—anyhow, she had the gaze of a jackal,—to fetch a leathern bottle of wine.—And I set to work.—'But thy sabre is spurious,' says he; 'here, take this genuine one. And now thou and I are friends.'—And you have lost your wager, gentlemen, so pay up."

A second legend concerning Mísha runs as follows. He was passionately fond of cards; but as he had no money and did not pay his gambling debts (although he was never a sharper), no one would any longer sit down to play with him. So one day he began to importune a brother officer, and insisted upon the latter's playing with him.

"But thou wilt be sure to lose, and thou wilt not pay."

"I will not pay in money, that's true—but I will shoot a hole through my left hand with this pistol here!"

"But what profit is there for me in that?"

"No profit whatever—but it's a curious thing, nevertheless."

This conversation took place after a carouse, in the presence of witnesses. Whether Mísha's proposal really did strike the officer as curious or not, —at all events, he consented. The cards were brought, the game began. Mísha was lucky; he won one hundred rubles. And thereupon his opponent smote himself on the forehead.

"What a blockhead I am!" he cried.—"On what a bait was I caught! If thou hadst lost, much thou wouldst have shot thyself through the hand!—so it's just an assault on my pocket!"

"That's where thou art mistaken," retorted Mísha:—"I have won—but I'll shoot the hole through my hand."

He seized his pistol, and bang! shot himself through the hand. The bullet went clear through . . . . and a week later the wound was completely healed!

On another occasion still, Mísha is riding

along the road by night with his comrades. . . .
And they see yawning, right by the side of the
road, a narrow ravine in the nature of a cleft,
dark, very dark, and the bottom of it not visible.

" Here now," says one comrade, " Mísha is
reckless enough about some things, but he will
not leap into this ravine."

" Yes, I will!"

" No, thou wilt not, because it is, probably, ten
fathoms deep, and thou mightest break thy neck."

His friend knew how to attack him—through
his vanity. . . . Mísha had a great deal of it.

" But I will leap, nevertheless! Wilt thou bet
on it? Ten rubles."

" All right!"

And before his comrade had managed to finish
the last word Mísha flew off his horse into the
ravine, and crashed down on the stones. They
were all fairly petrified with horror. . . . A
good minute passed, and they heard Mísha's voice
proceeding as though from the bowels of the
earth, and very dull:

" I 'm whole! I landed on sand. . . But the
descent was long! Ten rubles on you!"

" Climb out!" shouted his comrades.

" Yes, climb out!"—returned Mísha. " Damn
it! One can't climb out of here! You will have
to ride off now for ropes and lanterns. And in
the meanwhile, so that I may not find the waiting
tedious, toss me down a flask. . . ."

21

A RECKLESS CHARACTER

And so Mísha had to sit for five hours at the bottom of the ravine; and when they dragged him out, it appeared that he had a dislocated shoulder. But this did not daunt him in the least. On the following day a blacksmith bone-setter set his shoulder, and he used it as though nothing were the matter.

Altogether, his health was remarkable, unprecedented. I have already told you that until his death he preserved an almost childish freshness of complexion. He did not know what it was to be ill, in spite of all his excesses; the vigour of his constitution was not affected in a single instance. Where any other man would have fallen dangerously ill, or even have died, he merely shook himself like a duck in the water, and became more blooming than ever. Once—that also was in the Caucasus. . . . This legend is improbable, it is true, but from it one can judge what Mísha was regarded as capable of doing. . . . So then, once, in the Caucasus, when in a state of intoxication, he fell into a small stream that covered the lower part of his body; his head and arms remained exposed on the bank. The affair took place in winter; a rigorous frost set in; and when he was found on the following morning, his legs and body were visible beneath a stout crust of ice which had frozen over in the course of the night —and he never even had a cold in the head in consequence! On another occasion (this happened in Russia, near Orél,[1] and also during a severe frost), he chanced to go to a suburban eating-house in company with seven young theological students. These theological students were celebrating their graduation examination, and had invited Mísha, as a charming fellow, " a man with a sigh," as it was called then. They drank a great deal; and when, at last, the merry crew were preparing to depart, Mísha, dead drunk, was found to be already in a state of unconsciousness. The whole seven theological students had between them only one tróika sledge with a high back;[2]—where were they to put the helpless body? Then one of the young men, inspired by classical reminiscences, suggested that Mísha be tied by the feet to the back of the sledge, as Hector was to the chariot of Achilles! The suggestion was approved . . . . and bouncing over the hummocks, sliding sideways down the declivities, with his feet strung up in the air, and his head dragging through the snow, our Mísha traversed on his back the distance of two versts which separated the restaurant from the town, and never even so much as coughed or frowned. With such marvellous health had nature endowed him!

[1] Pronounced *Aryól*.—TRANSLATOR.
[2] Such a sledge, drawn by the national team of three horses, will hold five or six persons closely packed.—TRANSLATOR.

A RECKLESS CHARACTER

V

LEAVING the Caucasus, he presented himself once more in Moscow, in a Circassian coat, with cartridge-pouches on the breast, a dagger in his belt, and a tall fur cap on his head. From this costume he did not part until the end, although he was no longer in the military service, from which he had been dismissed for not reporting on time. He called on me, borrowed a little money . . . . and then began his " divings," his progress through the tribulations,[1] or, as he expressed it, " through the seven Semyóns ";[2] then began his sudden ab-

[1] The word he used, *mytárstvo,* has a peculiar meaning. It refers specifically to the experiences of the soul when it leaves the body. According to the teaching of divers ancient fathers of the church, the soul, as soon as it leaves the body, is confronted by accusing demons, who arraign it with all the sins, great and small, which it has committed during its earthly career. If its good deeds, alms, prayers, and so forth (added to the grace of God), offset the evil, the demons are forced to renounce their claims. These demons assault the soul in relays, each " trial," " suffering," or "tribulation" being a *mytárstvo.* One ancient authority enumerates twenty such trials. The soul is accompanied and defended in its trials by angels, who plead its cause. Eventually, they conduct it into the presence of God, who then assigns to it a temporary abode of bliss or woe until the day of judgment. The derivation of this curious and utterly untranslatable word is as follows: *Mytár* means a publican or tax-gatherer. As the publicans, under the Roman sway over the Jews, indulged in various sorts of violence, abuses, and inhuman conduct, calling every one to strict account, and even stationing themselves at the city gates to intercept all who came and went, *mytárstvo* represents, in general, the taxing or testing of the soul, which must pay a ransom before it is released from its trials and preliminary tribulations.—TRANSLATOR.

[2] A folk-tale narrates how the Tzar Arkhídei obtained his beauteous bride by the aid of seven brothers called " The Seven

sences and returns, the despatching of beautifully-
written letters addressed to all possible persons,
beginning with the Metropolitan and ending with
riding-masters and midwives! Then began the
visits to acquaintances and strangers! And here
is one point which must be noted: in making his
calls he did not cringe and did not importune; but,
on the contrary, he behaved himself in decorous
fashion, and even wore a cheery and pleasant
aspect, although an ingrained odour of liquor
accompanied him everywhere—and his Oriental
costume was gradually reduced to rags.

"Give—God will reward you—although I do
not deserve it," he was accustomed to say, smiling
brightly and blushing openly. "If you do not
give, you will be entirely in the right, and I shall
not be angry in the least. I shall support myself.
God will provide! For there are many, very
many people who are poorer and more worthy
than I!"

Mísha enjoyed particular success with women;
he understood how to arouse their compassion.
And do not think that he was or imagined himself
to be a Lovelace. . . Oh, no! In that respect he
was very modest. Whether he had inherited from
his parents such cold blood, or whether herein was
expressed his disinclination to do evil to any one,

Semyóns," who were his peasants. The bride was distant a ten
years' journey; but each of the brothers had a different "trade,"
by the combined means of which they were enabled to overcome
time and space and get the bride for their master.—TRANSLATOR.

—since, according to his ideas, to consort with a woman means inevitably to insult the woman,—I will not take it upon myself to decide; only, in his relations with the fair sex he was extremely delicate. The women felt this, and all the more willingly did they pity and aid him until he, at last, repelled them by his sprees and hard drinking, by the recklessness of which I have already spoken. . . . I cannot hit upon any other word.

On the other hand, in other respects he had already lost all delicacy and had gradually descended to the extreme depths of degradation. He once went so far that in the Assembly of Nobility of T * * * he placed on the table a jug with the inscription:

"Any one who finds it agreeable to tweak the nose of hereditary nobleman [1] Pólteff (whose authentic documents are herewith appended) may satisfy his desire, on condition that he puts a ruble in this jug."

And it is said that there were persons who did care to tweak the nobleman's nose! It is true that he first all but throttled one amateur who, having put but one ruble in the jug, tweaked his nose twice, and then made him sue for pardon; it is true also that he immediately distributed to other tatterdemalions a portion of the money thus se-

---

[1] The word used in Russian indicates not only that he was a hereditary noble, but that his nobility was ancient—a matter of some moment in a country where nobility, both personal and hereditary, can be won in the service of the state.—Translator.

cured . . . . but, nevertheless, what outrageous conduct!

In the course of his wanderings through the seven Semyóns he had also reached his ancestral nest, which he had sold for a song to a speculator and usurer well known at that period. The speculator was at home, and on learning of the arrival of the former owner, who had been transformed into a tramp, he gave orders that he was not to be admitted into the house, and that in case of need he was to be flung out by the scruff of the neck. Mísha declared that he would not enter the house, defiled as it was by the presence of a scoundrel; that he would allow no one to throw him out; but that he was on his way to the churchyard to salute the dust of his ancestors. This he did. At the churchyard he was joined by an old house-serf, who had formerly been his man-nurse. The speculator had deprived the old man of his monthly stipend and expelled him from the home farm; from that time forth the man sought shelter in the kennel of a peasant. Mísha had managed his estate for so short a time that he had not succeeded in leaving behind him a specially good memory of himself; but the old servitor had not been able to resist, nevertheless, and on hearing of his young master's arrival, he had immediately hastened to the churchyard, had found Mísha seated on the ground among the mortuary stones, had begged leave to kiss his hand in memory of old times, and had even melted into tears as he gazed at the rags wherewith the once petted limbs of his nursling were swathed. Mísha looked long and in silence at the old man.

"Timoféi!" he said at last.

Timoféi gave a start.

"What do you wish?"

"Hast thou a spade?"

"I can get one. . . . But what do you want with a spade, Mikhaílo Andréitch?"

"I want to dig a grave for myself here, Timoféi; and lie down here forever between my parents. For this is the only spot which is left to me in the world. Fetch the spade!"

"I obey," said Timoféi; and went off and brought it.

And Mísha immediately began to dig up the earth, while Timoféi stood by with his chin propped on his hand, repeating: "That's the only thing left for thee and me, master!"

And Mísha dug and dug, inquiring from time to time: "Life isn't worth living, is it, Timoféi?"

"It is not, dear little father."

The hole had already grown fairly deep. People saw Mísha's work and ran to report about it to the speculator-owner. At first the speculator flew into a rage, and wanted to send for the police. "What hypocrisy!" he said. But afterward, reflecting, probably, that it would be inconvenient to have a row with that lunatic, and that a scandal might be the result, he betook himself in person to the churchyard, and approaching the toiling Mísha, he made a polite obeisance to him. The latter continued to dig, as though he had not noticed his successor.

"Mikhaíl Andréitch," began the speculator, "permit me to inquire what you are doing there?"

"As you see—I am digging a grave for myself."

"Why are you doing that?"

"Because I do not wish to live any longer."

The speculator fairly flung apart his hands in surprise.—"You do not wish to live?"

Mísha cast a menacing glance at the speculator:—"Does that surprise you? Are not you the cause of it all? . . . Is it not you? . . . Is it not thou? [1] . . . Is it not thou, Judas, who hast robbed me, by taking advantage of my youth? Dost not thou skin the peasants? Is it not thou who hast deprived this decrepit old man of his daily bread? Is it not thou? . . . O Lord! Everywhere there is injustice, and oppression, and villainy. . . . So down with everything,— and with me also! I don't wish to live—I don't wish to live any longer in Russia!"—And the spade made swifter progress than ever in Mísha's hands.

"The devil knows the meaning of this!"

[1] The change to *thou* is made to express disrespect.—TRANSLATOR.

thought the speculator: "he actually is burying himself." — "Mikhaíl Andréitch," — he began afresh, "listen; I really am guilty toward you; people did not represent you properly to me."

Mísha went on digging.

"But why this recklessness?"

Mísha went on digging—and flung the dirt on the speculator, as much as to say: "Take that, earth-devourer!"

"Really, you have no cause for this. Will not you come to my house to eat and rest?"

Mísha raised his head a little. "Now you 're talking! And will there be anything to drink?"

The speculator was delighted.—"Good gracious! . . . . I should think so!"

"And dost thou invite Timoféi also?"

"But why . . . . well, I invite him also."

Mísha reflected.—"Only look out . . . . for thou didst turn me out of doors. . . . Don't think thou art going to get off with one bottle!"

"Do not worry . . . . there will be as much as you wish of everything."

Mísha flung aside his spade. . . . "Well, Timósha," he said, addressing his old man-nurse, "let us honour the host. . . . Come along!"

"I obey," replied the old man.

And all three wended their way toward the house.

The speculator knew with whom he had to deal. Mísha made him promise as a preliminary, it is

true, that he would " allow all privileges " to the
peasants;—but an hour later that same Mísha,
together with Timoféi, both drunk, danced a gal-
lopade through those rooms where the pious shade
of Andréi Nikoláitch seemed still to be hovering;
and an hour later still, Mísha, so sound asleep that
he could not be waked (liquor was his great weakness), was placed in a peasant-cart, together with
his kazák cap and his dagger, and sent off to the
town, five-and-twenty versts distant,—and there
was found under a fence. . . . Well, and Timoféi, who still kept his feet and merely hiccoughed,
was " pitched out neck and crop," as a matter of
course. The master had made a failure of his
attempt. So they might as well let the servant
pay the penalty!

VI

AGAIN considerable time elapsed and I heard
nothing of Mísha. . . . God knows where he
had vanished.—One day, as I was sitting before
the samovár at a posting-station on the T * * *
highway, waiting for horses, I suddenly heard,
under the open window of the station-room, a
hoarse voice uttering in French:—"*Monsieur
. . . . monsieur . . . . prenez pitié d'un pauvre
gentilhomme ruiné!*" . . . . I raised my head and
looked. . . . The kazák cap with the fur peeled
off, the broken cartridge-pouches on the tattered

Circassian coat, the dagger in a cracked sheath, the bloated but still rosy face, the dishevelled but still thick hair. . . . My God! It was Mísha! He had already come to begging alms on the highways!—I involuntarily uttered an exclamation. He recognised me, shuddered, turned away, and was about to withdraw from the window. I stopped him . . . . but what was there that I could say to him? Certainly I could not read him a lecture! . . . In silence I offered him a five-ruble bank-note. With equal silence he grasped it in his still white and plump, though trembling and dirty hand, and disappeared round the corner of the house.

They did not furnish me with horses very promptly, and I had time to indulge in cheerless meditations on the subject of my unexpected encounter with Mísha. I felt conscience-stricken that I had let him go in so unsympathetic a manner.—At last I proceeded on my journey, and after driving half a verst from the posting-station I observed, ahead of me on the road, a crowd of people moving along with a strange and as it were measured tread. I overtook this crowd,—and what did I see?—Twelve beggars, with wallets on their shoulders, were walking by twos, singing and skipping as they went,—and at their head danced Mísha, stamping time with his feet and saying: "Natchiki-tchikaldi, tchuk-

tchuk-tchuk!   Natchiki-tchikaldi,   tchuk-tchuk-
tchuk!"

As soon as my calash came on a level with him,
and he caught sight of me, he immediately began
to shout, " Hurrah! Halt, draw up in line! Eyes
front, my guard of the road!"

The beggars took up his cry and halted,—
while he, with his habitual laugh, sprang upon
the carriage-step, and again yelled: "Hurrah!"

"What is the meaning of this?" I asked, with
involuntary amazement.

"This? This is my squad, my army; all beggars, God's people, my friends! Each one of
them, thanks to your kindness, has quaffed a
cup of liquor: and now we are all rejoicing and
making merry! . . . Uncle! 'T is only with the
beggars and God's poor that one can live in
the world, you know . . . . by God, that 's so!"

I made him no reply . . . but this time he
seemed to me such a good-natured soul, his face
expressed such childlike ingenuousness . . . a
light suddenly seemed to dawn upon me, and
there came a prick at my heart. . . .

"Get into the calash with me," I said to him.
He was amazed. . . .

"What? Get into the calash?"

"Get in, get in!" I repeated. "I want to make
thee a proposition. Get in! . . . Drive on with
me."

"Well, you command."—He got in.—"Come,

and as for you, my dear friends, respected comrades," he added to the beggars: "good-bye! Until we meet again!"—Mísha took off his kazák cap and made a low bow.—The beggars all seemed to be dumbfounded. . . I ordered the coachman to whip up the horses, and the calash rolled on.

This is what I wished to propose to Mísha: the idea had suddenly occurred to me to take him into my establishment, into my country-house, which was situated about thirty versts from that posting-station,—to save him, or, at least, to make an effort to save him.

"Hearken, Mísha," said I; "wilt thou settle down with me? . . . Thou shalt have everything provided for thee, clothes and under-linen shall be made for thee, thou shalt be properly fitted out, and thou shalt receive money for tobacco and so forth, only on one condition: not to drink liquor! . . . . Dost thou accept?"

Mísha was even frightened with joy. He opened his eyes very wide, turned crimson, and suddenly falling on my shoulder, he began to kiss me and to repeat in a spasmodic voice:—"Uncle . . . benefactor . . . May God reward you! . . ." He melted into tears at last, and doffing his kazák cap, began to wipe his eyes, his nose, and his lips with it.

"Look out," I said to him. "Remember the condition—not to drink liquor!"

"Why, damn it!" he exclaimed, flourishing
both hands, and as a result of that energetic
movement I was still more strongly flooded with
that spirituous odour wherewith he was thoroughly impregnated. . . . "You see, dear uncle,
if you only knew my life. . . . If it were not
for grief, cruel Fate, you know. . . . But now I
swear,—I swear that I will reform, and will
prove . . . . Uncle, I have never lied—ask any
one you like if I have. . . . I am an honourable,
but an unhappy man, uncle; I have never known
kindness from any one. . . ."

At this point he finally dissolved in sobs. I
tried to soothe him and succeeded, for when we
drove up to my house Mísha had long been
sleeping the sleep of the dead, with his head resting on my knees.

VII

HE was immediately allotted a special room, and
also immediately, as the first measure, taken to
the bath, which was absolutely indispensable.
All his garments, and his dagger and tall kazák
cap and hole-ridden shoes, were carefully laid
away in the storehouse; clean linen was put on
him, slippers, and some of my clothing, which,
as is always the case with paupers, exactly fitted
his build and stature. When he came to the table,
washed, neat, fresh, he seemed so much touched,

and so happy, he was beaming all over with such
joyful gratitude, that I felt emotion and joy.
. . . . His face was completely transfigured.
Little boys of twelve wear such faces at Easter,
after the Communion, when, thickly pomaded,
clad in new round-jackets and starched collars,
they go to exchange the Easter greeting with
their parents. Mísha kept feeling of himself
cautiously and incredulously, and repeating:—
"What is this? . . . . Am not I in heaven?"
—And on the following day he announced that
he had not been able to sleep all night for rapture!

In my house there was then living an aged
aunt with her niece. They were both greatly
agitated when they heard of Mísha's arrival;
they did not understand how I could have invited him to my house! He bore a very bad
reputation. But, in the first place, I knew that
he was always very polite to ladies; and, in the
second place, I trusted to his promise to reform.
And, as a matter of fact, during the early days
of his sojourn under my roof Mísha not only
justified my expectations, but exceeded them;
and he simply enchanted my ladies. He played
picquet with the old lady; he helped her to wind
yarn; he showed her two new games of patience;
he accompanied the niece, who had a small voice,
on the piano; he read her French and Russian
poetry; he narrated diverting but decorous anec-

dotes to both ladies;—in a word, he was service-
able to them in all sorts of ways, so that they repeatedly expressed to me their surprise, while
the old woman even remarked: "How unjust
people sometimes are! . . . What all have not
they said about him . . . while he is so discreet
and polite . . . . poor Mísha!"

It is true that at table "poor Mísha" licked
his lips in a peculiarly-hasty way every time he
even looked at a bottle. But all I had to do was
to shake my finger, and he would roll up his eyes,
and press his hand to his heart . . . as much as
to say: "I have sworn. . . ."

"I am regenerated now!" he assured me.—
"Well, God grant it!" I thought to myself.
. . . . But this regeneration did not last long.

During the early days he was very loquacious
and jolly. But beginning with the third day he
quieted down, somehow, although, as before, he
kept close to the ladies and amused them. A
half-sad, half-thoughtful expression began to flit
across his face, and the face itself grew pale and
thin.

"Art thou ill?" I asked him.

"Yes," he answered;—"my head aches a little."

On the fourth day he became perfectly silent;
he sat in a corner most of the time, with dejectedly drooping head; and by his downcast aspect
evoked a feeling of compassion in the two ladies,

who now, in their turn, tried to divert him. At table he ate nothing, stared at his plate, and rolled bread-balls. On the fifth day the feeling of pity in the ladies began to be replaced by another—by distrust and even fear. Mísha had grown wild, he avoided people and kept walking along the wall, as though creeping stealthily, and suddenly darting glances around him, as though some one had called him. And what had become of his rosy complexion? It seemed to be covered with earth.

"Art thou still ill?" I asked him.

"No; I am well," he answered abruptly.

"Art thou bored?"

"Why should I be bored?"—But he turned away and would not look me in the eye.

"Or hast thou grown melancholy again?"—To this he made no reply.

On the following day my aunt ran into my study in a state of great excitement, and declared that she and her niece would leave my house if Mísha were to remain in it.

"Why so?"

"Why, we feel afraid of him. . . . He is not a man,—he is a wolf, a regular wolf. He stalks and stalks about, saying never a word, and has such a wild look. . . . He all but gnashes his teeth. My Kátya is such a nervous girl, as thou knowest. . . . She took a great interest in him the first day. . . . I am afraid for her and for myself. . . ."

A RECKLESS CHARACTER

I did not know what reply to make to my aunt. But I could not expel Mísha, whom I had invited in.

He himself extricated me from this dilemma.

That very day—before I had even left my study—I suddenly heard a dull and vicious voice behind me.

" Nikolái Nikoláitch, hey there, Nikolái Nikoláitch!"

I looked round. In the doorway stood Mísha, with a terrible, lowering, distorted visage.

"Nikolái Nikoláitch," he repeated . . . . (it was no longer "dear uncle").

"What dost thou want?"

"Let me go . . . . this very moment!"

"What?"

"Let me go, or I shall commit a crime,—set the house on fire or cut some one's throat."— Mísha suddenly fell to shaking.—"Order them to restore my garments, and give me a cart to carry me to the highway, and give me a trifling sum of money!"

"But art thou dissatisfied with anything?" I began.

"I cannot live thus!" he roared at the top of his voice.—"I cannot live in your lordly, thrice-damned house! I hate, I am ashamed to live so tranquilly! . . . How do *you* manage to endure it?!"

"In other words," I interposed, "thou wishest to say that thou canst not live without liquor. . . ."

39

"Well, yes! well, yes!" he yelled again.—
"Only let me go to my brethren, to my friends,
to the beggars! . . . Away from your noble,
decorous, repulsive race!"

I wanted to remind him of his promise on oath,
but the criminal expression of Mísha's face, his
unrestrained voice, the convulsive trembling of
all his limbs—all this was so frightful that I
made haste to get rid of him. I informed him
that he should receive his clothing at once, that
a cart should be harnessed for him; and taking
from a casket a twenty-ruble bank-note, I laid
it on the table. Mísha was already beginning
to advance threateningly upon me, but now he
suddenly stopped short, his face instantaneously
became distorted, and flushed up; he smote his
breast, tears gushed from his eyes, and he stammered,—"Uncle!—Angel! I am a lost man,
you see!—Thanks! Thanks!"—He seized the
bank-note and rushed out of the room.

An hour later he was already seated in a cart,
again clad in his Circassian coat, again rosy and
jolly; and when the horses started off he uttered
a yell, tore off his tall kazák cap, and waving it
above his head, he made bow after bow. Immediately before his departure he embraced me
long and warmly, stammering:—"Benefactor,
benefactor! . . . . It was impossible to save
me!" He even ran in to see the ladies, and kissed
their hands over and over again, went down on

his knees, appealed to God, and begged forgiveness! I found Kátya in tears later on.

But the coachman who had driven Mísha reported to me, on his return, that he had taken him to the first drinking establishment on the highway, and that there he "had got stranded," had begun to stand treat to every one without distinction, and had soon arrived at a state of inebriation.

Since that time I have never met Mísha, but I learned his final fate in the following manner.

VIII

THREE years later I again found myself in the country; suddenly a servant entered and announced that Madame Pólteff was inquiring for me. I knew no Madame Pólteff, and the servant who made the announcement was grinning in a sarcastic sort of way, for some reason or other. In reply to my questioning glance he said that the lady who was asking for me was young, poorly clad, and had arrived in a peasant-cart drawn by one horse which she was driving herself! I ordered that Madame Pólteff should be requested to do me the favour to step into my study.

I beheld a woman of five-and-twenty,—belonging to the petty burgher class, to judge from her attire,—with a large kerchief on her head.

Her face was simple, rather round in contour, not devoid of agreeability; her gaze was downcast and rather melancholy, her movements were embarrassed.

"Are you Madame Pólteff?" I asked, inviting her to be seated.

"Just so, sir," she answered, in a low voice, and without sitting down.—"I am the widow of your nephew, Mikhaíl Andréevitch Pólteff."

"Is Mikhaíl Andréevitch dead? Has he been dead long?—But sit down, I beg of you."

She dropped down on a chair.

"This is the second month since he died."

"And were you married to him long ago?"

"I lived with him one year in all."

"And whence come you now?"

"I come from the vicinity of Túla. . . . There is a village there called Známenskoe-Glúshkovo —perhaps you deign to know it. I am the daughter of the sexton there. Mikhaíl Andréitch and I lived there. . . . He settled down with my father. We lived together a year in all." The young woman's lips twitched slightly, and she raised her hand to them. She seemed to be getting ready to cry, but conquered herself, and cleared her throat.

"The late Mikhaíl Andréitch, before his death," she went on, "bade me go to you. 'Be sure to go,' he said. And he told me that I was to thank you for all your goodness, and transmit

42

to you . . . . this . . . . trifle" (she drew from her pocket a small package), "which he always carried on his person. . . . And Mikhaíl Andréitch said, would n't you be so kind as to accept it in memory—that you must not scorn it. . . . . 'I have nothing else to give him,' . . . meaning you . . . he said. . . ."

In the packet was a small silver cup with the monogram of Mikhaíl's mother. This tiny cup I had often seen in Mikhaíl's hands; and once he had even said to me, in speaking of a pauper, that he must be stripped bare, since he had neither cup nor bowl, "while I have this here," he said.

I thanked her, took the cup and inquired, "Of what malady did Mikhaíl Andréitch die?— Probably . . . ."

Here I bit my tongue . . . . but the young woman understood my unspoken thought. . . . She darted a swift glance at me, then dropped her eyes, smiled sadly, and immediately said: "Akh, no! He had abandoned that entirely from the time he made my acquaintance. . . . Only, what health had he?! . . . It was utterly ruined. As soon as he gave up drinking his malady immediately manifested itself. He became so steady: he was always wanting to help my father, either in the household affairs, or in the vegetable garden . . . or whatever other work happened to be on hand . . . . in spite of the fact that he was of noble birth. Only, where was he to get the strength? . . . And he would have liked to busy himself in the department of writing also,—he knew how to do that beautifully, as you are aware; but his hands shook so, and he could not hold the pen properly. . . . He was always reproaching himself: 'I 'm an idle dog,' he said. 'I have done no one any good, I have helped no one, I have not toiled!' He was very much afflicted over that same. . . . He used to say, 'Our people toil, but what are we doing? . . .' Akh, Nikolái Nikoláitch, he was a fine man—and he loved me . . . . and I . . . . Akh, forgive me. . . ."

Here the young woman actually burst into tears. I would have liked to comfort her, but I did not know how.

"Have you a baby?" I asked at last.

She sighed.—"No, I have not. . . . How could I have?"—And here tears streamed worse than before.

So this was the end of Mísha's wanderings through tribulations [old P. concluded his story]. —You will agree with me, gentlemen, as a matter of course, that I had a right to call him reckless; but you will probably also agree with me that he did not resemble the reckless fellows of the present day, although we must suppose that any philosopher would find traits of similarity between him and them. In both cases there is the thirst for self-annihilation, melancholy, dissatisfaction. . . . And what that springs from I will permit precisely that philosopher to decide.

THE DREAM

(1876)

THE DREAM

I

I WAS living with my mother at the time, in a small seaport town. I was just turned seventeen, and my mother was only thirty-five; she had married very young. When my father died I was only seven years old; but I remembered him well. My mother was a short, fair-haired woman, with a charming, but permanently-sad face, a quiet, languid voice, and timid movements. In her youth she had borne the reputation of a beauty, and as long as she lived she remained attractive and pretty. I have never beheld more profound, tender, and melancholy eyes. I adored her, and she loved me. . . . But our life was not cheerful; it seemed as though some mysterious, incurable and undeserved sorrow were constantly sapping the root of her existence. This sorrow could not be explained by grief for my father alone, great as that was, passionately as my mother had loved him, sacredly as she cherished his memory. . . . No! there was something else hidden there which I did not understand, but which I felt,—felt con-

49

fusedly and strongly as soon as I looked at those quiet, impassive eyes, at those very beautiful but also impassive lips, which were not bitterly compressed, but seemed to have congealed for good and all.

I have said that my mother loved me; but there were moments when she spurned me, when my presence was burdensome, intolerable to her. At such times she felt, as it were, an involuntary aversion for me—and was terrified afterward, reproaching herself with tears and clasping me to her heart. I attributed these momentary fits of hostility to her shattered health, to her unhappiness. . . . These hostile sentiments might have been evoked, it is true, in a certain measure, by some strange outbursts, which were incomprehensible even to me myself, of wicked and criminal feelings which occasionally arose in me. . . .

But these outbursts did not coincide with the moments of repulsion.—My mother constantly wore black, as though she were in mourning. We lived on a rather grand scale, although we associated with no one.

II

MY mother concentrated upon me all her thoughts and cares. Her life was merged in my life. Such relations between parents and children are not always good for the children . . . .

they are more apt to be injurious. Moreover I was my mother's only child . . . . and only children generally develop irregularly. In rearing them the parents do not think of themselves so much as they do of them. . . That is not practical. I did not get spoiled, and did not grow obstinate (both these things happen with only children), but my nerves were unstrung before their time; in addition to which I was of rather feeble health—I took after my mother, to whom I also bore a great facial resemblance. I shunned the society of lads of my own age; in general, I was shy of people; I even talked very little with my mother. I was fonder of reading than of anything else, and of walking alone— and dreaming, dreaming! What my dreams were about it would be difficult to say. It sometimes seemed to me as though I were standing before a half-open door behind which were concealed hidden secrets,—standing and waiting, and swooning with longing—yet not crossing the threshold; and always meditating as to what there was yonder ahead of me—and always waiting and longing . . . . or falling into slumber. If the poetic vein had throbbed in me I should, in all probability, have taken to writing verses; if I had felt an inclination to religious devoutness I might have become a monk; but there was nothing of the sort about me, and I continued to dream—and to wait.

THE DREAM

III

I HAVE just mentioned that I sometimes fell asleep under the inspiration of obscure thoughts and reveries. On the whole, I slept a great deal, and dreams played a prominent part in my life; I beheld visions almost every night. I did not forget them, I attributed to them significance, I regarded them as prophetic, I strove to divine their secret import. Some of them were repeated from time to time, which always seemed to me wonderful and strange. I was particularly perturbed by one dream. It seems to me that I am walking along a narrow, badly-paved street in an ancient town, between many-storied houses of stone, with sharp-pointed roofs. I am seeking my father who is not dead, but is, for some reason, hiding from us, and is living in one of those houses. And so I enter a low, dark gate, traverse a long courtyard encumbered with beams and planks, and finally make my way into a small chamber with two circular windows. In the middle of the room stands my father, clad in a dressing-gown and smoking a pipe. He does not in the least resemble my real father: he is tall, thin, black-haired, he has a hooked nose, surly, piercing eyes; in appearance he is about forty years of age. He is displeased because I have hunted him up; and I also am not in the least delighted at the meeting—and I stand still,

THE DREAM

in perplexity. He turns away slightly, begins
to mutter something and to pace to and fro with
short steps. . . . Then he retreats a little, without ceasing to mutter, and keeps constantly casting glances behind him, over his shoulder; the
room widens out and vanishes in a fog. . . . I
suddenly grow terrified at the thought that I am
losing my father again. I rush after him—but
I no longer see him, and can only hear his angry,
bear-like growl. . . . My heart sinks within me.
I wake up, and for a long time cannot get to
sleep again. . . . All the following day I think
about that dream and, of course, am unable to
arrive at any conclusion.

IV

THE month of June had come. The town in
which my mother and I lived became remarkably
animated at that season. A multitude of vessels
arrived at the wharves, a multitude of new faces
presented themselves on the streets. I loved at
such times to stroll along the quay, past the cof-
fee-houses and inns, to scan the varied faces of
the sailors and other people who sat under the
canvas awnings, at little white tables with pewter
tankards filled with beer.

One day, as I was passing in front of a coffee-
house, I caught sight of a man who immediately
engrossed my entire attention. Clad in a long
black coat of peasant cut, with a straw hat pulled

down over his eyes, he was sitting motionless, with his arms folded on his chest. Thin rings of black hair descended to his very nose; his thin lips gripped the stem of a short pipe. This man seemed so familiar to me, every feature of his swarthy, yellow face, his whole figure, were so indubitably stamped on my memory, that I could not do otherwise than halt before him, could not help putting to myself the question: "Who is this man? Where have I seen him?" He probably felt my intent stare, for he turned his black, piercing eyes upon me. . . . I involuntarily uttered a cry of surprise. . . .

This man was the father whom I had sought out, whom I had beheld in my dream!

There was no possibility of making a mistake, —the resemblance was too striking. Even the long-skirted coat, which enveloped his gaunt limbs, reminded me, in colour and form, of the dressing-gown in which my father had presented himself to me.

"Am not I dreaming?" I thought to myself. . . . . "No. . . . It is daylight now, a crowd is roaring round me, the sun is shining brightly in the blue sky, and I have before me, not a phantom, but a living man."

I stepped up to an empty table, ordered myself a tankard of beer and a newspaper, and seated myself at a short distance from this mysterious being.

THE DREAM

V

PLACING the sheets of the newspaper on a level with my face, I continued to devour the stranger with my eyes.—He hardly stirred, and only raised his drooping head a little from time to time. He was evidently waiting for some one. I gazed and gazed. . . . Sometimes it seemed to me that I had invented the whole thing, that in reality there was no resemblance whatever, that I had yielded to the semi-involuntary deception of the imagination . . . . but " he " would suddenly turn a little on his chair, raise his hand slightly, and again I almost cried aloud, again I beheld before me my " nocturnal " father! At last he noticed my importunate attention, and, first with surprise, then with vexation, he glanced in my direction, started to rise, and knocked down a small cane which he had leaned against the table. I instantly sprang to my feet, picked it up and handed it to him. My heart was beating violently.

He smiled in a constrained way, thanked me, and putting his face close to my face, he elevated his eyebrows and parted his lips a little, as though something had struck him.

"You are very polite, young man," he suddenly began, in a dry, sharp, snuffling voice.— "That is a rarity nowadays. Allow me to congratulate you. You have been well brought up."

55

THE DREAM

I do not remember precisely what answer I made to him; but the conversation between us was started. I learned that he was a fellow-countryman of mine, that he had recently returned from America, where he had lived many years, and whither he was intending to return shortly. He said his name was Baron . . . . I did not catch the name well. He, like my "nocturnal" father, wound up each of his remarks with an indistinct, inward growl. He wanted to know my name. . . . On hearing it he again showed signs of surprise. Then he asked me if I had been living long in that town, and with whom? I answered him that I lived with my mother.

" And your father? "

" My father died long ago. "

He inquired my mother's Christian name, and immediately burst into an awkward laugh—and then excused himself, saying that he had that American habit, and that altogether he was a good deal of an eccentric. Then he asked where we lived. I told him.

VI

THE agitation which had seized upon me at the beginning of our conversation had gradually subsided; I thought our intimacy rather strange —that was all. I did not like the smile with which the baron questioned me; neither did I like the expression of his eyes when he fairly stabbed them into me. . . . There was about them something rapacious and condescending . . . . something which inspired dread. I had not seen those eyes in my dream. The baron had a strange face! It was pallid, fatigued, and, at the same time, youthful in appearance, but with a disagreeable youthfulness! Neither had my "nocturnal" father that deep scar, which intersected his whole forehead in a slanting direction, and which I did not notice until I moved closer to him.

Before I had had time to impart to the baron the name of the street and the number of the house where we lived, a tall negro, wrapped up in a cloak to his very eyes, approached him from behind and tapped him softly on the shoulder. The baron turned round, said: "Aha! At last!" and nodding lightly to me, entered the coffee-house with the negro. I remained under the awning. I wished to wait until the baron should come out again, not so much for the sake of entering again into conversation with him (I really did not know what topic I could start with), as for the purpose of again verifying my first impression.—But half an hour passed; an hour passed. . . . The baron did not make his appearance. I entered the coffee-house, I made the circuit of all the rooms—but nowhere did I

see either the baron or the negro. . . . Both of
them must have taken their departure through
the back door.

My head had begun to ache a little, and with
the object of refreshing myself I set out along
the seashore to the extensive park outside the
town, which had been laid out ten years previously. After having strolled for a couple of
hours in the shade of the huge oaks and plain-
tain-trees, I returned home.

VII

OUR maid-servant flew to meet me, all tremulous with agitation, as soon as I made my appearance in the anteroom. I immediately divined, from the expression of her face, that
something unpleasant had occurred in our house
during my absence.—And, in fact, I learned that
half an hour before a frightful shriek had rung
out from my mother's bedroom. When the maid
rushed in she found her on the floor in a swoon
which lasted for several minutes. My mother had
recovered consciousness at last, but had been
obliged to go to bed, and wore a strange, frightened aspect; she had not uttered a word, she had
not replied to questions—she had done nothing
but glance around her and tremble. The servant had sent the gardener for a doctor. The
doctor had come and had prescribed a soothing

potion, but my mother had refused to say anything to him either. The gardener asserted that a few moments after the shriek had rung out from my mother's room he had seen a strange man run hastily across the flower-plots of the garden to the street gate. (We lived in a one-story house, whose windows looked out upon a fairly large garden.) The gardener had not been able to get a good look at the man's face; but the latter was gaunt, and wore a straw hat and a long-skirted coat. . . . " The baron's costume! " immediately flashed into my head. — The gardener had been unable to overtake him; moreover, he had been summoned, without delay, to the house and despatched for the doctor.

I went to my mother's room; she was lying in bed, whiter than the pillow on which her head rested. . . At sight of me she smiled faintly, and put out her hand to me. I sat down by her side, and began to question her; at first she persistently parried my questions; but at last she confessed that she had seen something which had frightened her greatly.

"Did some one enter here?" I asked.

"No," she answered hastily, "no one entered, but it seemed to me . . . . I thought I saw . . . . a vision. . . ."

She ceased speaking and covered her eyes with her hand. I was on the point of communicating to her what I had heard from the gardener—and my meeting with the baron also, by the way .... but, for some reason or other, the words died on my lips.

Nevertheless I did bring myself to remark to my mother that visions do not manifest themselves in the daylight. . . .

"Stop," she whispered, "please stop; do not torture me now. Some day thou shalt know...." Again she relapsed into silence. Her hands were cold, and her pulse beat fast and unevenly. I gave her a dose of her medicine and stepped a little to one side, in order not to disturb her.

She did not rise all day. She lay motionless and quiet, only sighing deeply from time to time, and opening her eyes in a timorous fashion.—Every one in the house was perplexed.

VIII

TOWARD night a slight fever made its appearance, and my mother sent me away. I did not go to my own chamber, however, but lay down in the adjoining room on the divan. Every quarter of an hour I rose, approached the door on tiptoe, and listened. . . . Everything remained silent—but my mother hardly slept at all that night. When I went into her room early in the morning her face appeared to me to be swollen, and her eyes were shining with an unnatural bril-

liancy. In the course of the day she became a
little easier, but toward evening the fever in-
creased again.

Up to that time she had maintained an obstinate silence, but now she suddenly began to talk
in a hurried, spasmodic voice. She was not de-
lirious, there was sense in her words, but there
was no coherency in them. Not long before
midnight she raised herself up in bed with a
convulsive movement (I was sitting beside her),
and with the same hurried voice she began to
narrate to me, continually drinking water in
gulps from a glass, feebly flourishing her hands,
and not once looking at me the while. . . . At
times she paused, exerted an effort over herself,
and went on again. . . . All this was strange, as
though she were doing it in her sleep, as though
she herself were not present, but as though some
other person were speaking with her lips, or
making her speak.

IX

"LISTEN to what I have to tell thee," she began.
"Thou art no longer a young boy; thou must
know all. I had a good friend. . . . She married a man whom she loved with all her heart,
and she was happy with her husband. But during the first year of their married life they both
went to the capital to spend a few weeks and

enjoy themselves. They stopped at a good hotel and went out a great deal to theatres and assemblies. My friend was very far from homely; every one noticed her, all the young men paid court to her; but among them was one in particular . . . an officer. He followed her unremittingly, and wherever she went she beheld his black, wicked eyes. He did not make her acquaintance, and did not speak to her even once; he merely kept staring at her in a very strange, insolent way. All the pleasures of the capital were poisoned by his presence. She began to urge her husband to depart as speedily as possible, and they had fully made up their minds to the journey. One day her husband went off to the club; some officers—officers who belonged to the same regiment as this man—had invited him to play cards. . . . For the first time she was left alone. Her husband did not return for a long time; she dismissed her maid and went to bed. . . . And suddenly a great dread came upon her, so that she even turned cold all over and began to tremble. It seemed to her that she heard a faint tapping on the other side of the wall—like the noise a dog makes when scratching—and she began to stare at that wall. In the corner burned a shrine-lamp; the chamber was all hung with silken stuff. . . . Suddenly something began to move at that point, rose, opened. . . . . And straight out of the wall, all black and long, stepped forth that dreadful man with the wicked eyes!

"She tried to scream and could not. She was benumbed with fright. He advanced briskly toward her, like a rapacious wild beast, flung something over her head, something stifling, heavy and white. . . . What happened afterward I do not remember. . . . I do not remember! It was like death, like murder. . . . When that terrible fog dispersed at last—when I . . . . my friend recovered her senses, there was no one in the room. Again—and for a long time—she was incapable of crying out, but she did shriek at last . . . . then again everything grew confused. . . .

"Then she beheld by her side her husband, who had been detained at the club until two o'clock. . . . . His face was distorted beyond recognition. He began to question her, but she said nothing. . . . Then she fell ill. . . . But I remember that when she was left alone in the room she examined that place in the wall. . . . Under the silken hangings there proved to be a secret door. And her wedding-ring had disappeared from her hand. This ring was of an unusual shape. Upon it seven tiny golden stars alternated with seven tiny silver stars; it was an ancient family heirloom. Her husband asked her what had become of her ring; she could make no reply. Her husband thought that she had dropped it somewhere, hunted everywhere for it, but nowhere could he find it. Gloom descended upon him, he decided to return home as speedily as possible, and as soon as the doctor permitted they quitted the capital. . . . But imagine! On the very day of their departure they suddenly encountered, on the street, a litter. . . . In that litter lay a man who had just been killed, with a cleft skull—and just imagine! that man was that same dreadful nocturnal visitor with the wicked eyes. . . . He had been killed over a game of cards!

"Then my friend went away to the country, and became a mother for the first time . . . . and lived several years with her husband. He never learned anything about that matter, and what could she say? She herself knew nothing. But her former happiness had vanished. Darkness had invaded their life—and that darkness was never dispelled. . . . They had no other children either before or after . . . . but that son. . . ."

My mother began to tremble all over, and covered her face with her hands.

"But tell me now," she went on, with redoubled force, "whether my friend was in any way to blame? With what could she reproach herself? She was punished, but had not she the right to declare, in the presence of God himself, that the punishment which overtook her was unjust? Then why can the past present itself to her, after the lapse of so many years, in so frightful an aspect, as though she were a sinner tortured by the gnawings of conscience? Macbeth slew Banquo, so it is not to be wondered at that he should have visions . . . . but I . . . ."

But my mother's speech became so entangled and confused that I ceased to understand her. . . . . I no longer had any doubt that she was raving in delirium.

X

ANY one can easily understand what a shattering effect my mother's narration produced upon me! I had divined, at her very first word, that she was speaking of herself, and not of any acquaintance of hers; her slip of the tongue only confirmed me in my surmise. So it really was my father whom I had sought out in my dream, whom I had beheld when wide awake! He had not been killed, as my mother had supposed, but merely wounded. . . . And he had come to her, and had fled, affrighted by her fright. Everything suddenly became clear to me; the feeling of involuntary repugnance for me which sometimes awoke in my mother, and her constant sadness, and our isolated life. . . . I remember that my head reeled, and I clutched at it with both hands, as though desirous of holding it firmly in its place. But one thought had become riveted in it like a nail. I made up my mind, without fail, at any cost, to find that man again! Why?

THE DREAM

With what object?—I did not account to myself for that; but to find him . . . . to find him—
that had become for me a question of life or
death!

On the following morning my mother regained
her composure at last . . . . the fever passed
off . . . . she fell asleep. Committing her to the
care of our landlord and landlady and the servants, I set out on my quest.

XI

First of all, as a matter of course, I betook myself to the coffee-house where I had met the
baron; but in the coffee-house no one knew him
or had even noticed him: he was a chance visitor.
The proprietors had noticed the negro—his figure had been too striking to escape notice; but
who he was, where he stayed, no one knew either.
Leaving my address, in case of an emergency, at
the coffee-house, I began to walk about the
streets and the water-front of the town, the
wharves, the boulevards; I looked into all the
public institutions, and nowhere did I find any
one who resembled either the baron or his companion. . . . As I had not caught the baron's
name, I was deprived of the possibility of appeal-
ing to the police; but I privately gave two or
three guardians of public order to understand
(they gazed at me in surprise, it is true, and did

66

not entirely believe me) that I would lavishly reward their zeal if they should be successful in coming upon the traces of those two individuals, whose personal appearance I tried to describe as minutely as possible.

Having strolled about in this manner until dinner-time, I returned home thoroughly worn out. My mother had got out of bed; but with her habitual melancholy there was mingled a new element, a sort of pensive perplexity, which cut me to the heart like a knife. I sat with her all the evening. We said hardly anything; she laid out her game of patience, I silently looked at her cards. She did not refer by a single word to her story, or to what had happened the day before. It was as though we had both entered into a compact not to touch upon those strange and terrifying occurrences. . . . She appeared to be vexed with herself and ashamed of what had involuntarily burst from her; but perhaps she did not remember very clearly what she had said in her semi-fevered delirium, and hoped that I would spare her. . . . And, in fact, I did spare her, and she was conscious of it; as on the preceding day she avoided meeting my eyes.

A frightful storm had suddenly sprung up out of doors. The wind howled and tore in wild gusts, the window-panes rattled and quivered; despairing shrieks and groans were borne through the air, as though something on high had broken loose and were flying with mad weeping over the shaking houses. Just before dawn I lost myself in a doze . . . . when suddenly it seemed to me as though some one had entered my room and called me, had uttered my name, not in a loud, but in a decided voice. I raised my head and saw no one; but, strange to relate! I not only was not frightened—I was delighted; there suddenly arose within me the conviction that now I should, without fail, attain my end. I hastily dressed myself and left the house.

XII

THE storm had subsided . . . . but its last flutterings could still be felt. It was early; there were no people in the streets; in many places fragments of chimneys, tiles, boards of fences which had been rent asunder, the broken boughs of trees, lay strewn upon the ground. . . . "What happened at sea last night?" I involuntarily thought at the sight of the traces left behind by the storm. I started to go to the port, but my feet bore me in another direction, as though in obedience to an irresistible attraction. Before ten minutes had passed I found myself in a quarter of the town which I had never yet visited. I was walking, not fast, but without stopping, step by step, with a strange sensation at my heart; I was expecting something remarkable, impossible, and, at the same time, I was convinced that that impossible thing would come to pass.

XIII

AND lo, it came to pass, that remarkable, that unexpected thing! Twenty paces in front of me I suddenly beheld that same negro who had spoken to the baron in my presence at the coffee-house! Enveloped in the same cloak which I had then noticed on him, he seemed to have popped up out of the earth, and with his back turned toward me was walking with brisk strides along the narrow sidewalk of the crooked alley! I immediately dashed in pursuit of him, but he redoubled his gait, although he did not glance behind him, and suddenly made an abrupt turn around the corner of a projecting house. I rushed to that corner and turned it as quickly as the negro had done. . . . Marvellous to relate! Before me stretched a long, narrow, and perfectly empty street; the morning mist filled it with its dim, leaden light,—but my gaze penetrated to its very extremity. I could count all its buildings . . . . and not a single living being was anywhere astir! The tall negro in the cloak had vanished as suddenly as he had appeared! I was amazed . . . . but only for a moment. Another feeling immediately took possession of me;

that street which stretched out before my eyes,
all dumb and dead, as it were,—I recognised it!
It was the street of my dream. I trembled and
shivered—the morning was so chilly—and instantly, without the slightest wavering, with a
certain terror of confidence, I went onward.

I began to seek with my eyes. . . . Yes, there
it is, yonder, on the right, with a corner projecting on the sidewalk—yonder is the house of my
dream, yonder is the ancient gate with the stone
scrolls on each side. . . . The house is not circular, it is true, but square . . . . but that is a
matter of no importance. . . . I knock at the
gate, I knock once, twice, thrice, ever more and
more loudly. . . . The gate opens slowly, with
a heavy screech, as though yawning. In front
of me stands a young serving-maid with a dishevelled head and sleepy eyes. She has evidently just waked up.

"Does the baron live here?" I inquire, as I
run a swift glance over the deep, narrow courtyard. . . . It is there; it is all there . . . . there
are the planks which I had seen in my dream.

"No," the maid answers me, "the baron does
not live here."

"What dost thou mean by that? It is impossible!"

"He is not here now. He went away yester-
day."

"Whither?"

" To America."

" To America!" I involuntarily repeated. " But he is coming back?"

The maid looked suspiciously at me.

"I don't know. Perhaps he will not come back at all."

" But has he been living here long?"

" No, not long; about a week. Now he is not here at all."

" But what was the family name of that baron?"

The maid-servant stared at me.

"Don't you know his name? We simply called him the baron. Hey, there! Piótr!" she cried, perceiving that I was pushing my way in. —" come hither: some stranger or other is asking all sorts of questions."

From the house there presented itself the shambling figure of a robust labourer.

"What 's the matter? What 's wanted?" he inquired in a hoarse voice,—and having listened to me with a surly mien, he repeated what the maid-servant had said.

" But who does live here?" I said.

" Our master."

" And who is he?"

" A carpenter. They are all carpenters in this street."

" Can he be seen?"

" Impossible now, he is asleep."

"And cannot I go into the house?"

"No; go your way."

"Well, and can I see your master a little later?"

"Why not? Certainly. He can always be seen. . . . That 's his business as a dealer. Only, go your way now. See how early it is."

"Well, and how about that negro?" I suddenly asked.

The labourer stared in amazement, first at me, then at the maid-servant.

"What negro?" he said at last.—"Go away, sir. You can come back later. Talk with the master."

I went out into the street. The gate was instantly banged behind me, heavily and sharply, without squeaking this time.

I took good note of the street and house and went away, but not home.—I felt something in the nature of disenchantment. Everything which had happened to me was so strange, so remarkable—and yet, how stupidly it had been ended! I had been convinced that I should behold in that house the room which was familiar to me—and in the middle of it my father, the baron, in a dressing-gown and with a pipe. . . . And instead of that, the master of the house was a carpenter, and one might visit him as much as one pleased,—and order furniture of him if one wished!

THE DREAM

But my father had gone to America! And what was left for me to do now? . . . Tell my mother everything, or conceal forever the very memory of that meeting? I was absolutely unable to reconcile myself to the thought that such a senseless, such a commonplace ending should be tacked on to such a supernatural, mysterious beginning!

I did not wish to return home, and walked straight ahead, following my nose, out of the town.

XIV

I WALKED along with drooping head, without a thought, almost without sensation, but wholly engrossed in myself.—A measured, dull and angry roar drew me out of my torpor. I raised my head: it was the sea roaring and booming fifty paces from me. Greatly agitated by the nocturnal storm, the sea was a mass of white-caps to the very horizon, and steep crests of long breakers were rolling in regularly and breaking on the flat shore. I approached it, and walked along the very line left by the ebb and flow on the yellow, ribbed sand, strewn with fragments of trailing seawrack, bits of shells, serpent-like ribbons of eel-grass. Sharp-winged gulls with pitiful cry, borne on the wind from the distant aerial depths, soared white as snow against the grey, cloudy sky, swooped down abruptly, and as though skipping from wave to wave, departed again and vanished like silvery flecks in the strips of swirling foam. Some of them, I noticed, circled persistently around a large isolated boulder which rose aloft in the midst of the monotonous expanse of sandy shores. Coarse seaweed grew in uneven tufts on one side of the rock; and at the point where its tangled stems emerged from the yellow salt-marsh, there was something black, and long, and arched, and not very large. . . . I began to look more intently. . . . . Some dark object was lying there—lying motionless beside the stone. . . . That object became constantly clearer and more distinct the nearer I approached. . . .

I was only thirty paces from the rock now. . . .

Why, that was the outline of a human body! It was a corpse; it was a drowned man, cast up by the sea! I went clear up to the rock.

It was the corpse of the baron, my father! I stopped short, as though rooted to the spot. Then only did I understand that ever since daybreak I had been guided by some unknown forces —that I was in their power,—and for the space of several minutes there was nothing in my soul save the ceaselesss crashing of the sea, and a dumb terror in the presence of the Fate which held me in its grip. . . .

THE DREAM

XV

He was lying on his back, bent a little to one
side, with his left arm thrown above his head . . . .
the right was turned under his bent body. The
sticky slime had sucked in the tips of his feet,
shod in tall sailor's boots; the short blue pea-
jacket, all impregnated with sea-salt, had not
unbuttoned; a red scarf encircled his neck in a
hard knot. The swarthy face, turned skyward.
seemed to be laughing; from beneath the up·
turned upper lip small close-set teeth were visible; the dim pupils of the half-closed eyes were
hardly to be distinguished from the darkened
whites; covered with bubbles of foam the dirt-
encrusted hair spread out over the ground and
laid bare the smooth forehead with the purplish
line of the scar; the narrow nose rose up like a
sharp, white streak between the sunken cheeks.
The storm of the past night had done its work.
. . . . He had not beheld America! The man
who had insulted my mother, who had marred
her life, my father—yes! my father, I could
cherish no doubt as to that—lay stretched out
helpless in the mud at my feet. I experienced
a sense of satisfied vengeance, and compassion,
and repulsion, and terror most of all . . . . of
twofold terror; terror of what I had seen, and
of what had come to pass. That evil, that crim-

75

inal element of which I have already spoken, those incomprehensible spasms rose up within me . . . . stifled me.

"Aha!" I thought to myself: "so that is why I am what I am. . . . That is where blood tells!" I stood beside the corpse and gazed and waited, to see whether those dead pupils would not stir, whether those benumbed lips would not quiver. No! everything was motionless; the very sea-weed, among which the surf had cast him, seemed to have congealed; even the gulls had flown away—there was not a fragment anywhere, not a plank or any broken rigging. There was emptiness everywhere . . . . only he—and I—and the foaming sea in the distance. I cast a glance behind me; the same emptiness was there; a chain of hillocks on the horizon . . . . that was all!

I dreaded to leave that unfortunate man in that loneliness, in the ooze of the shore, to be devoured by fishes and birds; an inward voice told me that I ought to hunt up some men and call them thither, if not to aid—that was out of the question—at least for the purpose of laying him out, of bearing him beneath an inhabited roof. . . . But indescribable terror suddenly took possession of me. It seemed to me as though that dead man knew that I had come thither, that he himself had arranged that last meeting—it even seemed as though I could hear that dull, familiar muttering. . . . I ran off to

one side . . . looked behind me once more. . . .
Something shining caught my eye; it brought
me to a standstill. It was a golden hoop on the
outstretched hand of the corpse. . . . I recognised my mother's wedding-ring. I remember
how I forced myself to return, to go close, to
bend down. . . I remember the sticky touch of
the cold fingers, I remember how I panted and
puckered up my eyes and gnashed my teeth, as
I tugged persistently at the ring. . . .

At last I got it off—and I fled—fled away,
in headlong flight,—and something darted after
me, and overtook me and caught me.

XVI

EVERYTHING which I had gone through and endured was, probably, written on my face when
I returned home. My mother suddenly rose upright as soon as I entered her room, and gazed
at me with such insistent inquiry that, after having unsuccessfully attempted to explain myself,
I ended by silently handing her the ring. She
turned frightfully pale, her eyes opened unusu-
ally wide and turned dim like *his*.—She uttered
a faint cry, seized the ring, reeled, fell upon my
breast, and fairly swooned there, with her head
thrown back and devouring me with those wide,
mad eyes. I encircled her waist with both arms,
and standing still on one spot, never stirring, I

slowly narrated everything, without the slightest reservation, to her, in a quiet voice: my dream and the meeting, and everything, everything. . . . She heard me out to the end, only her breast heaved more and more strongly, and her eyes suddenly grew more animated and drooped. Then she put the ring on her fourth finger, and, retreating a little, began to get out a mantilla and a hat. I asked where she was going. She raised a surprised glance to me and tried to answer, but her voice failed her. She shuddered several times, rubbed her hands as though endeavouring to warm herself, and at last she said: " Let us go at once thither."

" Whither, mother dear? "

" Where he is lying. . . . I want to see. . . . I want to know. . . . I shall identify. . . ."

I tried to persuade her not to go; but she was almost in hysterics. I understood that it was impossible to oppose her desire, and we set out.

XVII

AND lo, again I am walking over the sand of the dunes, but I am no longer alone, I am walking arm in arm with my mother. The sea has retreated, has gone still further away; it is quieting down; but even its diminished roar is menacing and ominous. Here, at last, the solitary rock has shown itself ahead of us—and there is the seaweed. I look intently, I strive to distinguish that rounded object lying on the ground—but I see nothing. We approach closer. I involuntarily retard my steps. But where is that black, motionless thing? Only the stalks of the seaweed stand out darkly against the sand, which is already dry. . . . We go to the very rock. . . . The corpse is nowhere to be seen, and only on the spot where it had lain there still remains a depression, and one can make out where the arms and legs lay. . . . Round about the seaweed seems tousled, and the traces of one man's footsteps are discernible; they go across the down, then disappear on reaching the flinty ridge.

My mother and I exchange glances and are ourselves frightened at what we read on our own faces. . . .

Can he have got up of himself and gone away?

"But surely thou didst behold him dead?" she asks in a whisper.

I can only nod my head. Three hours have not elapsed since I stumbled upon the baron's body. . . . Some one had discovered it and carried it away.—I must find out who had done it, and what had become of him.

But first of all I must attend to my mother.

XVIII

WHILE she was on her way to the fatal spot she was in a fever, but she controlled herself. The disappearance of the corpse had startled her as the crowning misfortune. She was stupefied. I feared for her reason. With great difficulty I got her home. I put her to bed again; again I called the doctor for her; but as soon as my mother partly recovered her senses she at once demanded that I should instantly set out in search of "that man." I obeyed. But, despite all possible measures, I discovered nothing. I went several times to the police-office, I visited all the villages in the neighbourhood, I inserted several advertisements in the newspapers, I made inquiries in every direction—all in vain! It is true that I did hear that a drowned man had been found at one of the hamlets on the seashore. . . . I immediately hastened thither, but he was already buried, and from all the tokens he did not resemble the Laron. I found out on what ship he had sailed for America. At first every one was positive that that ship had perished during the tempest; but several months afterward rumours began to circulate to the effect that it had been seen at anchor in the harbour of New York. Not knowing what to do, I set about hunting up the negro whom I had seen.—I offered him,

through the newspapers, a very considerable sum
of money if he would present himself at our house.
A tall negro in a cloak actually did come to the
house in my absence. . . . But after questioning
the servant-maid, he suddenly went away and returned no more.

And thus the trace of my . . . . my father
grew cold; thus did it vanish irrevocably in the
mute gloom. My mother and I never spoke of
him. Only, one day, I remember that she expressed surprise at my never having alluded before to my strange dream; and then she added:
"Of course, it really . . . ." and did not finish
her sentence.

My mother was ill for a long time, and after
her convalescence our former relations were not
reëstablished. She felt awkward in my presence
until the day of her death. . . . Precisely that,
awkward. And there was no way of helping her
in her grief. Everything becomes smoothed
down, the memories of the most tragic family
events gradually lose their force and venom; but
if a feeling of awkwardness has been set up
between two closely-connected persons, it is impossible to extirpate it!

I have never again had that dream which had
been wont so to disturb me; I no longer "search
for" my father; but it has sometimes seemed to
me—and it seems so to me to this day—that in my
sleep I hear distant shrieks, unintermittent, mel-

THE DREAM

ancholy plaints; they resound somewhere behind a lofty wall, across which it is impossible to clamber; they rend my heart—and I am utterly unable to comprehend what it is: whether it is a living man groaning, or whether I hear the wild, prolonged roar of the troubled sea. And now it passes once more into that beast-like growl—and I awake with sadness and terror in my soul.

FATHER ALEXYÉI S STORY

(1877)

FATHER ALEXYÉI'S STORY

TWENTY years ago I was obliged—in my capacity of private inspector—to make the circuit of all my aunt's rather numerous estates. The parish priests, with whom I regarded it as my duty to make acquaintance, proved to be individuals of pretty much one pattern, and made after one model, as it were. At length, in about the last of the estates which I was inspecting, I hit upon a priest who did not resemble his brethren. He was a very aged man, almost decrepit; and had it not been for the urgent entreaties of his parishioners, who loved and respected him, he would long before have petitioned to be retired that he might rest. Two peculiarities impressed me in Father Alexyéi (that was the priest's name). In the first place, he not only asked nothing for himself but announced plainly that he required nothing; and, in the second place, I have never beheld in any human face a more sorrowful, thoroughly indifferent—what is called an "overwhelmed"—expression. The features of that face were of the ordinary rustic type: a wrinkled forehead, small grey eyes, a large nose, a wedge-shaped beard, a swarthy, sunburned skin. . . . But the expression! . . . the expression! . . . In that dim gaze life barely burned, and sadly at that; and his voice also was, somehow, lifeless and dim.

I fell ill and kept my bed for several days. Father Alexyéi dropped in to see me in the evenings, not to chat, but to play "fool." [1] The game of cards seemed to divert him more than it did me. One day, after having been left "the fool" several times in succession (which delighted Father Alexyéi not a little), I turned the conversation on his past life, on the afflictions which had left on him such manifest traces. Father Alexyéi remained obdurate for a long time at first, but ended by relating to me his story. He must have taken a liking to me for some reason or other. Otherwise he would not have been so frank with me.

I shall endeavour to transmit his story in his own words. Father Alexyéi talked very simply and intelligently, without any seminary or provincial tricks and turns of speech. It was not the first time I had noticed that Russians, of all classes and callings, who have been violently shattered and humbled express themselves precisely in such language.

. . . . I HAD a good and sedate wife [thus he began], I loved her heartily, and we begat eight

[1] A simple card-game.—TRANSLATOR.

children. One of my sons became a bishop, and died not so very long ago, in his diocese. I shall now tell you about my other son,—Yákoff was his name. I sent him to the seminary in the town of T * * *, and soon began to receive the most comforting reports about him. He was the best pupil in all the branches! Even at home, in his boyhood, he had been distinguished for his diligence and discretion; a whole day would sometimes pass without one's hearing him . . . he would be sitting all the time over his book, reading. He never caused me and my wife[1] the slightest displeasure; he was a meek lad. Only sometimes he was thoughtful beyond his years, and his health was rather weak. Once something remarkable happened to him. He left the house at daybreak, on St. Peter's day,[2] and was gone almost all the morning. At last he returned. My wife and I ask him: "Where hast thou been?"

"I have been for a ramble in the forest," says he, "and there I met a certain little green old man, who talked a great deal with me, and gave me such savoury nuts!"

"What little green old man art thou talking about?" we ask him.

"I don't know," says he; "I never saw him

[1] The word used is *popadyá*, the feminine form of *pop(e)*, or priest. *Svyashtchénnik* is, however, more commonly used for priest. —TRANSLATOR.

[2] June 29 (O. S.), July 12 (N. S.).—TRANSLATOR.

before. He was a little old man with a hump, and he kept shifting from one to the other of his little feet, and laughing—and he was all green, just like a leaf."

"What," say we, "and was his face green also?"

"Yes, his face, and his hair, and even his eyes."

Our son had never lied to us; but this time my wife and I had our doubts.

"Thou must have fallen asleep in the forest, in the heat of the day, and have seen that old man in thy dreams."

"I wasn't asleep at all," says he. "Why, don't you believe me?" says he. "See here, I have one of the nuts left in my pocket."

Yákoff pulled the nut out of his pocket and showed it to us.—The kernel was small, in the nature of a chestnut, and rather rough; it did not resemble our ordinary nuts. I laid it aside, and intended to show it to the doctor . . . but it got lost. . . . I did not find it again.

Well, sir, so we sent him to the seminary, and, as I have already informed you, he rejoiced us by his success. So my spouse and I assumed that he would turn out a fine man! When he came for a sojourn at home it was a pleasure to look at him; he was so comely, and there was no mischief about him;—every one liked him, every one congratulated us. Only he was still rather thin of body, and there was no real good rosiness in his face. So then, he was already in his nineteenth year, and his education would soon be finished. When suddenly we receive from him a letter.—He writes to us: " Dear father and mother, be not wroth with me, permit me to be a layman;[1] my heart does not incline to the ecclesiastical profession, I dread the responsibility, I am afraid I shall sin—doubts have taken hold upon me! Without your parental permission and blessing I shall venture on nothing—but one thing I will tell you; I am afraid of myself, for I have begun to think a great deal."

I assure you, my dear sir, that this letter made me very sad,—as though a boar-spear had pricked my heart,—for I saw that I should have no one to take my place![2] My eldest son was a monk; and this one wanted to abandon his vocation altogether. I was also pained because priests from our family have lived in our parish for close upon two hundred years. But I thought to myself: " There 's no use in kicking against the pricks; evidently, so it was predestined for him. What sort of a pastor would he be if he has admitted doubt to his mind? " I took counsel with my wife, and wrote to him in the following sense:

---

[1] In former days the sons of priests generally became priests. It is still so, in a measure.—TRANSLATOR.

[2] Therefore, there would be no one to maintain his widow and daughters, unless some young man could be found to marry one of the daughters, be ordained, take the parish, and assume the support of the family.—TRANSLATOR.

FATHER ALEXYÉI'S STORY

"Think it over well, my son Yákoff; measure ten times before you cut off once—there are great difficulties in the worldly service, cold and hunger, and scorn for our caste! And thou must know beforehand that no one will lend a hand to aid; so see to it that thou dost not repine afterward. My desire, as thou knowest, has always been that thou shouldst succeed me; but if thou really hast come to cherish doubts as to thy calling and hast become unsteady in the faith, then it is not my place to restrain thee. The Lord's will be done! Thy mother and I will not refuse thee our blessing."

Yákoff answered me with a grateful letter. "Thou hast rejoiced me, dear father," said he. "It is my intention to devote myself to the profession of learning, and I have some protection; I shall enter the university and become a doctor, for I feel a strong bent for science." I read Yáshka's letter and became sadder than before; but I did not share my grief with any one. My old woman caught a severe cold about that time and died—from that same cold, or the Lord took her to Himself because He loved her, I know not which. I used to weep and weep because I was a lonely widower—but what help was there for that?[1] So it had to be, you know. And I would have been glad to go into the earth

[1] Parish priests (the White Clergy) must marry before they are ordained sub-deacon, and are not allowed to remarry in the Holy Catholic Church of the East.—TRANSLATOR.

. . . but it is hard . . . it will not open. And I was expecting my son; for he had notified me: "Before I go to Moscow," he said, "I shall look in at home." And he did come to the parental roof, but did not remain there long. It seemed as though something were urging him on; he would have liked, apparently, to fly on wings to Moscow, to his beloved university! I began to question him as to his doubts. "What was the cause of them?" I asked. But I did not get much out of him. One idea had pushed itself into his head, and that was the end of it! "I want to help my neighbours," he said.—Well, sir, he left me. I don't believe he took a penny with him, only a few clothes. He had such reliance on himself! And not without reason. He passed an excellent examination, matriculated as student, obtained lessons in private houses. . . . He was very strong on the ancient languages! And what think you? He took it into his head to send me money. I cheered up a little,—not on account of the money, of course,—I sent that back to him, and even scolded him; but I cheered up because I saw that the young fellow would make his way in the world. But my rejoicing did not last long. . . .

He came to me for his first vacation. . . . And, what marvel is this? I do not recognise my Yákoff! He had grown so tiresome and surly, —you could n't get a word out of him. And

his face had changed also: he had grown about
ten years older. He had been taciturn before,
there 's no denying that! At the slightest thing
he would grow shy and blush like a girl. . . .
But when he raised his eyes, you could see that
all was bright in his soul! But now it was quite
different. He was not shy, but he held aloof,
like a wolf, and was always looking askance.
He had neither a smile nor a greeting for any
one—he was just like a stone! If I undertook
to interrogate him, he would either remain silent or snarl. I began to wonder whether he
had taken to drink—which God forbid!—or had
conceived a passion for cards; or whether something in the line of a weakness for women had
happened to him. In youth love-longings act
powerfully,—well, and in such a large city as
Moscow bad examples and occasions are not lacking. But no; nothing of that sort was discernible. His drink was kvas [1] and water; he never
looked at the female sex—and had no intercourse
with people in general. And what was most bitter of all to me, he did not have his former confidence in me; a sort of indifference had made
its appearance, just as though everything belonging to him had become loathsome to him.
I turned the conversation on the sciences, on the

[1] A sourish, non-intoxicating beverage, prepared by putting water
on rye meal or the crusts of sour black rye bread and allowing
it to ferment.—TRANSLATOR.

university, but even there could get no real answer. He went to church, but he was not devoid of peculiarities there also; everywhere he was grim and scowling, but in church he seemed always to be grinning.

After this fashion he spent six weeks with me, then went back to Moscow. From Moscow he wrote to me twice, and it seemed to me, from his letters, as though he were regaining his sensibilities. But picture to yourself my surprise, my dear sir! Suddenly, in the very middle of the winter, just before the Christmas holidays, he presents himself before me!

"How didst thou get here? How is this? What's the matter? I know that thou hast no vacation at this time.—Dost thou come from Moscow?"—I ask.

"Yes."

"And how about . . . . the university?"

"I have left the university."

"Thou hast left it?"

"Just so."

"For good?"

"For good."

"But art thou ill, pray, Yákoff?"

"No, father," says he, "I am not ill; but just don't bother me and question me, dear father, or I will go away from here—and that's the last thou wilt ever see of me."

FATHER ALEXYÉI'S STORY

Yákoff tells me that he is not ill, but his face is such that I am fairly frightened. It was dreadful, dark—not human, actually!—His cheeks were drawn, his cheek-bones projected, he was mere skin and bone; his voice sounded as though it proceeded from a barrel . . . . while his eyes . . . O Lord and Master! what eyes!— menacing, wild, incessantly darting from side to side, and it was impossible to catch them; his brows were knit, his lips seemed to be twisted on one side. . . . What had happened to my Joseph Most Fair,[1] to my quiet lad? I cannot comprehend it. " Can he have gone crazy? " I say to myself. He roams about like a spectre by night, he does not sleep,—and then, all of a sudden, he will take to staring into a corner as though he were completely benumbed. . . . It was enough to scare one!

Although he had threatened to leave the house if I did not leave him in peace, yet surely I was his father! My last hope was ruined—yet I was to hold my tongue! So one day, availing myself of an opportunity, I began to entreat Yá-

[1] One of the ancient religious ballads sung by the " wandering cripples." Joseph (son of Jacob) is called by this appellation, and also a " tzarévitch," or king's son. For a brief account of these ballads see: " The Epic Songs of Russia " (Introduction), and Chapter I in " A Survey of Russian Literature " (I. F. Hapgood). This particular ballad is mentioned on page 22 of the last-named book.—TRANSLATOR.

(N. B. This note is placed here because there is no other book in English where any information whatever can be had concerning these ballads or this ballad.—I. F. H.)

koff with tears, I began to adjure him by the memory of his dead mother:

" Tell me," I said, " as thy father in the flesh and in the spirit, Yásha, what aileth thee? Do not kill me; explain thyself, lighten thy heart! Can it be that thou hast ruined some Christian soul? If so, repent! "

" Well, dear father," he suddenly says to me (this took place toward nightfall), " thou hast moved me to compassion. I will tell thee the whole truth. I have not ruined any Christian soul—but my own soul is going to perdition."

" How is that? "

" In this way. . . ." And thereupon Yákoff raised his eyes to mine for the first time.—" It is going on four months now," he began. . . . But suddenly he broke off and began to breathe heavily.

" What about the fourth month? Tell me, do not make me suffer! "

" This is the fourth month that I have been seeing him."

" Him? Who is he? "

" Why, the person . . . . whom it is awkward to mention at night."

I fairly turned cold all over and fell to quaking.

" What? ! " I said, " dost thou see *him?* "

" Yes."

" And dost thou see him now? "

" Yes."

" Where? "   And I did not dare to turn round, and we both spoke in a whisper.

" Why, yonder. . . ." and he indicated the spot with his eyes . . . . " yonder, in the corner."

I summoned up my courage and looked at the corner; there was nothing there.

" Why, good gracious, there is nothing there, Yákoff! "

" *Thou* dost not see him, but I do."

Again I glanced round . . . . again nothing. Suddenly there recurred to my mind the little old man in the forest who had given him the chestnut. " What does he look like? " I said. . . . . " Is he green? "

" No, he is not green, but black."

" Has he horns? "

" No, he is like a man,—only all black."

As Yákoff speaks he displays his teeth in a grin and turns as pale as a corpse, and huddles up to me in terror; and his eyes seem on the point of popping out of his head, and he keeps staring at the corner.

" Why, it is a shadow glimmering faintly," I say. " That is the blackness from a shadow, but thou mistakest it for a man."

" Nothing of the sort!—And I see his eyes: now he is rolling up the whites, now he is raising his hand, he is calling me."

" Yákoff, Yákoff, thou shouldst try to pray;

this obsession would disperse. Let God arise and His enemies shall be scattered!"

" I have tried," says he, " but it has no effect."

" Wait, wait, Yákoff, do not lose thy courage. I will fumigate with incense; I will recite a prayer; I will sprinkle holy water around thee."

Yákoff merely waved his hand. " I believe neither in thy incense nor in holy water; they don't help worth a farthing. I cannot get rid of him now. Ever since he came to me last summer, on one accursed day, he has been my constant visitor, and he cannot be driven away. Understand this, father, and do not wonder any longer at my behaviour—and do not torment me."

" On what day did he come to thee? " I ask him, and all the while I am making the sign of the cross over him. " Was it not when thou didst write about thy doubts? "

Yákoff put away my hand.

" Let me alone, dear father," says he, " don't excite me to wrath lest worse should come of it. I 'm not far from laying hands on myself, as it is."

You can imagine, my dear sir, how I felt when I heard that. . . . I remember that I wept all night. " How have I deserved such wrath from the Lord? " I thought to myself.

At this point Father Alexyéi drew from his pocket a checked handkerchief and began to blow his nose, and stealthily wiped his eyes, by the way.

A bad time began for us then [he went on]. I could think of but one thing: how to prevent him from running away, or—which the Lord forbid!—of actually doing himself some harm! I watched his every step, and was afraid to enter into conversation.—And there dwelt near us at that time a neighbour, the widow of a colonel, Márfa Sávishna was her name; I cherished a great respect for her, because she was a quiet, sensible woman, in spite of the fact that she was young and comely. I was in the habit of going to her house frequently, and she did not despise my vocation.[1] Not knowing, in my grief and anguish, what to do, I just told her all about it.—At first she was greatly alarmed, and even thoroughly frightened; but later on she became thoughtful. For a long time she deigned to sit thus, in silence; and then she expressed a wish to see my son and converse with him. And I felt that I ought without fail to comply with her wish; for it was not feminine curiosity which prompted it in this case, but something else.

On returning home I began to persuade Yákoff. "Come with me to see the colonel's widow," I said to him.

He began to flourish his legs and arms!

---

[1] Ecclesiastics are regarded as plebeians by the gentry or nobles in Russia.—TRANSLATOR.

"I won't go to her," says he, "not on any account! What shall I talk to her about?" He even began to shout at me. But at last I conquered him, and hitching up my little sledge, I drove him to Márfa Sávishna's, and, according to our compact, I left him alone with her. I was surprised at his having consented so speedily. Well, never mind,—we shall see. Three or four hours later my Yákoff returns.

"Well," I ask, "how did our little neighbour please thee?"

He made me no answer. I asked him again.

"She is a virtuous woman," I said.—"I suppose she was amiable with thee?"

"Yes," he says, "she is not like the others."

I saw that he seemed to have softened a little. And I made up my mind to question him then and there. . . .

"And how about the obsession?" I said.

Yákoff looked at me as though I had lashed him with a whip, and again made no reply. I did not worry him further, and left the room; and an hour later I went to the door and peeped through the keyhole. . . . And what do you think?—My Yásha was asleep! He was lying on the couch and sleeping. I crossed myself several times in succession. "May the Lord send Márfa Sávishna every blessing!" I said. "Evidently, she has managed to touch his embittered heart, the dear little dove!"

The next day I see Yákoff take his cap. . . .
I think to myself: "Shall I ask him whither he
is going?—But no, better not ask . . . . it certainly must be to her!" . . . . And, in point of
fact, Yákoff did set off for Márfa Sávishna's
house—and sat with her still longer than before;
and on the day following he did it again! Then
again, the next day but one! My spirits began
to revive, for I saw that a change was coming
over my son, and his face had grown quite different, and it was becoming possible to look
into his eyes: he did not turn away. He was
just as depressed as ever, but his former despair and terror had disappeared. But before
I had recovered my cheerfulness to any
great extent everything again broke off short!
Yákoff again became wild, and again it was
impossible to approach him. He sat locked
up in his little room, and went no more to the
widow's.

"Can it be possible," I thought, "that he has
hurt her feelings in some way, and she has forbidden him the house?—But no," I thought
. . . "although he is unhappy he would not
dare to do such a thing; and besides, she is not
that sort of woman."

At last I could endure it no longer, and I interrogated him: "Well, Yákoff, how about our
neighbour? . . . Apparently thou hast forgotten her altogether."

But he fairly roared at me:—"Our neighbour? Dost thou want *him* to jeer at me?"

"What?" I say.—Then he even clenched his fists and . . . got perfectly furious.

"Yes!" he says; and formerly he had only towered up after a fashion, but now he began to laugh and show his teeth.—"Away! Begone!"

To whom these words were addressed I know not! My legs would hardly bear me forth, to such a degree was I frightened. Just imagine: his face was the colour of red copper, he was foaming at the mouth, his voice was hoarse, exactly as though some one were choking him! . . . . And that very same day I went—I, the orphan of orphans—to Márfa Sávishna . . . . and found her in great affliction. Even her outward appearance had undergone a change: she had grown thin in the face. But she would not talk with me about my son. Only one thing she did say: that no human aid could effect anything in that case. "Pray, father," she said,—and then she presented me with one hundred rubles, —"for the poor and sick of your parish," she said. And again she repeated: "Pray!"— O Lord! As if I had not prayed without that —prayed day and night!

Here Father Alexyéi again pulled out his handkerchief, and again wiped away his tears, but not by stealth this time, and after resting for a little while, he resumed his cheerless narrative.

Yákoff and I then began to descend as a snow-ball rolls down hill, and both of us could see that an abyss lay at the foot of the hill; but how were we to hold back, and what measures could we take? And it was utterly impossible to conceal this; my entire parish was greatly disturbed, and said: " The priest's son has gone mad; he is possessed of devils,—and the authorities ought to be informed of all this."—And people infallibly would have informed the authorities had not my parishioners taken pity on me . . . . for which I thank them. In the meantime winter was drawing to an end, and spring was approaching.—And such a spring as God sent!— fair and bright, such as even the old people could not remember: the sun shone all day long, there was no wind, and the weather was warm! And then a happy thought occurred to me: to persuade Yákoff to go off with me to do reverence to Mitrofány, in Vorónezh. " If that last remedy is of no avail," I thought, " well, then, there is but one hope left—the grave! "

So I was sitting one day on the porch just before evening, and the sunset glow was flaming in the sky, and the larks were warbling, and the apple-trees were in bloom, and the grass was growing green. . . . I was sitting and meditating how I could communicate my intention to

Yákoff. Suddenly, lo and behold! he came out on the porch; he stood, gazed around, sighed, and sat down on the step by my side. I was even frightened out of joy, but I did nothing except hold my tongue. But he sits and looks at the sunset glow, and not a word does he utter either. But it seemed to me as though he had become softened, the furrows on his brow had been smoothed away, his eyes had even grown bright. . . . . A little more, it seemed, and a tear would have burst forth! On beholding such a change in him I—excuse me!—grew bold.

"Yákoff," I said to him, "do thou hearken to me without anger. . . ." And then I informed him of my intention; how we were both to go to Saint Mitrofány on foot; and it is about one hundred and fifty versts to Vorónezh from our parts; and how pleasant it would be for us two, in the spring chill, having risen before dawn, to walk and walk over the green grass, along the highway; and how, if we made proper obeisance and prayed before the shrine of the holy man, perhaps—who knows?—the Lord God would show mercy upon us, and he would receive healing, of which there had already been many instances. And just imagine my happiness, my dear sir!

"Very well," says Yákoff, only he does not turn round, but keeps on gazing at the sky.— "I consent. Let us go."

I was fairly stupefied. . . .

" My friend," I say, " my dear little dove, my benefactor!" . . . But he asks me:

" When shall we set out?"

" Why, to-morrow, if thou wilt," I say.

So on the following day we started. We slung wallets over our shoulders, took staves in our hands, and set forth. For seven whole days we trudged on, and all the while the weather favoured us, and was even downright wonderful! There was neither sultry heat nor rain; the flies did not bite, the dust did not make us itch. And every day my Yákoff acquired a better aspect. I must tell you that Yákoff had not been in the habit of seeing *that one* in the open air, but had felt him behind him, close to his back, or his shadow had seemed to be gliding alongside, which troubled my son greatly. But on this occasion nothing of that sort happened, and nothing made its appearance. We talked very little together . . . . but how greatly at our ease we felt—especially I! I saw that my poor boy was coming to life again. I cannot describe to you, my dear sir, what my feelings were then.—Well, we reached Vorónezh at last. We cleaned up ourselves and washed ourselves, and went to the cathedral, to the holy man. For three whole days we hardly left the temple. How many prayer-services we celebrated, how many candles we placed before the holy pictures! And everything was going well, everything was fine; the days were devout, the nights were tranquil; my Yákoff slept like an infant. He began to talk to me of his own accord. He would ask: "Dost thou see nothing, father dear?" and smile. "No, I see nothing," I would answer.— What more could be demanded? My gratitude to the saint was unbounded.

Three days passed; I said to Yákoff: "Well, now, dear son, the matter has been set in order; there's a festival in our street. One thing remains to be done; do thou make thy confession and receive the communion; and then, with God's blessing, we will go our way, and after having got duly rested, and worked a bit on the farm to increase thy strength, thou mayest bestir thyself and find a place—and Márfa Sávishna will certainly help us in that," I said.

"No," said Yákoff, "why should we trouble her? But I will take her a ring from Mitrofány's hand."

Thereupon I was greatly encouraged. "See to it," I said, "that thou takest a silver ring, not a gold one,—not a wedding-ring!"

My Yákoff flushed up and merely repeated that it was not proper to trouble her, but immediately assented to all the rest.—We went to the cathedral on the following day; my Yákoff made his confession, and prayed so fervently before it! And then he went forward to take the communion. I was standing a little to one side, and did not feel the earth under me for joy. . . . It is no sweeter for the angels in heaven! But as I look—what is the meaning of that?—My Yá-koff has received the communion, but does not go to sip the warm water and wine![1] He is standing with his back to me. . . . I go to him.

"Yákoff," I say, "why art thou standing here?"

He suddenly wheels round. Will you believe it, I sprang back, so frightened was I!—His face had been dreadful before, but now it had become ferocious, frightful! He was as pale as death, his hair stood on end, his eyes squinted. . . . . I even lost my voice with terror. I tried to speak and could not; I was perfectly be-numbed. . . . And he fairly rushed out of the church! I ran after him . . . . but he fled straight to the tavern where we had put up, flung his wallet over his shoulder, and away he flew!

"Whither?" I shouted to him. "Yákoff, what aileth thee? Stop, wait!"

But Yákoff never uttered a word in reply to me, but ran like a hare, and it was utterly im-possible to overtake him! He disappeared from

[1] In the Catholic Church of the East the communion is received fasting. A little to one side of the priest stands a cleric holding a platter of blessed bread, cut in small bits, and a porringer of warm water and wine, which (besides their symbolical significance) are taken by each communicant after the Holy Elements, in order that there may be something interposed between the sacrament and ordinary food.—TRANSLATOR.

sight. I immediately turned back, hired a cart, and trembled all over, and all I could say was: " O Lord! " and, " O Lord! " And I understood nothing: some calamity had descended upon us! I set out for home, for I thought, " He has certainly fled thither."—And so he had. Six versts out of the town I espied him; he was striding along the highway. I overtook him, jumped out of the cart, and rushed to him.

" Yásha! Yásha! "—He halted, turned his face toward me, but kept his eyes fixed on the ground and compressed his lips. And say what I would to him, he stood there just like a statue, and one could just see that he was breathing. And at last he trudged on again along the highway.—What was there to do? I followed him. . . .

Akh, what a journey that was, my dear sir! Great as had been our joy on the way to Vorónezh, just so great was the horror of the return! I would try to speak to him, and he would begin to gnash his teeth at me over his shoulder, precisely like a tiger or a hyena! Why I did not go mad I do not understand to this day! And at last, one night, in a peasant's chicken-house, he was sitting on the platform over the oven and dangling his feet and gazing about on all sides, when I fell on my knees before him and began to weep, and besought him with bitter entreaty:

"Do not slay thy old father outright," I said; "do not let him fall into despair—tell me what has happened to thee?"

He glanced at me as though he did not see who was before him, and suddenly began to speak, but in such a voice that it rings in my ears even now.

"Listen, daddy," said he. "Dost thou wish to know the whole truth? When I had taken the communion, thou wilt remember, and still held the particle [1] in my mouth, suddenly *he* (and that was in the church, in the broad daylight!) stood in front of me, just as though he had sprung out of the ground, and whispered to me . . . . (but he had never spoken to me before)—whispered: ' Spit it out, and grind it to powder! ' I did so; I spat it out, and ground it under foot. And now it must be that I am lost forever, for every sin shall be forgiven, save the sin against the Holy Spirit. . . ."

And having uttered these dreadful words, my son threw himself back on the platform and I dropped down on the floor of the hut. . . . My legs failed me. . . .

Father Alexyéi paused for a moment, and covered his eyes with his hand.

But why should I weary you longer [he went on], and myself? My son and I dragged ourselves home, and there he soon afterward ex-

[1] That is, the particle of bread dipped in the wine, which is placed in the mouth by the priest with the sacramental spoon.—Translator.

pired, and I lost my Yásha. For several days
before his death he neither ate nor drank, but
kept running back and forth in the room and
repeating that there could be no forgiveness for
his sin. . . . But he never saw *him* again. "He
has ruined my soul," he said; "and why should
he come any more now?" And when Yákoff
took to his bed, he immediately sank into unconsciousness, and thus, without repentance, like a
senseless worm, he went from this life to life eternal. . . .

But I will not believe that the Lord judged
harshly. . . .

And among other reasons why I do not believe it is, that he looked so well in his coffin; he
seemed to have grown young again and resembled the Yákoff of days gone by. His face was
so tranquil and pure, his hair curled in little
rings, and there was a smile on his lips. Márfa
Sávishna came to look at him, and said the same
thing. She encircled him all round with flowers,
and laid flowers on his heart, and set up the
gravestone at her own expense.

And I was left alone. . . . And that is why,
my dear sir, you have beheld such great grief on
my face. . . . It will never pass off—and it
cannot.

I wanted to speak a word of comfort to Father
Alexyéi . . . . but could think of none.

We parted soon after.

OLD PORTRAITS

(1881)

OLD PORTRAITS[1]

ABOUT forty versts from our village there
dwelt, many years ago, the great-uncle of
my mother, a retired Sergeant of the Guards
and a fairly wealthy landed proprietor, Alexyéi
Sergyéitch Telyégin, on his ancestral estate,
Sukhodól. He never went anywhere himself,
and therefore did not visit us; but I was sent
to pay my respects to him a couple of times a
year, at first with my governor, and later on
alone. Alexyéi Sergyéitch always received me
very cordially, and I spent three or four days
with him. He was already an old man when I
made his acquaintance; I remember that I was
twelve years old at my first visit, and he was
already over seventy. He had been born under
the Empress Elizabeth, in the last year of her
reign. He lived alone with his wife, Malánya
Pávlovna; she was ten years younger than he.
They had had two daughters who had been married long before, and rarely visited Sukhodól;

[1] Turgénieff labelled this story and "A Reckless Character,"
"Fragments from My Own Memoirs and Those of Other People."
In a foot-note he begs the reader not to mistake the "I" for
the author's own personality, as it was adopted merely for con-
venience of narration.—TRANSLATOR.

there had been quarrels between them and their parents,[1] and Alexyéi Sergyéitch hardly ever mentioned them.

I see that ancient, truly noble steppe home as though it stood before me now. Of one story, with a huge mezzanine,[2] erected at the beginning of the present century from wonderfully thick pine beams—such beams were brought at that epoch from the Zhízdrin pine forests; there is no trace of them nowadays!—it was very spacious and contained a multitude of rooms, which were decidedly low-ceiled and dark, it is true, and the windows were mere slits in the walls, for the sake of warmth. As was proper, the offices and the house-serfs' cottages surrounded the manor-house on all sides, and a park adjoined it, small but with fine fruit-trees, pellucid apples and seedless pears; for ten versts round about stretched out the flat, black-loam steppe. There was no lofty object for the eye: neither a tree nor a belfry; only here and there a windmill reared itself aloft with holes in its wings; it was a regular Sukhodól! (Dry Valley). Inside the house the rooms were filled with ordinary, plain furniture; rather unusual was a verst-post which stood on a window-sill in the hall, and bore the following inscription:

[1] The Russian expression is: "A black cat had run between them."—TRANSLATOR.

[2] In Russia a partial second story, over the centre, or the centre and ends of the main story, is called thus.—TRANSLATOR.

" If thou walkest 68 times around this hall,[1] thou wilt have gone a verst; if thou goest 87 times from the extreme corner of the drawing-room to the right corner of the billiard-room, thou wilt have gone a verst,"—and so forth. But what most impressed the guest who arrived for che first time was the great number of pictures hung on the walls, for the most part the work of so-called Italian masters: ancient landscapes, and mythological and religious subjects. But as all these pictures had turned very black, and had even become warped, all that met the eye was patches of flesh-colour, or a billowy red drapery on an invisible body—or an arch which seemed suspended in the air, or a dishevelled tree with blue foliage, or the bosom of a nymph with a large nipple, like the cover of a soup-tureen; a sliced watermelon, with black seeds; a turban, with a feather above a horse's head; or the gigantic, light-brown leg of some apostle or other, with a muscular calf and up-turned toes, suddenly protruded itself. In the drawing-room, in the place of honour, hung a portrait of the Empress Katherine II, full length, a copy from Lampi's well-known portrait—the object of special reverence, one may say adoration, for the master of the house. From the ceiling depended

[1] In Russian houses the " hall " is a combined ball-room, music-room, play-room, and exercising-ground; not the entrance hall.— TRANSLATOR.

crystal chandeliers in bronze fittings, very small and very dusty.

Alexyéi Sergyéitch himself was a very squat, pot-bellied, little old man, with a plump, but agreeable face all of one colour, with sunken lips and very vivacious little eyes beneath lofty eyebrows. He brushed his scanty hair over the back of his head; it was only since the year 1812 that he had discarded powder. Alexyéi Sergyéitch always wore a grey " redingote" with three capes which fell over his shoulders, a striped waistcoat, chamois-leather breeches and dark-red morocco short boots with a heart-shaped cleft, and a tassel at the top of the leg; he wore a white muslin neckerchief, a frill, lace cuffs, and two golden English " onions," [1] one in each pocket of his waistcoat. In his right hand he generally held an enamelled snuff-box with " Spanish " snuff, while his left rested on a cane with a silver handle which had been worn quite smooth with long use. Alexyéi Sergyéitch had a shrill, nasal voice, and was incessantly smiling, amiably, but somewhat patronisingly, not without a certain self-satisfied pompousness. He also laughed in an amiable manner, with a fine, thin laugh like a string of wax pearls. He was courteous and affable, in the ancient manner of Katherine's day, and moved his hands slowly and with a circular motion, also in ancient style.

[1] We should call such a watch a " turnip."—TRANSLATOR.

OLD PORTRAITS

On account of his weak legs he could not walk, but he was wont to trip with hurried little steps from one arm-chair to another arm-chair, in which he suddenly seated himself—or, rather, he fell into it, as softly as though he had been a pillow.

As I have already said, Alexyéi Sergyéitch never went anywhere, and associated very little with the neighbours, although he was fond of society,—for he was loquacious! He had plenty of society in his own house, it is true: divers Nikanór Nikanóritches, Sevastyéi Sevastyé-itches, Fedúlitches, and Mikhéitches, all poverty-stricken petty nobles, in threadbare kazák coats and short jackets, frequently from his own noble shoulders, dwelt beneath his roof, not to mention the poor gentlewomen in cotton-print gowns, with black kerchiefs on their shoulders, and worsted reticules in their tightly-clenched fingers,—divers Avdótiya Sávishnas, Pelagéya Mirónovnas, and plain Feklúskas and Arínkas, who received asylum in the women's wing. No less than fifteen persons ever sat down to Alexyéi Sergyéitch's table . . . . he was so hospitable! —Among all these parasites two individuals stood forth with special prominence: a dwarf named Janus or the Two-faced, a Dane,—or, as some asserted, of Jewish extraction,—and crazy Prince L. In contrast to the customs of that day the dwarf did not in the least serve as a butt for the guests, and was not a jester; on the contrary, he maintained constant silence, wore an irate and surly mien, contracted his brows in a frown, and gnashed his teeth as soon as any one addressed a question to him. Alexyéi Sergyéitch also called him a philosopher, and even respected him. At table he was always the first to be served after the guests and the master and mistress of the house.—" God has wronged him," Alexyéi Sergyéitch was wont to say: " that was the Lord's will; but it is not my place to wrong him."

" Why is he a philosopher? " I asked one day. (Janus did not like me. No sooner would I approach him, than he would begin to snarl and growl hoarsely, " Stranger! don't bother me! ")

" But God have mercy, why is n't he a philosopher? " replied Alexyéi Sergyéitch. " Just observe, my little gentleman, how finely he holds his tongue! "

" But why is he two-faced? "

" Because, my young sir, he has one face outside; there it is for you, ninny, and judge it. . . . But the other, the real one, he hides. And I am the only one who knows that face, and for that I love him. . . . Because 't is a good face. Thou, for example, gazest and beholdest nothing . . . . but even without words, I see when he is condemning me for anything; for he is strict! And always with reason. Which thing thou canst not understand, young sir; but just believe me, an old man!"

The true history of the two-faced Janus—whence he had come, how he had got into Alexyéi Sergyéitch's house—no one knew. On the other hand, the story of Prince L. was well known to all. As a young man of twenty, he had come from a wealthy and distinguished family to Petersburg, to serve in a regiment of the Guards; the Empress Katherine noticed him at the first Court reception, and halting in front of him and pointing to him with her fan, she said, in a loud voice, addressing one of her favourites: "Look, Adám Vasílievitch, see what a beauty! A regular doll!" The blood flew to the poor young fellow's head. On reaching home he ordered his calash to be harnessed up, and donning his ribbon of the Order of Saint Anna, he started out to drive all over the town, as though he had actually fallen into luck.—"Crush every one who does not get out of the way!" he shouted to his coachman.—All this was immediately brought to the Empress's knowledge; an order was issued that he was to be adjudged insane and given in charge of his two brothers; and the latter, without the least delay, carried him off to the country and chained him up in a stone bag.—As they were desirous to make use of his property, they did not release the unfortunate man even when he recovered his senses and came to himself, but continued to keep him incarcerated until he really did lose his mind.—But their wickedness profited them nothing. Prince L. outlived his brothers, and after long sufferings, found himself under the guardianship of Alexyéi Sergyéitch, who was a connection of his. He was a fat, perfectly bald man, with a long, thin nose and blue goggle-eyes. He had got entirely out of the way of speaking—he merely mumbled something unintelligible; but he sang the ancient Russian ballads admirably, having retained, to extreme old age, his silvery freshness of voice, and in his singing he enunciated every word clearly and distinctly. Something in the nature of fury came over him at times, and then he became terrifying. He would stand in one corner, with his face to the wall, and all perspiring and crimson,—crimson all over his bald head to the nape of his neck. Emitting a malicious laugh, and stamping his feet, he would issue orders that some one was to be castigated,—probably his brothers.—"Thrash!"—he yelled hoarsely, choking and coughing with laughter,—"scourge, spare not, thrash, thrash, thrash the monsters my malefactors! That's right! That's right!" Just before he died he greatly amazed and frightened Alexyéi Sergyéitch. He entered the latter's room all pale and quiet, and inclining his body in obeisance to the girdle, he first returned thanks for the asylum and oversight, and then requested that a priest might be sent for; for Death had come to him—he had beheld her—and he must pardon all men and whiten himself.

" How was it that thou didst see her? " muttered the astounded Alexyéi Sergyéitch, who now heard a coherent speech from him for the first time.—" What is she like? Has she a scythe? "

" No," replied Prince L.—" She 's a plain old woman in a loose gown—only she has but one eye in her forehead, and that eye has no lid."

And on the following day Prince L. actually expired, after having fulfilled all his religious obligations and taken leave of every one intelligently and with emotion.

" That 's the way I shall die also," Alexyéi Sergyéitch was wont to remark. And, in fact, something similar happened with him—of which, later on.

But now let us return to our former subject. Alexyéi Sergyéitch did not consort with the neighbours, as I have already said; and they did not like him any too well, calling him eccentric, arrogant, a mocker, and even a Martinist who did not recognise the authorities, without themselves understanding, of course, the meaning of the last word. To a certain extent the neighbours were right. Alexyéi Sergyéitch had resided for nearly seventy years in succession in his Sukhodól, having almost no dealings whatever with the superior authorities, with the military officials, or the courts. "The court is for the bandit, the military officer for the soldier," he was wont to say; 'but I, God be thanked, am neither a bandit nor a soldier." Alexyéi Sergyéitch really was somewhat eccentric, but the soul within him was not of the petty sort. I will narrate a few things about him.

I never found out authoritatively what were his political views, if, indeed, one can apply to him such a very new-fangled expression; but he was, in his way, rather an aristocrat than a nobly-born master of serfs. More than once he complained because God had not given him a son and heir "for the honour of the race, for the continuation of the family." On the wall of his study hung the genealogical tree of the Telyégins, with very profuse branches, and multitudinous circles in the shape of apples, enclosed in a gilt frame.

"We Telyégins,"[1] he said, "are a very ancient stock, existing from remote antiquity; there have been a great many of us Telyégins, but we have not run after foreigners, we have not bowed our backs, we have not wearied ourselves by standing on the porches of the mighty, we have not nourished ourselves on the courts, we have not earned

---

[1] The author is slightly sarcastic in the name he has chosen for this family, which is derived from *telyéga*, a peasant-cart.— TRANSLATOR.

wages, we have not pined for Moscow, we have not intrigued in Peter;[1] we have sat still, each on his place, his own master on his own land . . . . thrifty, domesticated birds, my dear sir!—Although I myself have served in the Guards, yet it was not for long, I thank you!"

Alexyéi Sergyéitch preferred the olden days. —" Things were freer then, more seemly, I assure you on my honour! But ever since the year one thousand and eight hundred " (why precisely from that year he did not explain), " this warring and this soldiering have come into fashion, my dear fellow. These military gentlemen have mounted upon their heads some sort of plumes made of cocks' tails, and made themselves like cocks; they have drawn their necks up tightly, very tightly . . . . they speak in hoarse tones, their eyes are popping out of their heads—and how can they help being hoarse? The other day some police corporal or other came to see me.—' I have come to you, Your Well-Born,' quoth he . . . . (A pretty way he had chosen to surprise me! . . . . for I know myself that I am well-born . . . .) ' I have a matter of business with you.' But I said to him: ' Respected sir, first undo the hooks on thy collar. Otherwise, which God forbid, thou wilt sneeze! Akh, what will become of thee! What will become of thee!—Thou wilt burst like a puff-ball. . . . And I shall be responsible for it!' And how they drink, those military gentlemen—o-ho-ho! I generally give orders that they shall be served with champagne from the Don, because Don champagne and Pontacq are all the same to them; it slips down their throats so smoothly and so fast—how are they to distinguish the difference? And here 's another thing: they have begun to suck that sucking-bottle, to smoke tobacco. A military man will stick that same sucking-bottle under his moustache, between his lips, and emit smoke through his nostrils, his mouth, and even his ears —and think himself a hero! There are my horrid sons-in-law, for example; although one of them is a senator, and the other is some sort of a curator, they suck at the sucking-bottle also,—and yet they regard themselves as clever men! . . . ."

Alexyéi Sergyéitch could not endure smoking tobacco, nor dogs, especially small dogs.— " Come, if thou art a Frenchman, then keep a lap-dog. Thou runnest, thou skippest hither and thither, and it follows thee, with its tail in the air . . . . but of what use is it to fellows like me?"—He was very neat and exacting. He never spoke of the Empress Katherine otherwise than with enthusiasm, and in a lofty, somewhat bookish style: " She was a demi-god, not a human being!—Only contemplate yon smile, my good sir," he was wont to add, pointing at the Lampi portrait, " and admit that she was a demi-god! I, in my lifetime, have been so happy as to have been vouchsafed the bliss of beholding yon smile, and to all eternity it will never be erased from my heart!"—And thereupon he would impart anecdotes from the life of Katherine such as it has never been my lot to read or hear anywhere. Here is one of them. Alexyéi Sergyéitch did not permit the slightest hint at the failings of the great Empress. "Yes, and in conclusion," he cried: "is it possible to judge her as one judges other people?—One day, as she was sitting in her powder-mantle, at the time of her morning toilet, she gave orders that her hair should be combed out. . . . And what happened? The waiting-woman passes the comb through it, and electric sparks fly from it in a perfect shower!—Then she called to her the body physician, Rodgerson, who was present on duty, and says to him: 'I know that people condemn me for certain actions; but dost thou see this electricity? Consequently, with such a nature and constitution as mine, thou mayest thyself judge, for thou art a physician, that it is unjust to condemn me, but they should understand me!'"

The following incident was ineffaceably retained in the memory of Alexyéi Sergyéitch. He was standing one day on the inner watch in the palace, and he was only sixteen years of age. And lo, the Empress passes him—he presents arms. . . . "And she," cried Alexyéi Sergyéitch, again with rapture, " smiling at my youth and my zeal, deigned to give me her hand to kiss, and patted me on the cheek, and inquired who I was, and whence I came, and from what family? And then . . . ." (here the old man's voice generally broke) . . . " then she bade me give my mother her compliments and thank her for rearing her children so well. And whether I was in heaven or on earth, and how and whither she withdrew,—whether she soared up on high, or passed into another room,—I know not to this day! "

I often tried to question Alexyéi Sergyéitch about those olden days, about the men who surrounded the Empress. . . . But he generally evaded the subject. " What 's the use of talking about old times? "—he said . . . . " one only tortures himself. One says to himself,—' Thou wert a young man then, but now thy last teeth have vanished from thy mouth.' And there 's no denying it—the old times were good . . . . well, and God be with them! And as for those men—I suppose, thou fidgety child, that thou art talking about the accidental men? Thou hast seen a bubble spring forth on water? So long as it is whole and lasts, what beautiful colours play upon it! Red and yellow and blue; all one can say is, ' 'T is a rainbow or a diamond! '—But it soon bursts, and no trace of it remains. And that 's what those men were like."

" Well, and how about Potyómkin? " I asked one day.

Alexyéi Sergyéitch assumed a pompous mien. —" Potyómkin, Grigóry Alexándritch, was a statesman, a theologian, a nursling of Katherine's, her offspring, one must say. . . . But enough of that, my little sir! "

Alexyéi Sergyéitch was a very devout man and went to church regularly, although it was beyond his strength. There was no superstition perceptible in him; he ridiculed signs, the evil eye, and other " twaddle," yet he did not like it when a hare ran across his path, and it was not quite agreeable for him to meet a priest.[1] He was very respectful to ecclesiastical persons, nevertheless, and asked their blessing, and even kissed their hand every time, but he talked with them reluctantly.—" They emit a very strong odour," he explained; " but I, sinful man that I am, have grown effeminate beyond measure;—their hair is so long [2] and oily, and they comb it out in all directions, thinking thereby to show me respect, and they clear their throats loudly in the middle of conversation, either out of timidity or because they wish to please me in that way also. Well, but they remind me of my hour of death. But

[1] Both these are bad omens, according to superstitious Russians. —TRANSLATOR.

[2] Priests and monks in Russia wear their hair and beards long to resemble the pictures of Christ. Missionaries in foreign lands are permitted to conform to the custom of the country and cut it short.—TRANSLATOR.

be that as it may, I want to live a while longer.
Only, little sir, don't repeat these remarks of
mine; respect the ecclesiastical profession—only
fools do not respect it; and I am to blame for
talking nonsense in my old age."

Alexyéi Sergyéitch had received a scanty education,[1] like all nobles of that epoch; but he had
completed it, to a certain degree, by reading. He
read only Russian books of the end of the last
century; he considered the newer writers un-
leavened and weak in style. During his reading
he placed beside him, on a round, one-legged
little table, a silver jug filled with a special effer-
vescent kvas flavoured with mint, whose pleasant odour disseminated itself through all the
rooms. He placed large, round spectacles on the
tip of his nose; but in his later years he did not
so much read as stare thoughtfully over the rims
of the spectacles, elevating his brows, mowing
with his lips and sighing. Once I caught him
weeping, with a book on his knees, which greatly
surprised me, I admit.

He recalled the following wretched doggerel:

> O all-conquering race of man!
> Rest is unknown to thee!
> Thou findest it only
> When thou swallowest the dust of the grave. . . .
> Bitter, bitter is this rest!
> Sleep, ye dead. . . . But weep, ye living!

[1] "Had been educated on copper coins" is the Russian expression. That is, had received a cheap education.—TRANSLATOR.

OLD PORTRAITS

These verses were composed by a certain Górmitch-Gormítzky, a roving poetaster, whom
Alexyéi Sergyéitch had harboured in his house
because he seemed to him a delicate and even
subtle man; he wore shoes with knots of ribbon,
pronounced his *o's* broadly, and, raising his eyes
to heaven, he sighed frequently. In addition
to all these merits, Górmitch-Gormítzky spoke
French passably well, for he had been educated
in a Jesuit college, while Alexyéi Sergyéitch only
" understood " it. But having once drunk himself dead-drunk in a dram-shop, this same subtle
Gormítzky displayed outrageous violence. He
thrashed " to flinders " Alexyéi Sergyéitch's
valet, the cook, two laundresses who happened
along, and even an independent carpenter, and
smashed several panes in the windows, yelling
lustily the while: " Here now, I 'll just show
these Russian sluggards, these unlicked kat-
zápy! " [1] — And what strength that puny little
man displayed! Eight men could hardly control
him! For this turbulence Alexyéi Sergyéitch
gave orders that the rhymster should be flung out
of the house, after he had preliminarily been
rolled in the snow (it happened in the winter),
to sober him.

" Yes," Alexyéi Sergyéitch was wont to say,
" my day is over; the horse is worn out. I used
to keep poets at my expense, and I used to buy

[1] The nickname generally applied by the Little Russians
to the Great Russians.—TRANSLATOR.

129

pictures and books from the Jews—and my
geese were quite as good as those of Mukhán,
and I had genuine slate-coloured tumbler-pi-
geons. . . . I was an amateur of all sorts of
things! Except that I never was a dog-fancier,
because of the drunkenness and the clownishness!
I was mettlesome, untamable! God forbid that
a Telyégin should be anything but first-class
in everything! And I had a splendid horse-
breeding establishment. . . And those horses
came . . . . whence, thinkest thou, my little sir?
—From those very renowned studs of the Tzar
Iván Alexyéitch, the brother of Peter the Great.
. . . . I 'm telling you the truth! All stallions,
dark brown in colour, with manes to their
knees, tails to their hoofs. . . . Lions! Vanity
of vanities, all is vanity! But what 's the
use of regretting it? Every man has his limit
fixed for him.—You cannot fly higher than
heaven, nor live in the water, nor escape from
the earth. . . . Let us live on a while longer, at
any rate! ''

And again the old man smiled and took a
pinch of his Spanish tobacco.

His peasants loved him. Their master was
kind, according to them, and not a heart-breaker.
—Only, they also repeated that he was a worn-
out steed. Formerly Alexyéi Sergyéitch had
gone into everything himself: he had ridden out
into the fields, and to the flour-mill, and to the

oil-mill and the storehouses, and looked in to the peasants' cottages; every one was familiar with his racing-drozhky,[1] upholstered in crimson plush and drawn by a well-grown horse with a broad blaze extending clear across its forehead, named "Lantern"—from that same famous breeding establishment. Alexyéi Sergyéitch drove him himself with the ends of the reins wound round his fists. But when his seventieth birthday came the old man gave up everything, and entrusted the management of his estate to the peasant bailiff Antíp, of whom he secretly stood in awe and called Micromegas (memories of Voltaire!), or simply "robber."

"Well, robber, hast thou gathered a big lot of stolen goods?" he would say, looking the robber straight in the eye.

"Everything is according to your grace," Antíp would reply merrily.

"Grace is all right, only just look out for thyself, Micromegas! Don't dare to touch my peasants, my subjects behind my back! They will make complaint . . . . my cane is not far off, seest thou?"

"I always keep your little cane well in mind, dear little father Alexyéi Sergyéitch," replied Antíp-Micromegas, stroking his beard.

[1] The racing-drozhky is frequently used in the country. It consists of a plank, without springs, mounted on four small wheels of equal size. The driver sits flat on the plank, which may or may not be upholstered.—TRANSLATOR.

"That's right, keep it in mind!" and master and bailiff laughed in each other's faces.

With his house-serfs, with his serfs in general, with his "subjects" (Alexyéi Sergyéitch loved that word), he dealt gently.—"Because, judge for thyself, little nephew, if thou hast nothing of thine own save the cross on thy neck,[1] and that a brass one, don't hanker after other folks' things. . . . What sense is there in that?" There is no denying the fact that no one even thought of the so-called problem of the serfs at that epoch; and it could not disturb Alexyéi Sergyéitch. He very calmly ruled his "subjects"; but he condemned bad landed proprietors and called them the enemies of their class.

He divided the nobles in general into three categories: the judicious, "of whom there are not many"; the profligate, "of whom there is a goodly number"; and the licentious, "of whom there are enough to dam a pond." And if any one of them was harsh and oppressive to his subjects, that man was guilty in the sight of God, and culpable in the sight of men!—Yes; the house-serfs led an easy life in the old man's house; the "subjects behind his back" were less well off, as a matter of course, despite the cane wherewith he threatened Micromegas.—And how many there were of them—of those house-

[1] The baptismal cross.—Translator.

serfs—in his manor! And for the most part
they were old, sinewy, hairy, grumbling, stoop-
shouldered, clad in long-skirted nankeen kaftans,
and imbued with a strong acrid odour! And in
the women's department nothing was to be
heard but the trampling of bare feet, and the
rustling of petticoats.—The head valet was
named Irinárkh, and Alexyéi Sergyéitch always
summoned him with a long-drawn-out call: " I-ri-
na-a-árkh! "—He called the others: " Young fellow! Boy! What subject is there?!"—He
could not endure bells. " God have mercy, this
is no tavern!" And what amazed me was, that
no matter at what time Alexyéi Sergyéitch called
his valet, the man instantly presented himself,
just as though he had sprung out of the earth,
and placing his heels together, and putting his
hands behind his back, stood before his master
a grim and, as it were, an irate but zealous servant!

Alexyéi Sergyéitch was lavish beyond his
means; but he did not like to be called " benefactor."—" What sort of a benefactor am I to
you, sir? . . . I 'm doing myself a favour, not
you, my good sir!" (When he was angry or indignant he always called people " you.")—" To
a beggar give once, give twice, give thrice," he
was wont to say. . . . " Well, and if he returns
for the fourth time—give to him yet again, only
add therewith: ' My good man, thou shouldst

work with something else besides thy mouth all the time.' "

" Uncle," I used to ask him, " what if the beggar should return for the fifth time after that? "

" Why, then, do thou give to him for the fifth time."

The sick people who appealed to him for aid he had cured at his own expense, although he himself did not believe in doctors, and never sent for them.—" My deceased mother," he asserted, " used to heal all maladies with olive-oil and salt; she both administered it internally and rubbed it on externally, and everything passed off splendidly. And who was my mother? She had her birth under Peter the First—only think of that! "

Alexyéi Sergyéitch was a Russian man in every respect; he loved Russian viands, he loved Russian songs, but the accordion, " a factory invention," he detested; he loved to watch the maidens in their choral songs, the women in their dances. In his youth, it was said, he had sung rollickingly and danced with agility. He loved to steam himself in the bath,—and steamed himself so energetically that Irinárkh, who served him as bath-attendant, thrashed him with a birch-besom soaked in beer, rubbed him down with shredded linden bark,[1] then with a bit of woollen

[1] The bath-besom is made of birch-twigs with the leaves attached, and is soaked in hot water (or in beer) to keep it soft. The mas-

cloth, rolled a soap bladder over his master's shoulders,—this faithfully-devoted Irinárkh was accustomed to say every time, as he climbed down from the shelf as red as "a new brass statue": "Well, for this time I, the servant of God, Irinárkh Tolobýeeff, am still whole. . . . . What will happen next time?"

And Alexýei Sergyéitch spoke splendid Russian, somewhat old-fashioned, but piquant and pure as spring water, constantly interspersing his speech with his pet words: "honour bright," "God have mercy," "at any rate," "sir," and "little sir." . . . .

Enough concerning him, however. Let us talk about Alexýei Sergyéitch's spouse, Malánya Pávlovna.

Malánya Pávlovna was a native of Moscow, and had been accounted the greatest beauty in town, *la Vénus de Moscou*.—When I knew her she was already a gaunt old woman, with delicate but insignificant features, little curved hare-like teeth in a tiny little mouth, with a multitude of tight little curls on her forehead, and dyed eyebrows. She constantly wore a pyramidal cap with rose-coloured ribbons, a high ruff around her neck, a short white gown and prunella shoes with red heels; and over her gown she wore a

sage administered with the besom is delightful. The peasants often use besoms of nettles, as a luxury. The shredded linden bark is used as a sponge.—TRANSLATOR.

jacket of blue satin, with the sleeve depending from the right shoulder. She had worn precisely such a toilet on St. Peter's day, 1789! On that day, being still a maiden, she had gone with her relatives to the Khodýnskoe Field,[1] to see the famous prize-fight arranged by the Orlóffs.

"And Count Alexyéi Grigórievitch . . . ." (oh, how many times did I hear that tale!), . . . "having descried me, approached, made a low obeisance, holding his hat in both hands, and spake thus: ' My stunning beauty, why dost thou allow that sleeve to hang from thy shoulder? Is it that thou wishest to have a match at fisti-cuffs with me? . . . With pleasure; only I tell thee beforehand that thou hast vanquished me —I surrender!—and I am thy captive!'—and every one stared at us and marvelled."

And so she had worn that style of toilet ever since.

" Only, I wore no cap then, but a hat *à la ber-gère de Trianon;* and although I was powdered, yet my hair gleamed through it like gold! "

Malánya Pávlovna was stupid to sanctity, as the saying goes; she chattered at random, and did not herself quite know what issued from her mouth—but it was chiefly about Orlóff.—Or-lóff had become, one may say, the principal in-

---

[1] The great manœuvre plain, near which the Moscow garrison is lodged, in the vicinity of Petróvsky Park and Palace. Here the disaster took place during the coronation festivities of the present Emperor.—TRANSLATOR.

terest of her life. She usually entered—no! she floated into—the room, moving her head in a measured way like a peacock, came to a halt in the middle of it, with one foot turned out in a strange sort of way, and holding the pendent sleeve in two fingers (that must have been the pose which had pleased Orlóff once on a time), she looked about her with arrogant carelessness, as befits a beauty,—she even sniffed and whispered " The idea! " exactly as though some important cavalier-adorer were besieging her with compliments,—then suddenly walked on, clattering her heels and shrugging her shoulders.—She also took Spanish snuff out of a tiny bonbon box, scooping it out with a tiny golden spoon, and from time to time, especially when a new person made his appearance, she raised—not to her eyes, but to her nose (her vision was excellent)—a double lorgnette in the shape of a pair of horns, showing off and twisting about her little white hand with one finger standing out apart.

How many times did Malánya Pávlovna describe to me her wedding in the Church of the Ascension, " which is on the Arbát Square—such a fine church!—and all Moscow was present at it . . . . there was such a crush! 'T was frightful! There were equipages drawn by six horses, golden carriages, runners . . . . one of Count Zavadóvsky's runners even fell under the wheels!

And the bishop himself married us,[1] and what
an address he delivered! Everybody wept—
wherever I looked there was nothing but tears,
tears . . . . and the Governor-General's horses
were tiger-coloured. . . . And how many,
many flowers people brought! . . . They overwhelmed us with flowers! And one foreigner,
a rich, very rich man, shot himself for love on
that occasion, and Orlóff was present also. . . .
And approaching Alexyéi Sergyéitch he congratulated him and called him a lucky dog. . . .
' Thou art a lucky dog, brother gaper!' he said.
And in reply Alexyéi Sergyéitch made such a
wonderful obeisance, and swept the plume of his
hat along the floor from left to right . . . as
much as to say: ' There is a line drawn now,
Your Radiance, between you and my spouse
which you must not step across!'—And Orlóff,
Alexyéi Grigórievitch, immediately understood
and lauded him.—Oh, what a man he was! What
a man! And then, on another occasion, Alexis
and I were at a ball in his house—I was already
married—and what magnificent diamond but-

[1] It is very rarely that a bishop performs the marriage ceremony.
All bishops are monks; and monks are not supposed to perform
ceremonies connected with the things which they have renounced.
The exceptions are when monks are appointed parish priests (as in
some of the American parishes, for instance), and, therefore, must
fulfil the obligations of a married parish priest; or when the
chaplain-monk on war-ships is called upon, at times, to minister
to scattered Orthodox, in a port which has no settled priest.—
TRANSLATOR.

tons he wore! And I could not restrain myself, but praised them. 'What splendid diamonds you have, Count!' And thereupon he took a knife from the table, cut off one button and presented it to me—saying: ' You have in your eyes, my dear little dove, diamonds a hundredfold finer; just stand before the mirror and compare them.' And I did stand there, and he stood beside me.—' Well? Who is right?'—says he—and keeps rolling his eyes all round me. And then Alexyéi Sergyéitch was greatly dismayed; but I said to him: ' Alexis,' I said to him, ' please do not be dismayed; thou shouldst know me better!' And he answered me: ' Be at ease, Mélanie!'—And those same diamonds I now have encircling a medallion of Alexyéi Grigórievitch —I think, my dear, that thou hast seen me wear it on my shoulder on festival days, on a ribbon of St. George—because he was a very brave hero, a cavalier of the Order of St. George: he burned the Turks! " [1]

Notwithstanding all this, Malánya Pávlovna was a very kind woman; she was easy to please. —" She does n't nag you, and she does n't sneer at you," the maids said of her.—Malánya Pávlovna was passionately fond of all sweets, and a special old woman, who occupied herself with nothing but the preserves, and therefore was

---

[1] The Order of St. George, with its black and orange ribbon, must be won by great personal bravery—like the Victoria Cross.—
TRANSLATOR.

called the preserve-woman, brought to her, half
a score of times in a day, a Chinese plate now
with candied rose-leaves, again with barberries in
honey, or orange sherbet. Malánya Pávlovna
feared solitude—dreadful thoughts come then—
and was almost constantly surrounded by female hangers-on whom she urgently entreated:
" Talk, talk! Why do you sit there and do nothing but warm your seats? "—and they began
to twitter like canary-birds. Being no less devout than Alexyéi Sergyéitch, she was very fond
of praying; but as, according to her own words,
she had not learned to recite prayers well, she
kept for that purpose the widow of a deacon,
who prayed so tastily! She would never stum-
ble to all eternity! And, in fact, that deacon's
widow understood how to utter prayerful words
in an irrepressible sort of way, without a break
even when she inhaled or exhaled her breath—
and Malánya Pávlovna listened and melted with
emotion. She had another widow also attached
to her service; the latter's duty consisted in telling her stories at night,—" but only old ones,"
entreated Malánya Pávlovna, " those I already
know; all the new ones are spurious."

Malánya Pávlovna was very frivolous and
sometimes suspicious. All of a sudden she would
take some idea into her head. She did not like
the dwarf Janus, for example; it always seemed
to her as though he would suddenly start in and

begin to shriek: "But do you know who I am? A Buryát Prince! So, then, submit!"—And if she did not, he would set fire to the house out of melancholy. Malánya Pávlovna was as lavish as Alexyéi Sergyéitch; but she never gave money —she did not wish to soil her pretty little hands —but kerchiefs, ear-rings, gowns, ribbons, or she would send a patty from the table, or a bit of the roast, or if not that, a glass of wine. She was also fond of regaling the peasant-women on holidays. They would begin to dance, and she would click her heels and strike an attitude.

Alexyéi Sergyéitch was very well aware that his wife was stupid; but he had trained himself, almost from the first year of his married life, to pretend that she was very keen of tongue and fond of saying stinging things. As soon as she got to chattering he would immediately shake his little finger at her and say: "Okh, what a naughty little tongue! What a naughty little tongue! Won't it catch it in the next world! It will be pierced with red-hot needles!"—But Malánya Pávlovna did not take offence at this; on the contrary, she seemed to feel flattered at hearing such remarks—as much as to say: "Well, I can't help it! It is n't my fault that I was born witty!"

Malánya Pávlovna worshipped her husband, and all her life remained an exemplary and faithful wife. But there had been an "object" in her life also, a young nephew, a hussar, who had been slain, so she assumed, in a duel on her account—but, according to more trustworthy information, he had died from a blow received on the head from a billiard-cue, in tavern company. The water-colour portrait of this " object " was preserved by her in a secret casket. Malánya Pávlovna crimsoned to the very ears every time she alluded to Kapítonushka—that was the " object's " name;—while Alexyéi Sergyéitch scowled intentionally, again menaced his wife with his little finger and said, " Trust not a horse in the meadow, a wife in the house! Okh, that Kapítonushka, Kupidónushka!"—Then Malánya Pávlovna bristled up all over and exclaimed:

" Alexis, shame on you, Alexis!—You yourself probably flirted with divers little ladies in your youth—and so you take it for granted . . . ."

" Come, that will do, that will do, Malániushka," Alexyéi Sergyéitch interrupted her, with a smile;—" thy gown is white, and thy soul is whiter still! "

" It is whiter, Alexis; it is whiter! "

" Okh, what a naughty little tongue, on my honour, what a naughty little tongue! " repeated Alexyéi Sergyéitch, tapping her on the cheek.

To mention Malánya Pávlovna's " convictions " would be still more out of place than to mention those of Alexyéi Sergyéitch; but I once chanced to be the witness of a strange manifestation of my aunt's hidden feelings. I once chanced, in the course of conversation, to mention the well-known Sheshkóvsky.[1] Malánya Pávlovna suddenly became livid in the face,—as livid as a corpse,—turned green, despite the layer of paint and powder, and in a dull, entirely-genuine voice (which very rarely happened with her —as a general thing she seemed always somewhat affected, assumed an artificial tone and lisped) said: " Okh! whom hast thou mentioned! And at nightfall, into the bargain!—Don't utter that name! " I was amazed; what significance could that name possess for such an inoffensive and innocent being, who would not have known how to devise, much less to execute, anything reprehensible?—This alarm, which revealed itself after a lapse of nearly half a century, induced in me reflections which were not altogether cheerful.

Alexyéi Sergyéitch died in his eighty-eighth year, in the year 1848, which evidently disturbed even him. And his death was rather strange. That morning he had felt well, although he no longer quitted his arm-chair at all. But suddenly he called to his wife: " Malániushka, come hither! "

" What dost thou want, Alexis? "

" It is time for me to die, that 's what, my darling."

[1] Head of the Secret Service under Alexander I.—TRANSLATOR.

"God be with you, Alexyéi Sergyéitch! Why so?"

"This is why. In the first place, one must show moderation; and more than that; I was looking at my legs a little while ago . . . they were strange legs—and that settles it!—I looked at my hands—and those were strange also! I looked at my belly—and the belly belonged to some one else!—Which signifies that I am devouring some other person's life.[1] Send for the priest; and in the meanwhile, lay me on my bed, from which I shall not rise again."

Malánya Pávlovna was in utter consternation, but she put the old man to bed, and sent for the priest. Alexyéi Sergyéitch made his confession, received the holy communion, took leave of the members of his household, and began to sink into a stupor. Malánya Pávlovna was sitting beside his bed.

"Alexis!" she suddenly shrieked, "do not frighten me, do not close thy dear eyes! Hast thou any pain?"

The old man looked at his wife.—"No, I have no pain . . . . but I find it . . . . rather difficult . . . . difficult to breathe." Then, after a brief pause:—"Malániushka," he said, "now life has galloped past—but dost thou remember our wedding . . . . what a fine young couple we were?"

---

[1] That is, living too long.—Translator.

"We were, my beauty, Alexis my incomparable one!"

Again the old man remained silent for a space.

"And shall we meet again in the other world, Malániushka?"

"I shall pray to God that we may, Alexis."—And the old woman burst into tears.

"Come, don't cry, silly one; perchance the Lord God will make us young again there—and we shall again be a fine young pair!"

"He will make us young, Alexis!"

"Everything is possible to Him, to the Lord," remarked Alexyéi Sergyéitch.—"He is a worker of wonders!—I presume He will make thee a clever woman also. . . . Come, my dear, I was jesting; give me thy hand to kiss."

"And I will kiss thine."

And the two old people kissed each other's hands.

Alexyéi Sergyéitch began to quiet down and sink into a comatose state. Malánya Pávlovna gazed at him with emotion, brushing the tears from her eyelashes with the tip of her finger. She sat thus for a couple of hours.

"Has he fallen asleep?" asked in a whisper the old woman who knew how to pray so tastily, peering out from behind Irinárkh, who was standing as motionless as a pillar at the door, and staring intently at his dying master.

"Yes," replied Malánya Pávlovna, also in a

whisper. And suddenly Alexyéi Sergyéitch opened his eyes.

"My faithful companion," he stammered, "my respected spouse, I would like to bow myself to thy feet for all thy love and faithfulness —but how am I to rise? Let me at least sign thee with the cross."

Malánya Pávlovna drew nearer, bent over. . . . But the hand which had been raised fell back powerless on the coverlet, and a few moments later Alexyéi Sergyéitch ceased to be.

His daughters with their husbands only arrived in time for the funeral; neither one of them had any children. Alexyéi Sergyéitch had not discriminated against them in his will, although he had not referred to them on his death-bed.

"My heart is locked against them," he had said to me one day. Knowing his kind-heartedness, I was surprised at his words.—It is a difficult matter to judge between parents and children.—"A vast ravine begins with a tiny rift," Alexyéi Sergyéitch had said to me on another occasion, referring to the same subject. "A wound an arshín long will heal over, but if you cut off so much as a nail, it will not grow again!"

I have an idea that the daughters were ashamed of their eccentric old folks.

A month later Malánya Pávlovna expired

also. She hardly rose from her bed again after the day of Alexyéi Sergyéitch's death, and did not array herself; but they buried her in the blue jacket, and with the medal of Orlóff on her shoulder, only minus the diamonds. The daughters shared those between them, under the pretext that those diamonds were to be used for the setting of holy pictures; but as a matter of fact they used them to adorn their own persons.

And now how vividly do my old people stand before me, and what a good memory I cherish of them! And yet, during my very last visit to them (I was already a student at the time) an incident occurred which injected some discord into the harmoniously-patriarchal mood with which the Telyégin house inspired me.

Among the number of the household serfs was a certain Iván, nicknamed " Sukhíkh—the coachman, or the little coachman, as he was called, on account of his small size, in spite of his years, which were not few. He was a tiny scrap of a man, nimble, snub-nosed, curly-haired, with a perennial smile on his infantile countenance, and little, mouse-like eyes. He was a great joker and buffoon; he was able to acquire any trick; he set off fireworks, snakes, played all card-games, galloped his horse while standing erect on it, flew higher than any one else in the swing, and even knew how to present Chinese shadows. There was no one who could

amuse children better than he, and he would
have been only too glad to occupy himself with
them all day long. When he got to laughing
he set the whole house astir. People would answer him from this point and that—every one
would join in. . . They would both abuse him
and laugh.—Iván danced marvellously—especially "the fish."—The chorus would thunder
out a dance tune, the young fellow would
step into the middle of the circle, and begin to
leap and twist about and stamp his feet, and
then come down with a crash on the ground—
and there represent the movements of a fish
which has been thrown out of the water upon the
dry land; and he would writhe about this way
and that, and even bring his heels up to his neck;
and then, when he sprang to his feet and began
to shout, the earth would simply tremble beneath him! Alexyéi Sergyéitch was extremely
fond of choral songs and dances, as I have already said; he could never refrain from shouting: "Send hither Vániushka! the little coachman! Give us 'the fish,' be lively!"—and a
minute later he would whisper in ecstasy: "Akh,
what a devil of a man he is!"

Well, then,—on my last visit this same Iván
Sukhíkh comes to me in my room, and without
uttering a word plumps down on his knees.

"What is the matter with thee, Iván?"

"Save me, master!"

" Why, what 's the trouble? "

And thereupon Iván related to me his grief.

He had been swapped twenty years previously by the Messrs. Sukhóy for another serf, a man belonging to the Telyégins—he had simply been exchanged, without any formalities and documents. The man who had been given in exchange for him had died, but the Messrs. Sukhóy had forgotten all about Iván and had left him in Alexyéi Sergyéitch's house as his property; his nickname alone served as a reminder of his origin.[1]—But lo and behold! his former owners had died also, their estate had fallen into other hands, and the new owner, concerning whom rumours were in circulation to the effect that he was a cruel man, a torturer, having learned that one of his serfs was to be found at Alexyéi Sergyéitch's without any passport and right, began to demand his return; in case of refusal he threatened to have recourse to the courts and a penalty—and he did not threaten idly, as he himself held the rank of Privy Councillor,[2] and had great weight in the government.[3] Iván, in his affright, darted to Alexyéi Sergyéitch. The old man was sorry for his dancer, and he offered to buy Iván from the privy councillor

[1] *Sukhóy,* dry; *Sukhíkh,* genitive plural (proper names are declinable), meaning, " one of the Sukhóys."—TRANSLATOR.

[2] The third from the top in the Table of Ranks instituted by Peter the Great.—TRANSLATOR.

[3] Corresponding, in a measure, to an American State.—TRANSLATOR.

at a good price; but the privy councillor would not hear of such a thing; he was a Little Russian and obstinate as the devil. The poor fellow had to be surrendered.

" I have got used to living here, I have made myself at home here, I have eaten bread here, and here I wish to die," Iván said to me—and there was no grin on his face now; on the contrary, he seemed turned into stone. . . . " But now I must go to that malefactor. . . . Am I a dog that I am to be driven from one kennel to another with a slip-noose round my neck—and a ' take that '? Save me, master; entreat your uncle,—remember how I have always amused you. . . . Or something bad will surely come of it; the matter will not pass off without sin."

" Without what sin, Iván? "

" Why, I will kill that gentleman.—When I arrive I shall say to him: ' Let me go back, master; otherwise, look out, beware . . . . I will kill you.' "

If a chaffinch or a bullfinch could talk and had begun to assure me that it would claw another bird, it would not have caused me greater astonishment than did Iván on that occasion.—What! Ványa Sukhíkh, that dancer, jester, buffoon, that favourite of the children, and a child himself —that kindest-hearted of beings—a murderer! What nonsense! I did not believe him for a single moment. I was startled in the extreme that he should have been able to utter such a word! Nevertheless, I betook myself to Alexyéi Sergyéitch. I did not repeat to him what Iván had said to me, but I tried in every way to beg him to see whether he could not set the matter right.

"My little sir," the old man replied to me, "I would be only too delighted, but how can I?— I have offered that Topknot[1] huge remuneration. I offered him three hundred rubles, I assure thee on my honour! but in vain. What is one to do? We had acted illegally, on faith, after the ancient fashion . . . . and now see what a bad thing has come of it! I am sure that Topknot will take Iván from me by force the first thing we know; he has a strong hand, the Governor eats sour cabbage-soup with him—the Topknot will send a soldier! I 'm afraid of those soldiers! In former days, there 's no denying it, I would have defended Iván,—but just look at me now, how decrepit I have grown. How am I to wage war?"—And, in fact, during my last visit I found that Alexyéi Sergyéitch had aged very greatly; even the pupils of his eyes had acquired a milky hue—like that in infants—and on his lips there appeared not the discerning smile of former days, but that strainedly-sweet, unconscious smirk which never

[1] The Great Russians' scornful nickname for a Little Russian.—TRANSLATOR.

leaves the faces of very old people even in their sleep.

I imparted Alexyéi Sergyéitch's decision to Iván. He stood a while, held his peace, and shook his head.—" Well," he said at last, " what is fated to be cannot be avoided. Only my word is firm. That is to say: only one thing remains for me . . . play the wag to the end.—Master, please give me something for liquor! " I gave it; he drank himself drunk—and on that same day he danced " the fish " in such wise that the maidens and married women fairly squealed with delight, so whimsically amusing was he.

The next day I went home, and three months later—when I was already in Petersburg—I learned that Iván had actually kept his word!— He had been sent to his new master; his master had summoned him to his study and announced to him that he was to serve as his coachman, that he entrusted him with a tróika of Vyátka horses,[1] and that he should exact a strict account from him if he treated them badly, and, in general, if he were not punctual.—" I 'm not fond of jesting," he said.—Iván listened to his master, first made obeisance to his very feet, and then informed him that it was as his mercy liked, but he could not be his servant.—" Release me on quit-

[1] Each coachman has his own pair or tróika of horses to attend to, and has nothing to do with any other horses which may be in the stable.—Translator.

rent, Your High-Born," he said, " or make a soldier of me; otherwise there will be a catastrophe before long."

The master flared up.—" Akh, damn thee! What is this thou darest to say to me?—Know, in the first place, that I am ' Your Excellency,' and not ' Your High-Born '; in the second place, thou art beyond the age, and thy size is not such that I can hand thee over as a soldier; and, in conclusion,—what calamity art thou threatening me with? Art thou preparing to commit arson? "

" No, your Excellency, not to commit arson."

" To kill me, then, pray? "

Iván maintained a stubborn silence.—" I will not be your servant," he said at last.

" Here, then, I 'll show thee," roared the gentleman, " whether thou wilt be my servant or not!"—And after having cruelly flogged Iván, he nevertheless ordered that the tróika of Vyátka horses should be placed in his charge, and appointed him a coachman at the stables.

Iván submitted, to all appearances; he began to drive as coachman. As he was a proficient in that line his master speedily took a fancy to him,—the more so as Iván behaved very discreetly and quietly, and the horses throve under his care; he tended them so that they became as plump as cucumbers,—one could never leave off admiring them! The master began to drive out more frequently with him than with the other coachmen. He used to ask: " Dost thou remember, Iván, how unpleasant was thy first meeting with me? I think thou hast got rid of thy folly? " But to these words Iván never made any reply.

So, then, one day, just before the Epiphany, the master set out for the town with Iván in his tróika with bells, in a broad sledge lined with rugs. The horses began to ascend a hill at a walk, while Iván descended from the box and went back to the sledge, as though he had dropped something.—The cold was very severe. The master sat there all wrapped up, and with his beaver cap drawn down over his ears. Then Iván pulled a hatchet out from under the skirts of his coat, approached his master from behind, knocked off his cap, and saying: " I warned thee, Piótr Petróvitch—now thou hast thyself to thank for this! "—he laid open his head with one slash. Then he brought the horses to a standstill, put the cap back on his murdered master's head, and again mounting the box, he drove him to the town, straight to the court-house.

" Here 's the general from Sukhóy for you, murdered; and I killed him.—I told him I would do it, and I have done it. Bind me! "

They seized Iván, tried him, condemned him to the knout and then to penal servitude.—The merry, bird-like dancer reached the mines—and there vanished forever. . . .

Yes; involuntarily—although in a different sense,—one repeats with Alexyéi Sergyéitch:— "The old times were good . . . . well, yes, but God be with them! I want nothing to do with them!"

THE SONG OF LOVE
TRIUMPHANT

(1881)

THE SONG OF LOVE TRIUMPHANT

MDXLII

DEDICATED TO THE MEMORY OF GUSTAVE FLAUBERT

Wage du zu irren und zu träumen!

SCHILLER.

THE following is what I read in an Italian manuscript:

I

ABOUT the middle of the sixteenth century there dwelt in Ferrara— (it was then flourishing under the sceptre of its magnificent dukes, the patrons of the arts and of poetry) —there dwelt two young men, named Fabio and Muzio. Of the same age and nearly related, they were almost never separated; a sincere friendship had united them since their early childhood, and a similarity of fate had strengthened this bond. Both belonged to ancient families; both were wealthy, independent, and without family; the tastes and inclinations of both were similar. Muzio occupied himself with music, Fabio with painting. All Ferrara was proud of them as the finest ornaments of the Court, of society, and of the city. But in personal appearance they did not resemble each other, although both were distinguished for their stately, youthful beauty. Fabio was the taller of the two, white of complexion, with ruddy-gold hair, and had blue eyes. Muzio, on the contrary, had a swarthy face, black hair, and in his dark-brown eyes there was not that merry gleam, on his lips not that cordial smile, which Fabio had; his thick eyebrows overhung his narrow eyelids, while Fabio's golden brows rose in slender arches on his pure, smooth forehead. Muzio was less animated in conversation also; nevertheless both friends were equally favoured by the ladies; for not in vain were they models of knightly courtesy and lavishness.

At one and the same time with them there dwelt in Ferrara a maiden named Valeria. She was considered one of the greatest beauties in the city, although she was to be seen only very rarely, as she led a retired life and left her house only to go to church;—and on great festivals for a walk. She lived with her mother, a noblyborn but not wealthy widow, who had no other children. Valeria inspired in every one whom she met a feeling of involuntary amazement and of equally involuntary tender respect: so modest was her mien, so little aware was she, to all appearance, of the full force of her charms. Some persons, it is true, thought her rather pale; the glance of her eyes, which were almost always lowered, expressed a certain shyness and even timidity; her lips smiled rarely, and then but slightly; hardly ever did any one hear her voice. But a rumour was in circulation to the effect that it was very beautiful, and that, locking herself in her chamber, early in the morning, while everything in the city was still sleeping, she loved to warble ancient ballads to the strains of a lute, upon which she herself played. Despite the pallor of her face, Valeria was in blooming health; and even the old people, as they looked on her, could not refrain from thinking:—" Oh, how happy will be that young man for whom this bud still folded in its petals, still untouched and virgin, shall at last unfold itself!"

II

Fabio and Muzio beheld Valeria for the first time at a sumptuous popular festival, got up at the command of the Duke of Ferrara, Ercole, son of the famous Lucrezia Borgia, in honour of some distinguished grandees who had arrived from Paris on the invitation of the Duchess, the daughter of Louis XII, King of France. Side by side with her mother sat Valeria in the centre of an elegant tribune, erected after drawings by Palladius on the principal square of Ferrara for the most honourable ladies of the city. Both

Fabio and Muzio fell passionately in love with her that day; and as they concealed nothing from each other, each speedily learned what was going on in his comrade's heart. They agreed between themselves that they would both try to make close acquaintance with Valeria, and if she should deign to choose either one of them the other should submit without a murmur to her decision.

Several weeks later, thanks to the fine reputation which they rightfully enjoyed, they succeeded in penetrating into the not easily accessible house of the widow; she gave them permission to visit her. From that time forth they were able to see Valeria almost every day and to converse with her;—and with every day the flame kindled in the hearts of both young men blazed more and more vigorously. But Valeria displayed no preference for either of them, although their presence evidently pleased her. With Muzio she occupied herself with music; but she chatted more with Fabio: she was less shy with him. At last they decided to learn their fate definitely, and sent to Valeria a letter wherein they asked her to explain herself and say on whom she was prepared to bestow her hand. Valeria showed this letter to her mother, and informed her that she was content to remain unmarried; but if her mother thought it was time for her to marry, she would wed the man of her mother's choice. The honourable widow shed a few tears at the thought of parting from her beloved child; but there was no reason for rejecting the suitors: she considered them both equally worthy of her daughter's hand. But as she secretly preferred Fabio, and suspected that he was more to Valeria's taste also, she fixed upon him. On the following day Fabio learned of his happiness: and all that was left to Muzio was to keep his word and submit.

This he did; but he was not able to be a witness to the triumph of his friend, his rival. He immediately sold the greater part of his property, and collecting a few thousand ducats, he set off on a long journey to the Orient. On taking leave of Fabio he said to him that he would not return until he should feel that the last traces of passion in him had vanished. It was painful for Fabio to part from the friend of his childhood and his youth . . . . but the joyful anticipation of approaching bliss speedily swallowed up all other sentiments—and he surrendered himself completely to the transports of happy love.

He soon married Valeria, and only then did he learn the full value of the treasure which it had fallen to his lot to possess. He had a very beautiful villa at a short distance from Ferrara; he removed thither with his wife and her mother. A bright time then began for them. Wedded life displayed in a new and captivating light all

Valeria's perfections. Fabio became a remarkable artist,—no longer a mere amateur, but a master. Valeria's mother rejoiced and returned thanks to God as she gazed at the happy pair. Four years flew by unnoticed like a blissful dream. One thing alone was lacking to the young married couple, one thing caused them grief: they had no children . . . . but hope had not deserted them. Toward the end of the fourth year a great, and this time a genuine grief, visited them: Valeria's mother died, after an illness of a few days.

Valeria shed many tears; for a long time she could not reconcile herself to her loss. But another year passed; life once more asserted its rights and flowed on in its former channel. And, lo! one fine summer evening, without having forewarned any one, Muzio returned to Ferrara.

III

DURING the whole five years which had elapsed since his departure, no one had known anything about him. All rumours concerning him had died out, exactly as though he had vanished from the face of the earth. When Fabio met his friend on one of the streets in Ferrara he came near crying out aloud, first from fright, then from joy, and immediately invited him to his villa. There, in the garden, was a spacious, detaehed pavilion; he suggested that his friend should settle down in that pavilion. Muzio gladly accepted, and that same day removed thither with his servant, a dumb Malay—dumb but not deaf, and even, judging from the vivacity of his glance, a very intelligent man. . . . His tongue had been cut out. Muzio had brought with him scores of chests filled with divers precious things which he had collected during his prolonged wanderings.

Valeria was delighted at Muzio's return; and he greeted her in a cheerfully-friendly but composed manner. From everything it was obvious that he had kept the promise made to Fabio. In the course of the day he succeeded in installing himself in his pavilion; with the aid of his Malay he set out the rarities he had brought—rugs, silken tissues, garments of velvet and brocade, weapons, cups, dishes, and beakers adorned with enamel, articles of gold and silver set with pearls and turquoises, carved caskets of amber and ivory, faceted flasks, spices, perfumes, pelts of wild beasts, the feathers of unknown birds, and a multitude of other objects, the very use of which seemed mysterious and incomprehensible. Among the number of all these precious things there was one rich pearl necklace which Muzio had received from the Shah of Persia for a certain great and mysterious service; he asked Valeria's permission to place this necklace on her neck with his own hand; it seemed to her heavy, and as though endowed with a strange sort of warmth . . . . it fairly adhered to the skin. Toward evening, after dinner, as they sat on the terrace of the villa, in the shade of oleanders and laurels, Muzio began to narrate his adventures. He told of the distant lands which he had seen, of mountains higher than the clouds, of rivers like unto seas; he told of vast buildings and temples, of trees thousands of years old, of rainbow-hued flowers and birds; he enumerated the cities and peoples he had visited . . . . (their very names exhaled something magical). All the Orient was familiar to Muzio: he had traversed Persia and Arabia, where the horses are more noble and beautiful than all other living creatures; he had penetrated the depths of India, where is a race of people resembling magnificent plants; he had attained to the confines of China and Tibet, where a living god, the Dalai Lama by name, dwells upon earth in the form of a speechless man with narrow eyes. Marvellous were his tales! Fabio and Valeria listened to him as though enchanted.

In point of fact, Muzio's features had undergone but little change: swarthy from childhood, his face had grown still darker,—had been burned beneath the rays of a more brilliant sun, —his eyes seemed more deeply set than of yore,

that was all; but the expression of that face had
become different: concentrated, grave, it did not
grow animated even when he alluded to the dan-
gers to which he had been subjected by night in
the forests, deafened by the roar of tigers, by
day on deserted roads where fanatics lie in wait
for travellers and strangle them in honour of
an iron goddess who demands human blood.
And Muzio's voice had grown more quiet and
even; the movements of his hands, of his whole
body, had lost the flourishing ease which is peculiar to the Italian race.

With the aid of his servant, the obsequiously-
alert Malay, he showed his host and hostess several tricks which he had been taught by the
Brahmins of India. Thus, for example, having
preliminarily concealed himself behind a curtain,
he suddenly appeared sitting in the air, with his
legs doubled up beneath him, resting the tips of
his fingers lightly on a bamboo rod set upright,
which not a little amazed and even alarmed
Fabio and Valeria. . . "Can it be that he is a
magician?" the thought occurred to her.—But
when he set to calling out tame snakes from
a covered basket by whistling on a small flute,—
when, wiggling their fangs, their dark, flat heads
made their appearance from beneath the motley
stuff, Valeria became frightened and begged
Muzio to hide away those horrors as quickly as
possible.

At supper Muzio regaled his friends with wine of Shiraz from a round flask with a long neck; extremely fragrant and thick, of a golden hue, with greenish lights, it sparkled mysteriously when poured into the tiny jasper cups. In taste it did not resemble European wines: it was very sweet and spicy; and, quaffed slowly, in small sips, it produced in all the limbs a sensation of agreeable drowsiness. Muzio made Fabio and Valeria drink a cup apiece, and drank one himself. Bending over her cup, he whispered something and shook his fingers. Valeria noticed this; but as there was something strange and unprecedented in all Muzio's ways in general, and in all his habits, she merely thought: " I wonder if he has not accepted in India some new faith, or whether they have such customs there? "— Then, after a brief pause, she asked him: " Had he continued to occupy himself with music during the time of his journeys? "— In reply Muzio ordered the Malay to bring him his Indian violin. It resembled those of the present day, only, instead of four strings it had three; a bluish snake-skin was stretched across its top, and the slender bow of reed was semi-circular in form, and on its very tip glittered a pointed diamond.

Muzio first played several melancholy airs,— which were, according to his assertion, popular ballads,—strange and even savage to the Italian ear; the sound of the metallic strings was plaintive and feeble. But when Muzio began the last song, that same sound suddenly strengthened, quivered powerfully and resonantly; the passionate melody poured forth from beneath the broadly-handled bow,—poured forth with beautiful undulations, like the snake which had covered the top of the violin with its skin; and with so much fire, with so much triumphant joy did this song beam and blaze that both Fabio and Valeria felt a tremor at their heart, and the tears started to their eyes . . . . while Muzio, with his head bent down and pressed against his violin, with pallid cheeks, and brows contracted into one line, seemed still more concentrated and serious than ever, and the diamond at the tip of the bow scattered ray-like sparks in its flight, as though it also were kindled with the fire of that wondrous song. And when Muzio had finished and, still holding the violin tightly pressed between his chin and his shoulder, dropped his hand which held the bow—"What is that? What hast thou been playing to us?" Fabio exclaimed. —Valeria uttered not a word, but her whole being seemed to repeat her husband's question. Muzio laid the violin on the table, and lightly shaking back his hair, said, with a courteous smile: "That? That melody . . . . that song I heard once on the island of Ceylon. That song is known there, among the people, as the song of happy, satisfied love."

"Repeat it," whispered Fabio.

"No; it is impossible to repeat it," replied Muzio. "And it is late now. Signora Valeria ought to rest; and it is high time for me also. . . . I am weary."

All day long Muzio had treated Valeria in a respectfully-simple manner, like a friend of long standing; but as he took leave he pressed her hand very hard, jamming his fingers into her palm, staring so intently into her face the while that she, although she did not raise her eyelids, felt conscious of that glance on her suddenly-flushing cheeks. She said nothing to Muzio, but drew away her hand, and when he was gone she stared at the door through which he had made his exit. She recalled how, in former years also, she had been afraid of him . . . . and now she was perplexed. Muzio went off to his pavilion; the husband and wife withdrew to their bed-chamber.

IV

VALERIA did not soon fall asleep; her blood was surging softly and languidly, and there was a faint ringing in her head . . . . from that strange wine, as she supposed, and, possibly, also from Muzio's tales, from his violin playing. . . . Toward morning she fell asleep at last, and had a remarkable dream.

It seems to her that she enters a spacious room

with a low, vaulted ceiling. . . . She has never
seen such a room in her life. All the walls are
set with small blue tiles bearing golden patterns;
slender carved pillars of alabaster support the
marble vault; this vault and the pillars seem
semi-transparent. . . . A   pale,   rose-coloured
light penetrates the room from all directions,
illuminating all the objects mysteriously and
monotonously; cushions of gold brocade lie on
a narrow rug in the very middle of the floor,
which is as smooth as a mirror. In the corners, barely visible, two tall incense-burners,
representing monstrous animals, are smoking;
there are no windows anywhere; the door,
screened by a velvet drapery, looms silently
black in a niche of the wall. And suddenly this
curtain softly slips aside, moves away . . . .
and Muzio enters. He bows, opens his arms,
smiles. . . . His harsh arms encircle Valeria's
waist; his dry lips have set her to burning all
over. . . . She falls prone on the cushions. . . .

    *   *   *   *   *

Moaning with fright, Valeria awoke after long
efforts.—Still not comprehending where she is
and what is the matter with her, she half raises
herself up in bed and looks about her. . . . A
shudder runs through her whole body. . . .
Fabio is lying beside her. He is asleep; but his
face, in the light of the round, clear moon, is as
pale as that of a corpse . . . . it is more melan-

choly than the face of a corpse. Valeria awoke
her husband—and no sooner had he cast a glance
at her than he exclaimed: " What is the matter
with thee? "

" I have seen . . . I have seen a dreadful
dream," she whispered, still trembling. . . .

But at that moment, from the direction of the
pavilion, strong sounds were wafted to them—
and both Fabio and Valeria recognised the melody which Muzio had played to them, calling it
the Song of Love Triumphant.—Fabio cast a
glance of surprise at Valeria. . . . She closed
her eyes, and turned away—and both, holding
their breath, listened to the song to the end.
When the last sound died away the moon went
behind a cloud, it suddenly grew dark in the
room. . . . The husband and wife dropped
their heads on their pillows, without exchanging
a word, and neither of them noticed when the
other fell asleep.

V

ON the following morning Muzio came to breakfast; he seemed pleased, and greeted Valeria
merrily. She answered him with confusion,—
scrutinised him closely, and was startled by that
pleased, merry face, those piercing and curious
eyes. Muzio was about to begin his stories

again . . . . but Fabio stopped him at the first word.

"Evidently, thou wert not able to sleep in a new place? My wife and I heard thee playing the song of last night."

"Yes? Did you hear it?"—said Muzio.—"I did play it, in fact; but I had been asleep before that, and I had even had a remarkable dream."

Valeria pricked up her ears.—"What sort of a dream?" inquired Fabio.

"I seemed," replied Muzio, without taking his eyes from Valeria, "to see myself enter a spacious apartment with a vaulted ceiling, decorated in Oriental style. Carved pillars supported the vault; the walls were covered with tiles, and although there were no windows nor candles, yet the whole room was filled with a rosy light, just as though it had all been built of transparent stone. In the corners Chinese incense-burners were smoking; on the floor lay cushions of brocade, along a narrow rug. I entered through a door hung with a curtain, and from another door directly opposite a woman whom I had once loved made her appearance. And she seemed to me so beautiful that I became all aflame with my love of days gone by . . . ."

Muzio broke off significantly. Valeria sat motionless, only paling slowly . . . . and her breathing grew more profound.

"Then," pursued Muzio, "I woke up and played that song."

"But who was the woman?" said Fabio.

"Who was she? The wife of an East Indian. I met her in the city of Delhi. . . . She is no longer among the living. She is dead."

"And her husband?" asked Fabio, without himself knowing why he did so.

"Her husband is dead also, they say. I soon lost sight of them."

"Strange!" remarked Fabio.—"My wife also had a remarkable dream last night— which she did not relate to me," added Fabio.

But at this point Valeria rose and left the room. Immediately after breakfast Muzio also went away, asserting that he was obliged to go to Ferrara on business, and that he should not return before evening.

VI

SEVERAL weeks before Muzio's return Fabio had begun a portrait of his wife, depicting her with the attributes of Saint Cecilia.—He had made noteworthy progress in his art; the famous Luini, the pupil of Leonardo da Vinci, had come to him in Ferrara, and aiding him with his own advice, had also imparted to him the precepts of his great master. The portrait was almost finished; it only remained for him to complete the

face by a few strokes of the brush, and then
Fabio might feel justly proud of his work.

When Muzio departed to Ferrara, Fabio betook himself to his studio, where Valeria was generally awaiting him; but he did not find her
there; he called to her—she did not respond. A
secret uneasiness took possession of Fabio; he
set out in quest of her. She was not in the house;
Fabio ran into the garden—and there, in one
of the most remote alleys, he descried Valeria.
With head bowed upon her breast, and hands
clasped on her knees, she was sitting on a bench,
and behind her, standing out against the dark
green of a cypress, a marble satyr, with face distorted in a malicious smile, was applying his
pointed lips to his reed-pipes. Valeria was
visibly delighted at her husband's appearance,
and in reply to his anxious queries she said that
she had a slight headache, but that it was of no
consequence, and that she was ready for the sitting. Fabio conducted her to his studio, posed
her, and took up his brush; but, to his great vexation, he could not possibly finish the face as he
would have liked. And that not because it was
somewhat pale and seemed fatigued . . . . no;
but he did not find in it that day the pure, holy
expression which he so greatly loved in it, and
which had suggested to him the idea of representing Valeria in the form of Saint Cecilia. At last
he flung aside his brush, told his wife that he

was not in the mood, that it would do her good to lie down for a while, as she was not feeling quite well, to judge by her looks,—and turned his easel so that the portrait faced the wall. Valeria agreed with him that she ought to rest, and repeating her complaint of headache, she retired to her chamber.

Fabio remained in the studio. He felt a strange agitation which was incomprehensible even to himself. Muzio's sojourn under his roof, a sojourn which he, Fabio, had himself invited, embarrassed him. And it was not that he was jealous . . . . was it possible to be jealous of Valeria?—but in his friend he did not recognise his former comrade. All that foreign, strange, new element which Muzio had brought with him from those distant lands—and which, apparently, had entered into his very flesh and blood,—all those magical processes, songs, strange beverages, that dumb Malay, even the spicy odour which emanated from Muzio's garments, from his hair, his breath,—all this inspired in Fabio a feeling akin to distrust, nay, even to timidity. And why did that Malay, when serving at table, gaze upon him, Fabio, with such disagreeable intentness? Really, one might suppose that he understood Italian. Muzio had said concerning him, that that Malay, in paying the penalty with his tongue, had made a great sacrifice, and in compensation now possessed great power.—What power? And how could he have acquired it at the cost of his tongue? All this was very strange! Very incomprehensible!

Fabio went to his wife in her chamber; she was lying on the bed fully dressed, but was not asleep.—On hearing his footsteps she started, then rejoiced again to see him, as she had done in the garden. Fabio sat down by the bed, took Valeria's hand, and after a brief pause, he asked her, "What was that remarkable dream which had frightened her during the past night? And had it been in the nature of that dream which Muzio had related?"

Valeria blushed and said hastily—"Oh, no! no! I saw . . . some sort of a monster, which tried to rend me."

"A monster? In the form of a man?" inquired Fabio.

"No, a wild beast . . . . a wild beast!"—And Valeria turned away and hid her flaming face in the pillows. Fabio held his wife's hand for a while longer; silently he raised it to his lips, and withdrew.

The husband and wife passed a dreary day. It seemed as though something dark were hanging over their heads . . . . but what it was, they could not tell. They wanted to be together, as though some danger were menacing them;—but what to say to each other, they did not know.

Fabio made an effort to work at the portrait, to read Ariosto, whose poem, which had recently made its appearance in Ferrara, was already famous throughout Italy; but he could do nothing. . . . . Late in the evening, just in time for supper, Muzio returned.

VII

HE appeared calm and contented—but related few stories; he chiefly interrogated Fabio concerning their mutual acquaintances of former days, the German campaign, the Emperor Charles; he spoke of his desire to go to Rome, to have a look at the new Pope. Again he offered Valeria wine of Shiraz—and in reply to her refusal he said, as though to himself, "It is not necessary now."

On returning with his wife to their bedroom Fabio speedily fell asleep . . . . and waking an hour later was able to convince himself that no one shared his couch: Valeria was not with him. He hastily rose, and at the selfsame moment he beheld his wife, in her night-dress, enter the room from the garden. The moon was shining brightly, although not long before a light shower had passed over.—With widely-opened eyes, and an expression of secret terror on her impassive face, Valeria approached the bed, and fumbling for it with her hands, which were outstretched in front of her, she lay down hurriedly and in silence. Fabio asked her a question, but she made no reply; she seemed to be asleep. He touched her, and felt rain-drops on her clothing, on her hair, and grains of sand on the soles of her bare feet. Then he sprang up and rushed into the garden through the half-open door. The moonlight, brilliant to harshness, inundated all objects. Fabio looked about him and descried on the sand of the path traces of two pairs of feet; one pair was bare; and those tracks led to an arbour covered with jasmin, which stood apart, between the pavilion and the house. He stopped short in perplexity; and lo! suddenly the notes of that song which he had heard on the preceding night again rang forth! Fabio shuddered, and rushed into the pavilion. . . . Muzio was standing in the middle of the room, playing on his violin. Fabio darted to him.

" Thou hast been in the garden, thou hast been out, thy clothing is damp with rain."

" No . . . . I do not know . . . . I do not think . . . . that I have been out of doors . . . ." replied Muzio, in broken accents, as though astonished at Fabio's advent, and at his agitation.

Fabio grasped him by the arm.—" And why art thou playing that melody again? Hast thou had another dream? "

Muzio glanced at Fabio with the same surprise as before, and made no answer.

" Come, answer me! "

> "The moon is steel, like a circular shield . . .
> The river gleams like a snake . . . .
> The friend is awake, the enemy sleeps—
> The hawk seizes the chicken in his claws . . . .
> Help! "

mumbled Muzio, in a singsong, as though in
state of unconsciousness.

Fabio retreated a couple of paces, fixed h
eyes on Muzio, meditated for a space . . . . an
returned to his house, to the bed-chamber.

With her head inclined upon her shoulder, an
her arms helplessly outstretched, Valeria wa
sleeping heavily. He did not speedily succeed i
waking her . . . . but as soon as she saw hi
she flung herself on his neck, and embraced hi
convulsively; her whole body was quivering.

" What aileth thee, my dear one, what ailet
thee? " said Fabio repeatedly, striving to sootl
her.

But she continued to lie as in a swoon on h
breast. " Akh, what dreadful visions I see! " sl
whispered, pressing her face against him.

Fabio attempted to question her . . . . bu
she merely trembled. . . .

The window-panes were reddening with th
first gleams of dawn when, at last, she fell aslee
in his arms.

VIII

ON the following day Muzio disappeared early
in the morning, and Valeria informed her husband that she intended to betake herself to the
neighbouring monastery, where dwelt her spiritual father—an aged and stately monk, in whom
she cherished unbounded confidence. To Fabio's
questions she replied that she desired to alleviate
by confession her soul, which was oppressed with
the impressions of the last few days. As he
gazed at Valeria's sunken visage, as he listened to
her faint voice, Fabio himself approved of her
plan: venerable Father Lorenzo might be able to
give her useful advice, disperse her doubts. . . .
Under the protection of four escorts, Valeria
set out for the monastery, but Fabio remained
at home; and while awaiting the return of his
wife, he roamed about the garden, trying to
understand what had happened to her, and feeling the unremitting terror and wrath and pain
of indefinite suspicions. . . More than once he
entered the pavilion; but Muzio had not returned, and the Malay stared at Fabio like a
statue, with an obsequious inclination of his head,
and a far-away grin—at least, so it seemed to
Fabio—a far-away grin on his bronze countenance.

In the meantime Valeria had narrated every-

thing in confession to her confessor, being les
ashamed than frightened. The confessor lis
tened to her attentively, blessed her, absolved he
from her involuntary sins,—but thought to him
self: " Magic, diabolical witchcraft . . . . thing
cannot be left in this condition " . . . . and ac
companied Valeria to her villa, ostensibly for th
purpose of definitely calming and comforting
her.

At the sight of the confessor Fabio was some
what startled; but the experienced old man had
already thought out beforehand how he ough
to proceed. On being left alone with Fabio, h
did not, of course, betray the secrets of the con
fessional; but he advised him to banish from hi
house, if that were possible, his invited gues
who, by his tales, songs, and his whole conduct
had upset Valeria's imagination. Moreover, ir
the old man's opinion, Muzio had not been firn
in the faith in days gone by, as he now recalled
to mind; and after having sojourned so long ir
regions not illuminated by the light of Christian
ity, he might have brought thence the infectior
of false doctrines; he might even have dabbled ir
magic; and therefore, although old friendship
did assert its rights, still wise caution pointed to
parting as indispensable.

Fabio thoroughly agreed with the venerable
monk. Valeria even beamed all over when her
husband communicated to her her confessor's

counsel; and accompanied by the good wishes of both husband and wife, and provided with rich gifts for the monastery and the poor, Father Lorenzo wended his way home.

Fabio had intended to have an explanation with Muzio directly after supper, but his strange guest did not return to supper. Then Fabio decided to defer the interview with Muzio until the following day, and husband and wife withdrew to their bed-chamber.

IX

VALERIA speedily fell asleep; but Fabio could not get to sleep. In the nocturnal silence all that he had seen, all that he had felt, presented itself to him in a still more vivid manner; with still greater persistence did he ask himself questions, to which, as before, he found no answer. Was Muzio really a magician? And had he already poisoned Valeria? She was ill . . . . but with what malady? While he was engrossed in painful meditations, with his head propped on his hand and restraining his hot breathing, the moon again rose in the cloudless sky; and together with its rays, through the semi-transparent window-panes, in the direction of the pavilion, there began to stream in—or did Fabio merely imagine it?—there began to stream in a breath resembling a faint, perfumed current of air. . . .

Now an importunate, passionate whisper began
to make itself heard . . . and at that same moment he noticed that Valeria was beginning to
stir slightly. He started, gazed; she rose, thrust
first one foot, then the other from the bed, and,
like a somnambulist, with her dull eyes strained
straight ahead, and her arms extended before
her, she advanced toward the door into the garden! Fabio instantly sprang through the other
door of the bedroom, and briskly running round
the corner of the house, he closed the one which
led into the garden. . . . He had barely succeeded in grasping the handle when he felt some
one trying to open the door from within, throwing their force against it . . . . more and more
strongly . . . . then frightened moans resounded.

*   *   *   *   *

"But Muzio cannot have returned from the
town, surely," flashed through Fabio's head, and
he darted into the pavilion. . . .

What did he behold?

Coming to meet him, along the path brilliantly
flooded with the radiance of the moonlight, also
with arms outstretched and lifeless eyes staring
widely—was Muzio. . . . Fabio ran up to him,
but the other, without noticing him, walked on,
advancing with measured steps, and his impassive face was smiling in the moonlight like the
face of the Malay. Fabio tried to call him by
name . . . . but at that moment he heard a win-

dow bang in the house behind him. . . . He glanced round. . . .

In fact, the window of the bedroom was open from top to bottom, and with one foot thrust across the sill stood Valeria in the window . . . and her arms seemed to be seeking Muzio, her whole being was drawn toward him.

Unspeakable wrath flooded Fabio's breast in a suddenly-invading torrent.—"Accursed sorcerer!" he yelled fiercely, and seizing Muzio by the throat with one hand, he fumbled with the other for the dagger in his belt, and buried its blade to the hilt in his side.

Muzio uttered a piercing shriek, and pressing the palm of his hand to the wound, fled, stumbling, back to the pavilion. . . . But at that same instant, when Fabio stabbed him, Valeria uttered an equally piercing shriek and fell to the ground like one mowed down.

Fabio rushed to her, raised her up, carried her to the bed, spoke to her. . . .

For a long time she lay motionless; but at last she opened her eyes, heaved a deep sigh, convulsively and joyously, like a person who has just been saved from inevitable death,—caught sight of her husband, and encircling his neck with her arms, pressed herself to his breast.

"Thou, thou, it is thou," she stammered. Gradually the clasp of her arms relaxed, her head sank backward, and whispering, with a blissful smile:—" Thank God, all is over. . . . But how weary I am!"—she fell into a profound but not heavy slumber.

X

FABIO sank down beside her bed, and never taking his eyes from her pale, emaciated, but already tranquil face, he began to reflect upon what had taken place . . . . and also upon how he ought to proceed now. What was he to do? If he had slain Muzio—and when he recalled how deeply the blade of his dagger had penetrated he could not doubt that he had done so—then it was impossible to conceal the fact. He must bring it to the knowledge of the Duke, of the judges . . . . but how was he to explain, how was he to narrate such an incomprehensible affair? He, Fabio, had slain in his own house his relative, his best friend! People would ask, "What for? For what cause? . . ." But what if Muzio were not slain?—Fabio had not the strength to remain any longer in uncertainty, and having made sure that Valeria was asleep, he cautiously rose from his arm-chair, left the house, and directed his steps toward the pavilion. All was silent in it; only in one window was a light visible. With sinking heart he opened the outer door—(a trace of bloody fingers still clung to it, and on the sand of the path drops of blood made black patches) —traversed the first dark chamber . . . . and halted on the threshold, petrified with astonishment.

In the centre of the room, on a Persian rug, with a brocade cushion under his head, covered with a wide scarlet shawl with black figures, lay Muzio, with all his limbs stiffly extended. His face, yellow as wax, with closed eyes and lids which had become blue, was turned toward the ceiling, and no breath was to be detected: he seemed to be dead. At his feet, also enveloped in a scarlet shawl, knelt the Malay. He held in his left hand a branch of some unfamiliar plant, resembling a fern, and bending slightly forward, he was gazing at his master, never taking his eyes from him. A small torch, thrust into the floor, burned with a greenish flame, and was the only light in the room. Its flame did not flicker nor smoke.

The Malay did not stir at Fabio's entrance, but merely darted a glance at him and turned his eyes again upon Muzio. From time to time he raised himself a little, and lowered the branch, waving it through the air,—and his dumb lips slowly parted and moved, as though uttering inaudible words. Between Muzio and the Malay there lay upon the floor the dagger with which Fabio had stabbed his friend. The Malay smote the blood-stained blade with his bough. One minute passed . . . . then another. Fabio approached the Malay, and bending toward him, he said in a low voice: " Is he dead? "—The Malay bowed his head, and disengaging his right hand from beneath the shawl, pointed imperiously to the door. Fabio was about to repeat his question, but the imperious hand repeated its gesture, and Fabio left the room, raging and marvelling but submitting.

He found Valeria asleep, as before, with a still more tranquil face. He did not undress, but seated himself by the window, propped his head on his hand, and again became immersed in thought. The rising sun found him still in the same place. Valeria had not wakened.

XI

FABIO was intending to wait until she should awake, and then go to Ferrara—when suddenly some one tapped lightly at the door of the bed-room. Fabio went out and beheld before him his aged major-domo, Antonio.

" Signor," began the old man, " the Malay has just informed us that Signor Muzio is ailing and desires to remove with all his effects to the town; and therefore he requests that you will furnish him with the aid of some persons to pack his things—and that you will send, about dinner-time, both pack- and saddle-horses and a few men as guard. Do you permit? "

"Did the Malay tell thee that?" inquired Fabio. "In what manner? For he is dumb."

"Here, signor, is a paper on which he wrote all this in our language, very correctly."

"And Muzio is ill, sayest thou?"

"Yes, very ill, and he cannot be seen."

"Has not a physician been sent for?"

"No; the Malay would not allow it."

"And was it the Malay who wrote this for thee?"

"Yes, it was he."

Fabio was silent for a space.

"Very well, take the necessary measures," he said at last.

Antonio withdrew.

Fabio stared after his servant in perplexity. —"So he was not killed?"—he thought . . . . and he did not know whether to rejoice or to grieve.—"He is ill?"—But a few hours ago he had beheld him a corpse!

Fabio returned to Valeria. She was awake, and raised her head. The husband and wife exchanged a long, significant look.

"Is he already dead?" said Valeria suddenly. —Fabio shuddered.

"What . . . he is not?—Didst thou . . . . Has he gone away?" she went on.

Fabio's heart was relieved.—"Not yet; but he is going away to-day."

"And I shall never, never see him again?"

" Never."

" And those visions will not be repeated?"

" No."

Valeria heaved another sigh of relief; a blissful smile again made its appearance on her lips. She put out both hands to her husband.

" And we shall never speak of him, never, hearest thou, my dear one. And I shall not leave this room until he is gone. But now do thou send me my serving-women . . . . and stay: take that thing!"—she pointed to a pearl necklace which lay on the night-stand, the necklace which Muzio had given her,—" and throw it immediately into our deep well. Embrace me—I am thy Valeria —and do not come to me until . . . . that man is gone."

Fabio took the necklace—its pearls seemed to have grown dim—and fulfilled his wife's behest. Then he began to roam about the garden, gazing from a distance at the pavilion, around which the bustle of packing was already beginning. Men were carrying out chests, lading horses . . . . but the Malay was not among them. An irresistible feeling drew Fabio to gaze once more on what was going on in the pavilion. He recalled the fact that in its rear façade there was a secret door through which one might penetrate to the interior of the chamber where Muzio had been lying that morning. He stole up to that door, found it unlocked, and pushing aside the folds of a heavy curtain, darted in an irresolute glance.

XII

Muzio was no longer lying on the rug. Dressed in travelling attire, he was sitting in an arm-chair, but appeared as much of a corpse as at Fabio's first visit. The petrified head had fallen against the back of the chair, the hands lay flat, motionless, and yellow on the knees. His breast did not heave. Round about the chair, on the floor strewn with dried herbs, stood several flat cups filled with a dark liquid which gave off a strong, almost suffocating odour,—the odour of musk. Around each cup was coiled a small, copper-coloured serpent, which gleamed here and there with golden spots; and directly in front of Muzio, a couple of paces distant from him, rose up the tall figure of the Malay, clothed in a motley-hued mantle of brocade, girt about with a tiger's tail, with a tall cap in the form of a horned tiara on his head.

But he was not motionless: now he made devout obeisances and seemed to be praying, again he drew himself up to his full height, even stood on tiptoe; now he threw his hands apart in broad and measured sweep, now he waved them urgently in the direction of Muzio, and seemed to be menacing or commanding with them, as he contracted his brows in a frown and stamped his foot. All these movements evidently cost him great effort, and even caused him suffering: he breathed heavily, the sweat streamed from his

face. Suddenly he stood stock-still on one spot,
and inhaling the air into his lungs and scowling,
he stretched forward, then drew toward him his
clenched fists, as though he were holding reins in
them . . . . and to Fabio's indescribable horror,
Muzio's head slowly separated itself from the
back of the chair and reached out after the Malay's hands. . . . The Malay dropped his hands,
and Muzio's head again sank heavily backward;
the Malay repeated his gestures, and the obedient head repeated them after him. The dark
liquid in the cups began to seethe with a faint
sound; the very cups themselves emitted a faint
tinkling, and the copper snakes began to move
around each of them in undulating motion.
Then the Malay advanced a pace, and elevating
his eyebrows very high and opening his eyes until they were of huge size, he nodded his head
at Muzio . . . . and the eyelids of the corpse
began to flutter, parted unevenly, and from beneath them the pupils, dull as lead, revealed
themselves. With proud triumph and joy—a
joy that was almost malicious—beamed the face
of the Malay; he opened his lips widely, and
from the very depths of his throat a prolonged
roar wrested itself with an effort. . . . Muzio's
lips parted also, and a faint groan trembled on
them in reply to that inhuman sound.

But at this point Fabio could endure it no
longer: he fancied that he was witnessing some

devilish incantations! He also uttered a shriek and started off at a run homeward, without looking behind him,—homeward as fast as he could go, praying and crossing himself as he ran.

XIII

THREE hours later Antonio presented himself before him with the report that everything was ready, all the things were packed, and Signor Muzio was preparing to depart. Without uttering a word in answer to his servant, Fabio stepped out on the terrace, whence the pavilion was visible. Several pack-horses were grouped in front of it; at the porch itself a powerful black stallion, with a roomy saddle adapted for two riders, was drawn up. There also stood the servants with bared heads and the armed escort. The door of the pavilion opened and, supported by the Malay, Muzio made his appearance. His face was deathlike, and his arms hung down like those of a corpse,—but he walked . . . . yes! he put one foot before the other, and once mounted on the horse, he held himself upright, and got hold of the reins by fumbling. The Malay thrust his feet into the stirrups, sprang up behind him on the saddle, encircled his waist with his arm,— and the whole procession set out. The horses proceeded at a walk, and when they made the turn in front of the house, Fabio fancied that on Mu-

zio's dark countenance two small white patches
gleamed. . . . Could it be that he had turned his
eyes that way?—The Malay alone saluted him
. . . . mockingly, but as usual.

Did Valeria see all this? The shutters of her
windows were closed . . . . but perhaps she was
standing behind them.

XIV

At dinner-time she entered the dining-room, and
was very quiet and affectionate; but she still
complained of being weary. Yet there was no
agitation about her, nor any of her former constant surprise and secret fear; and when, on the
day after Muzio's departure, Fabio again set
about her portrait, he found in her features that
pure expression, the temporary eclipse of which
had so disturbed him . . . . and his brush flew
lightly and confidently over the canvas.

Husband and wife began to live their life as of
yore. Muzio had vanished for them as though
he had never existed. And both Fabio and Va
leria seemed to have entered into a compact not
to recall him by a single sound, not to inquire
about his further fate; and it remained a mystery
for all others as well. Muzio really did vanish, a
though he had sunk through the earth. One day
Fabio thought himself bound to relate to Valeria
precisely what had occurred on that fateful night

194

LOVE TRIUMPHANT

. . . . but she, probably divining his intention, held her breath, and her eyes narrowed as though she were anticipating a blow. . . . And Fabio understood her: he did not deal her that blow.

One fine autumnal day Fabio was putting the finishing touches to the picture of his Cecilia; Valeria was sitting at the organ, and her fingers were wandering over the keys. . . . Suddenly, contrary to her own volition, from beneath her fingers rang out that Song of Love Triumphant which Muzio had once played,—and at that same instant, for the first time since her marriage, she felt within her the palpitation of a new, germinating life. . . . Valeria started and stopped short. . . .

What was the meaning of this? Could it be . . .

WITH this word the manuscript came to an end.

CLARA MÍLITCH

(1882)

CLARA MÍLITCH

A TALE

I

IN the spring of 1878 there lived in Moscow,
in a small wooden house on Shabólovka
Street, a young man five-and-twenty years of
age, Yákoff Arátoff by name. With him lived
his aunt, an old maid, over fifty years of age, his
father's sister, Platonída Ivánovna. She managed his housekeeping and took charge of his ex-
penditures, of which Arátoff was utterly incapable. He had no other relations. Several years
before, his father, a petty and not wealthy noble
of the T * * * government, had removed to Moscow, together with him and Platonída Ivánovna
who, by the way, was always called Platósha; and
her nephew called her so too. When he quitted
the country where all of them had constantly
dwelt hitherto, old Arátoff had settled in the capital with the object of placing his son in the university, for which he had himself prepared him;
he purchased for a trifling sum a small house on
one of the remote streets, and installed himself
therein with all his books and "preparations."

And of books and preparations he had many, for he was a man not devoid of learning . . . . " a supernatural eccentric," according to the words of his neighbours. He even bore among them the reputation of a magician: he had even received the nickname of " the insect-observer." He busied himself with chemistry, mineralogy, entomology, botany, and medicine; he treated voluntary patients with herbs and metallic powders of his own concoction, after the method of Paracelsus. With those same powders he had sent into the grave his young, pretty, but already too delicate wife, whom he had passionately loved, and by whom he had had an only son. With those same metallic powders he had wrought considerable havoc with the health of his son also, which, on the contrary, he had wished to reinforce, as he detected in his organisation anæmia and a tendency to consumption inherited from his mother. The title of " magician " he had acquired, among other things, from the fact that he considered himself a great-grandson—not in the direct line, of course—of the famous Bruce, in whose honour he had named his son Yákoff.[1] He was the sort of man who is called " very good-natured," but of a melancholy temperament, fussy, and timid, with a predilection for everything that was mysterious

---

[1] Yákoff (James) Daniel Bruce, a Russian engineer, of Scottish extraction, born in Moscow, 1670, became Grand Master of the Artillery in 1711, and died in 1735.—TRANSLATOR.

or mystical. . . . " Ah!" uttered in a half-whisper was his customary exclamation; and he died with that exclamation on his lips, two years after his removal to Moscow.

His son Yákoff did not, in outward appearance, resemble his father, who had been homely in person, clumsy and awkward; he reminded one rather of his mother. There were the same delicate, pretty features, the same soft hair of ash-blonde hue, the same plump, childish lips, and large, languishing, greenish-grey eyes, and feathery eyelashes. On the other hand in disposition he resembled his father; and his face, which did not resemble his father's, bore the stamp of his father's expression; and he had angular arms, and a sunken chest, like old Arátoff, who, by the way, should hardly be called an old man, since he did not last to the age of fifty. During the latter's lifetime Yákoff had already entered the university, in the physico-mathematical faculty; but he did not finish his course,—not out of idleness, but because, according to his ideas, a person can learn no more in the university than he can teach himself at home; and he did not aspire to a diploma, as he was not intending to enter the government service. He avoided his comrades, made acquaintance with hardly any one, was especially shy of women, and lived a very isolated life, immersed in his books. He was shy of women, although he had a very tender heart, and was captivated by beauty. . . . He even acquired the luxury of an English keepsake, and (Oh, for shame!) admired the portraits of divers, bewitching Gulnares and Medoras which "adorned" it. . . . . But his inborn modesty constantly restrained him. At home he occupied his late father's study, which had also been his bedroom; and his bed was the same on which his father had died.

The great support of his whole existence, his unfailing comrade and friend, was his aunt, that Platósha, with whom he exchanged barely ten words a day, but without whom he could not take a step. She was a long-visaged, long-toothed being, with pale eyes in a pale face, and an unvarying expression partly of sadness, partly of anxious alarm. Eternally attired in a grey gown, and a grey shawl which was redolent of camphor, she wandered about the house like a shadow, with noiseless footsteps; she sighed, whispered prayers—especially one, her favourite, which consisted of two words: "Lord, help!"— and managed the housekeeping very vigorously, hoarding every kopék and buying everything herself. She worshipped her nephew; she was constantly fretting about his health, was constantly in a state of alarm, not about herself but about him, and as soon as she thought there was anything the matter with him, she would quietly approach and place on his writing-table a cup of herb-tea, or stroke his back with her hands, which were as soft as wadding.

This coddling did not annoy Yákoff, but he did not drink the herb-tea, and only nodded approvingly. But neither could he boast of his health. He was extremely sensitive, nervous, suspicious; he suffered from palpitation of the heart, and sometimes from asthma. Like his father, he believed that there existed in nature and in the soul of man secrets, of which glimpses may sometimes be caught, though they cannot be understood; he believed in the presence of certain forces and influences, sometimes well-disposed but more frequently hostile . . . . and he also believed in science,—in its dignity and worth. Of late he had conceived a passion for photography. The odour of the ingredients used in that connection greatly disturbed his old aunt,—again not on her own behalf, but for Yásha's sake, on account of his chest. But with all his gentleness of disposition he possessed no small portion of stubbornness, and he diligently pursued his favourite occupation. " Platósha " submitted, and merely sighed more frequently than ever, and whispered " Lord, help! " as she gazed at his fingers stained with iodine.

Yákoff, as has already been stated, shunned his comrades; but with one of them he struck up a rather close friendship, and saw him frequently, even after that comrade, on leaving the university, entered the government service, which, however, was not very exacting: to use his own words, he had "tacked himself on" to the building of the Church of the Saviour[1] without, of course, knowing anything whatever about architecture. Strange to say, that solitary friend of Arátoff's, Kupfer by name, a German who was Russified to the extent of not knowing a single word of German, and even used the epithet "German"[2] as a term of opprobrium,—that friend had, to all appearance, nothing in common with him. He was a jolly, rosy-cheeked young fellow with black, curly hair, loquacious, and very fond of that feminine society which Arátoff so shunned. Truth to tell, Kupfer breakfasted and dined with him rather often, and even—as he was not a rich man—borrowed small sums of money from him; but it was not that which made the free-and-easy German so diligently frequent the little house on Shabólovka Street. He had taken a liking to Yákoff's spiritual purity, his "ideality,"—possibly as a contrast to what he daily encountered and beheld;—or, perhaps, in that same attraction toward "ideality" the young man's German blood revealed itself. And Yákoff liked Kupfer's good-natured frankness; and in addi-

---

[1] The great cathedral in commemoration of the Russian triumph in the war of 1812, which was begun in 1837, and completed in 1883.—TRANSLATOR.

[2] *Nyémetz,* "the dumb one," meaning any one unable to speak Russian (hence, any foreigner), is the specific word for a German. —TRANSLATOR.

tion to this, his tales of the theatres, concerts, and balls which he constantly attended—in general of that alien world into which Yákoff could not bring himself to penetrate—secretly interested and even excited the young recluse, yet without arousing in him a desire to test all this in his own experience. And Platósha liked Kupfer; she sometimes thought him too unceremonious, it is true; but instinctively feeling and understanding that he was sincerely attached to her beloved Yásha, she not only tolerated the noisy visitor, but even felt a kindness for him.

II

AT the time of which we are speaking, there was in Moscow a certain widow, a Georgian Princess, —a person of ill-defined standing and almost a suspicious character. She was about forty years of age; in her youth she had, probably, bloomed with that peculiar oriental beauty, which so quickly fades; now she powdered and painted herself, and dyed her hair a yellow hue. Various, not altogether favourable, and not quite definite, rumours were in circulation about her; no one had known her husband—and in no one city had she lived for any length of time. She had neither children nor property; but she lived on a lavish scale,—on credit or otherwise. She held a salon, as the saying is, and received a decidedly mixed company—chiefly composed of young men. Her whole establishment, beginning with her own toilette, furniture, and table, and ending with her equipage and staff of servants, bore a certain stamp of inferiority, artificiality, transitoriness . . . but neither the Princess herself nor her guests, apparently, demanded anything better. The Princess was reputed to be fond of music and literature, to be a patroness of actors and artists; and she really did take an 'interest in these " questions," even to an enthusiastic degree—and even to a pitch of rapture which was not altogether simulated. She indubitably did possess the æsthetic chord. Moreover, she was very accessible, amiable, devoid of pretensions, of affectation, and—a fact which many did not suspect—in reality extremely kind, tenderhearted and obliging. . . . Rare qualities, and therefore all the more precious, precisely in individuals of that stamp.

" A frivolous woman!" one clever person said concerning her, " and she will infallibly get into paradise! For she forgives everything—and everything will be forgiven her!"—It was also said concerning her that when she disappeared from any town, she always left behind her as many creditors as persons whom she had loaded with benefits. A soft heart can be pressed in any direction you like.

Kupfer, as was to be expected, was a visitor at

her house, and became very intimate with her . . .
altogether too intimate, so malicious tongues asserted. But he always spoke of her not only in a
friendly manner, but also with respect; he lauded
her as a woman of gold—interpret that as you
please!—and was a firm believer in her love for
art, and in her comprehension of art!—So then,
one day after dinner, at the Arátoffs', after having discussed the Princess and her evening gath-
erings, he began to urge Yákoff to break in upon
his life of an anchorite for once, and permit him,
Kupfer, to introduce him to his friend. At first
Yákoff would not hear to anything of the sort.

"Why, what idea hast thou got into thy
head?" exclaimed Kupfer at last. "What sort of
a presentation is in question? I shall simply take
thee, just as thou art now sitting there, in thy
frock-coat, and conduct thee to her evening.
They do not stand on ceremony in the least there,
brother! Here now, thou art learned, and thou
art fond of music" (there actually was in Arátoff's study a small piano, on which he occasionally struck a few chords in diminished sevenths)
—"and in her house there is any quantity of that
sort of thing! . . . And there thou wilt meet
sympathetic people, without any airs! And, in
conclusion, it is not right that at thy age, with thy
personal appearance" (Arátoff dropped his eyes
and waved his hand)—"yes, yes, with thy personal appearance, thou shouldst shun society, the

world, in this manner! I 'm not going to take thee
to call on generals, seest thou! Moreover, I don't
know any generals myself! . . . . Don't be
stubborn, my dear fellow! Morality is a good
thing, a thing worthy of respect. . . . But why
give thyself up to asceticism? Assuredly, thou
art not preparing to become a monk!"

Arátoff continued, nevertheless, to resist; but
Platonída Ivánovna unexpectedly came to Kupfer's assistance. Although she did not quite understand the meaning of the word "asceticism,"
still she also thought that it would not be a bad
idea for Yáshenka to divert himself, to take a
look at people,—and show himself.—"The more
so," she added, "that I have confidence in Feódor
Feódoritch! He will not take thee to any bad
place! . . . ."

"I 'll restore him to thee in all his pristine purity!" cried Kupfer, at whom Platonída Ivánovna,
in spite of her confidence, kept casting uneasy
glances; Arátoff blushed to his very ears—but he
ceased to object.

It ended in Kupfer taking him, on the following day, to the Princess's evening assembly. But
Arátoff did not remain there long. In the first
place, he found at her house about twenty guests,
men and women, who were, presumably, sympathetic, but who were strangers to him, nevertheless; and this embarrassed him, although he was
obliged to talk very little: but he feared this most

of all. In the second place, he did not like the
hostess herself, although she welcomed him very
cordially and unaffectedly. Everything about
her displeased him; her painted face, and her
churned-up curls, and her hoarsely-mellifluous
voice, her shrill laugh, her way of rolling up her
eyes, her too *décolleté* bodice—and those plump,
shiny fingers with a multitude of rings! . . .
Slinking off into a corner, he now swiftly ran his
eyes over the faces of all the guests, as though he
did not even distinguish one from another; again
he stared persistently at his own feet. But when,
at last, an artist who had just come to town, with
a drink-sodden countenance, extremely long hair,
and a bit of glass under his puckered brow, seated
himself at the piano, and bringing down his hands
on the keys and his feet on the pedals, with a
flourish, began to bang out a fantasia by Liszt on
a Wagnerian theme, Arátoff could stand it no
longer, and slipped away, bearing in his soul a
confused and oppressive impression, athwart
which, nevertheless, there pierced something
which he did not understand, but which was significant and even agitating.

III

Kupfer came on the following day to dinner; but
he did not enlarge upon the preceding evening,
he did not even reproach Arátoff for his hasty

flight, and merely expressed regret that he had not waited for supper, at which champagne had been served! (of Nízhegorod[1] fabrication, we may remark in parenthesis).

Kupfer probably understood that he had made a mistake in trying to rouse his friend, and that Arátoff was a man who positively was not adapted to that sort of society and manner of life. On his side, Arátoff also did not allude to the Princess or to the night before. Platonída Ivánovna did not know whether to rejoice at the failure of this first attempt or to regret it. She decided, at last, that Yásha's health might suffer from such expeditions, and regained her complacency. Kupfer went away directly after dinner, and did not show himself again for a whole week. And that not because he was sulking at Arátoff for the failure of his introduction,—the good-natured fellow was incapable of such a thing,—but he had, evidently, found some occupation which engrossed all his time, all his thoughts;—for thereafter he rarely came to the Arátoff's', wore an abstracted aspect, and soon vanished.
. . . . Arátoff continued to live on as before; but some hitch, if we may so express ourselves, had secured lodgment in his soul. He still recalled something or other, without himself being quite aware what it was precisely,—and that "something" referred to the evening which he had

[1] Short for Nízhni Nóvgorod.—TRANSLATOR.

spent at the Princess's house. Nevertheless, he had not the slightest desire to return to it; and society, a section of which he had inspected in her house, repelled him more than ever. Thus passed six weeks.

And lo! one morning, Kupfer again presented himself to him, this time with a somewhat embarrassed visage.

" I know," he began, with a forced laugh, " that thy visit that evening was not to thy taste; but I hope that thou wilt consent to my proposal nevertheless . . . and wilt not refuse my request."

" What art thou talking about? " inquired Arátoff.

"See here," pursued Kupfer, becoming more and more animated; " there exists here a certain society of amateurs and artists, which from time to time organises readings, concerts, even theatrical representations, for philanthropic objects. . . ."

"And the Princess takes part?" interrupted Arátoff.

" The Princess always takes part in good works—but that is of no consequence. We have got up a literary and musical morning . . . . and at that performance thou mayest hear a young girl . . . . a remarkable young girl!—We do not quite know, as yet, whether she. will turn out a Rachel or a Viardot . . . . for she sings splendidly, and declaims and acts. . . . She has talent of the first class, my dear fellow! I am not exaggerating.—So here now . . . wilt not thou take a ticket?—Five rubles if thou wishest the first row."

"And where did this wonderful young girl come from?" asked Arátoff.

Kupfer grinned.—"That I cannot say. . . . Of late she has found an asylum with the Princess. The Princess, as thou knowest, is a patron of all such people. . . . And it is probable that thou sawest her that evening."

Arátoff started inwardly, faintly . . . . but made no answer.

"She has even acted somewhere in country districts," went on Kupfer, "and, on the whole, she was created for the theatre. Thou shalt see for thyself!"

"Is her name Clara?" asked Arátoff.

"Yes, Clara . . . ."

"Clara!" interrupted Arátoff again.—"It cannot be!"

"Why not?—Clara it is, . . . Clara Mílitch; that is not her real name . . . . but that is what she is called. She is to sing a romance by Glinka . . . . and one by Tchaikóvsky, and then she will recite the letter from 'Evgény Onyégin'[1]— Come now! Wilt thou take a ticket?"

---

[1] The famous letter from the heroine, Tatyána, to the hero, Evgény Onyégin, in Púshkin's celebrated poem. The music to the opera of the same name, which has this poem for its basis, is by Tchaikóvsky.—TRANSLATOR.

"But when is it to be?"

"To-morrow . . . . to-morrow, at half-past one, in a private hall, on Ostozhyónka Street. . . . I will come for thee. A ticket at five rubles? . . . Here it is. . . . No, this is a three-ruble ticket.— Here it is.—And here is the affiche.[1]—I am one of the managers."

Arátoff reflected. Platonída Ivánovna entered the room at that moment and, glancing at his face, was suddenly seized with agitation.— "Yásha," she exclaimed, "what ails thee? Why art thou so excited? Feódor Feódorovitch, what hast thou been saying to him?"

But Arátoff did not give his friend a chance to answer his aunt's question, and hastily seizing the ticket which was held out to him, he ordered Platonída Ivánovna to give Kupfer five rubles on the instant.

She was amazed, and began to blink her eyes. . . . Nevertheless, she handed Kupfer the money in silence. Yáshenka had shouted at her in a very severe manner.

"She's a marvel of marvels, I tell thee!" cried Kupfer, darting toward the door.—"Expect me to-morrow!"

"Has she black eyes?" called Arátoff after him.

[1] Advertisements of theatres, concerts, and amusements in general, are not published in the daily papers, but in an *affiche,* printed every morning, for which a separate subscription is necessary.— TRANSLATOR.

"As black as coal!" merrily roared Kupfer, and disappeared.

Arátoff went off to his own room, while Platonída Ivánovna remained rooted to the spot, repeating: "Help, Lord! Lord, help!"

IV

THE large hall in a private house on Ostozhyónka Street was already half filled with spectators when Arátoff and Kupfer arrived. Theatrical representations were sometimes given in that hall, but on this occasion neither stage-scenery nor curtain were visible. Those who had organised the "morning" had confined themselves to erecting a platform at one end, placing thereon a piano and a couple of music-racks, a few chairs, a table with a carafe of water and a glass, and hanging a curtain of red cloth over the door which led to the room set apart for the artists. In the first row the Princess was already seated, clad in a bright green gown; Arátoff placed himself at some distance from her, after barely exchanging a bow with her. The audience was what is called motley; it consisted chiefly of young men from various institutions of learning. Kupfer, in his quality of a manager, with a white ribbon on the lapel of his dress-coat, bustled and fussed about with all his might; the Princess was visibly excited, kept looking about her, launching smiles in

all directions, and chatting with her neighbours
. . . . there were only men in her immediate vicinity.

The first to make his appearance on the platform was a flute-player of consumptive aspect, who spat out . . . . that is to say, piped out a piece which was consumptive like himself. Two persons shouted "Bravo!" Then a fat gentleman in spectacles, very sedate and even grim of aspect, recited in a bass voice a sketch by Shtchedrín;[1] the audience applauded the sketch, not him.— Then the pianist, who was already known to Arátoff, presented himself, and pounded out the same Liszt fantasia; the pianist was favoured with a recall. He bowed, with his hand resting on the back of a chair, and after each bow he tossed back his hair exactly like Liszt! At last, after a decidedly long intermission, the red cloth over the door at the rear of the platform moved, was drawn widely apart, and Clara Mílitch made her appearance. The hall rang with applause. With unsteady steps she approached the front of the platform, came to a halt, and stood motionless, with her large, red, ungloved hands crossed in front of her, making no curtsey, neither bending her head nor smiling.

She was a girl of nineteen, tall, rather broad-shouldered, but well built. Her face was swarthy,

---

[1] M. E. Saltikóff wrote his famous satires under the name of Shtchedrín.—TRANSLATOR.

partly Hebrew, partly Gipsy in type; her eyes were small and black beneath thick brows which almost met, her nose was straight, slightly up-turned, her lips were thin with a beautiful but sharp curve; she had a huge braid of black hair, which was heavy even to the eye, a low, impassive, stony brow, tiny ears . . . . her whole counte-nance was thoughtful, almost surly. A passion-ate, self-willed nature,—not likely to be either kindly or even intelligent,—but gifted, was mani-fested by everything about her.

For a while she did not raise her eyes, but sud-denly gave a start and sent her intent but not attentive glance, which seemed to be buried in herself, along the rows of spectators.

"What tragic eyes!" remarked a certain grey-haired fop, who sat behind Arátoff, with the face of a courtesan from Revel,—one of Moscow's well-known first-nighters and rounders. The fop was stupid and intended to utter a bit of non-sense . . . . but he had spoken the truth! Ará-toff, who had never taken his eyes from Clara since she had made her appearance, only then re-called that he actually had seen her at the Prin-cess's; and had not only seen her, but had even noticed that she had several times looked at him with particular intentness out of her dark, watch-ful eyes. And on this occasion also . . . . or did he merely fancy that it was so?—on catching sight of him in the first row, she seemed to be delighted, seemed to blush—and again she gazed intently at him. Then, without turning round, she retreated a couple of paces in the direction of the piano, at which the accompanist, the long-haired foreigner, was already seated. She was to execute Glinka's romance, " As soon as I recognised thee . . . ." She immediately began to sing, without altering the position of her hands and without glancing at the notes. Her voice was soft and resonant,—a contralto,—she pronounced her words distinctly and forcibly, and sang monotonously, without shading but with strong expression.

" The lass sings with conviction," remarked the same fop who sat behind Arátoff,—and again he spoke the truth.

Shouts of " Bis!" " Bravo!" resounded all about, but she merely darted a swift glance at Arátoff, who was neither shouting nor clapping, —he had not been particularly pleased by her singing,—made a slight bow and withdrew, without taking the arm of the hairy pianist which he had crooked out like a cracknel. She was recalled . . . . but it was some time before she made her appearance, advanced to the piano with the same uncertain tread as before, and after whispering a couple of words to her accompanist, who was obliged to get and place on the rack before him not the music he had prepared but something else, —she began Tchaikóvsky's romance: " No, only he who hath felt the thirst of meeting". . . .

217

This romance she sang in a different way from
the first—in an undertone, as though she were
weary . . . and only in the line before the last,
"He will understand how I have suffered,"—did
a ringing, burning cry burst from her. The last
line, "And how I suffer . . . ." she almost
whispered, sadly prolonging the final word. This
romance produced a slighter impression on the
audience than Glinka's; but there was a great
deal of applause. . . . Kupfer, in particular,
distinguished himself: he brought his hands together in a peculiar manner, in the form of a cask,
when he clapped, thereby producing a remarkably sonorous noise. The Princess gave him a
large, dishevelled bouquet, which he was to present to the songstress; but the latter did not appear to perceive Kupfer's bowed figure, and his
hand outstretched with the bouquet, and she
turned and withdrew, again without waiting for
the pianist, who had sprung to his feet with still
greater alacrity than before to escort her, and
who, being thus left in the lurch, shook his hair
as Liszt himself, in all probability, never shook
his!

During the whole time she was singing Arátoff had been scanning Clara's face. It seemed
to him that her eyes, athwart her contracted
lashes, were again turned on him. But he was
particularly struck by the impassiveness of that
face, that forehead, those brows, and only when

she uttered her passionate cry did he notice a row of white, closely-set teeth gleaming warmly from between her barely parted lips. Kupfer stepped up to him.

"Well, brother, what dost thou think of her?" he asked, all beaming with satisfaction.

"She has a fine voice," replied Arátoff, "but she does not know how to sing yet, she has had no real school." (Why he said this and what he meant by "school" the Lord only knows!)

Kupfer was surprised.—"She has no school," he repeated slowly. . . . "Well, now. . . . She can still study. But on the other hand, what soul! But just wait until thou hast heard her recite Tatyána's letter."

He ran away from Arátoff, and the latter thought: "Soul! With that impassive face!"— He thought that she bore herself and moved like a hypnotised person, like a somnambulist. . . . And, at the same time, she was indubitably. . . . Yes! she was indubitably staring at him.

Meanwhile the "morning" went on. The fat man in spectacles presented himself again; despite his serious appearance he imagined that he was a comic artist and read a scene from Gógol, this time without evoking a single token of approbation. The flute-player flitted past once more; again the pianist thundered; a young fellow of twenty, pomaded and curled, but with traces of tears on his cheeks, sawed out some va-

riations on his fiddle. It might have appeared
strange that in the intervals between the recita-
tions and the music the abrupt notes of a French
horn were wafted, now and then, from the artists'
room; but this instrument was not used, nevertheless. It afterward came out that the amateur
who had offered to perform on it had been seized
with a panic at the moment when he should have
made his appearance before the audience. So at
last, Clara Mílitch appeared again.

She held in her hand a small volume of Púshkin; but during her reading she never once glanced
at it. . . . She was obviously frightened; the little
book shook slightly in her fingers. Arátoff also
observed the expression of dejection which *now*
overspread her stern features. The first line: " I
write to you . . . what would you more?" she
uttered with extreme simplicity, almost ingenuously,—stretching both arms out in front of
her with an ingenuous, sincere, helpless gesture.
Then she began to hurry a little; but beginning
with the line: "Another! Nay! to none on
earth could I have given e'er my heart!" she regained her self-possession, and grew animated;
and when she reached the words: "All, all life
hath been a pledge of faithful meeting thus with
thee,"—her hitherto rather dull voice rang out en-
thusiastically and boldly, and her eyes riveted
themselves on Arátoff with a boldness and direct-
ness to match. She went on with the same enthu-

siasm, and only toward the close did her voice
again fall, and in it and in her face her previous
dejection was again depicted. She made a complete muddle, as the saying is, of the last four
lines,—the little volume of Púshkin suddenly
slipped from her hands, and she beat a hasty retreat.

The audience set to applauding and recalling
her in desperate fashion. . . . One theological
student,—a Little Russian,—among others, bellowed so loudly: "Muíluitch! Muíluitch!"[1] that
his neighbour politely and sympathetically
begged him to "spare himself, as a future proto-
deacon!"[2] But Arátoff immediately rose and
betook himself to the entrance. Kupfer overtook
him. . . .

"Good gracious, whither art thou going?"
he yelled:—"I'll introduce thee to Clara if thou
wishest—shall I?"

"No, thanks," hastily replied Arátoff, and set
off homeward almost at a run.

[1] The Little Russians (among other peculiarities of pronunciation
attached to their dialect) use the guttural instead of the clear *i.*—
Translator.

[2] A bishop or priest in the Russian Church is not supposed to
speak loudly, no matter how fine a voice he may possess. The
deacon, on the contrary, or the proto-deacon (attached to a cathedral) is supposed to have a huge voice, and, especially at certain
points, to roar at the top of his lungs. He sometimes cracks
his voice—which is what the sympathetic neighbour was hinting
at here.—Translator.

V

STRANGE emotions, which were not clear even to himself, agitated him. In reality, Clara's recitation had not altogether pleased him either . . . . altogether he could not tell precisely why. It had troubled him, that recitation, it had seemed to him harsh, unmelodious. . . . Somehow it seemed to have broken something within him, to have exerted some sort of violence. And those importunate, persistent, almost insolent glances—what had caused them? What did they signify?

Arátoff's modesty did permit him even a momentary thought that he might have pleased that strange young girl, that he might have inspired her with a sentiment akin to love, to passion! . . . And he had imagined to himself quite otherwise that as yet unknown woman, that young girl, to whom he would surrender himself wholly, and who would love him, become his bride, his wife. . . . He rarely dreamed of this: he was chaste both in body and soul;—but the pure image which rose up in his imagination at such times was evoked under another form,—the form of his dead mother, whom he barely remembered, though he cherished her portrait like a sacred treasure. That portrait had been painted in water-colours, in a rather inartistic manner, by a friendly neighbour, but the likeness was striking, as every one averred. The woman, the young girl, whom as yet he did not so much as venture to expect, must possess just such a tender profile, just such kind, bright eyes, just such silky hair, just such a smile, just such a clear understanding. . . .

But this was a black-visaged, swarthy creature, with coarse hair, and a moustache on her lip; she must certainly be bad-tempered, giddy. . . . "A gipsy" (Arátoff could not devise a worse expression)—what was she to him?

And in the meantime, Arátoff was unable to banish from his mind that black-visaged gipsy, whose singing and recitation and even whose personal appearance were disagreeable to him. He was perplexed, he was angry with himself. Not long before this he had read Walter Scott's romance "Saint Ronan's Well" (there was a complete edition of Walter Scott's works in the library of his father, who revered the English romance-writer as a serious, almost a learned author). The heroine of that romance is named Clara Mowbray. A poet of the '40's, Krásoff, wrote a poem about her, which wound up with the words:

"Unhappy Clara! foolish Clara!
Unhappy Clara Mowbray!"

Arátoff was acquainted with this poem also. . . . And now these words kept incessantly recurring to his memory. . . . "Unhappy Clara! foolish Clara! . . ." (That was why he had been so surprised when Kupfer mentioned Clara Mílitch to him.) Even Platósha noticed, not precisely a change in Yákoff's frame of mind—as a matter of fact, no change had taken place—but something wrong about his looks, in his remarks. She cautiously interrogated him about the literary morning at which he had been present;— she whispered, sighed, scrutinised him from in front, scrutinised him from the side, from behind —and suddenly, slapping her hands on her thighs, she exclaimed:

"Well, Yásha!—I see what the trouble is!"

"What dost thou mean?" queried Arátoff in his turn.

"Thou hast certainly met at that morning some one of those tail-draggers" (that was what Platonída Ivánovna called all ladies who wore fashionable gowns). . . . "She has a comely face—and she puts on airs like *this*,—and twists her face like *this*" (Platósha depicted all this in her face), "and she makes her eyes go round like this . . . " (she mimicked this also, describing huge circles in the air with her forefinger). . . . "And it made an impression on thee, because thou art not used to it. . . . But that does not signify anything, Yásha . . . . it does not signify a-any-thing! Drink a cup of herb-tea when thou goest to bed, and that will be the end of it! . . . . Lord, help!"

Platósha ceased speaking and took herself off.
. . . She probably had never made such a long
and animated speech before since she was born
. . . . but Arátoff thought:

"I do believe my aunt is right. . . . It is all
because I am not used to such things. . . ." (He
really had attracted the attention of the female
sex to himself for the first time . . . . at any rate,
he had never noticed it before.)   "I must not indulge myself."

So he set to work at his books, and drank some
linden-flower tea when he went to bed, and even
slept well all that night, and had no dreams.
On the following morning he busied himself with
his photography, as though nothing had happened. . . .

But toward evening his spiritual serenity was
again disturbed.

VI

To wit: a messenger brought him a note, written
in a large, irregular feminine hand, which ran as
follows:

"If you guess who is writing to you, and if it
does not bore you, come to-morrow, after dinner,
to the Tver boulevard—about five o'clock—and
wait. You will not be detained long. But it is
very important. Come."

There was no signature. Arátoff instantly divined who his correspondent was, and that was

225

precisely what disturbed him.—"What nonsense!" he said, almost aloud. "This is too much!
Of course I shall not go."—Nevertheless, he ordered the messenger to be summoned, and from
him he learned merely that the letter had been
handed to him on the street by a maid. Having
dismissed him, Arátoff reread the letter, and
flung it on the floor. . . . But after a while he
picked it up and read it over again; a second time
he cried: "Nonsense!" He did not throw the
letter on the floor this time, however, but put it
away in a drawer.

Arátoff went about his customary avocations,
busying himself now with one, now with another;
but his work did not make progress, was not a success. Suddenly he noticed that he was waiting
for Kupfer, that he wanted to interrogate him, or
even communicate something to him. . . . But
Kupfer did not make his appearance. Then Arátoff got Púshkin and read Tatyána's letter and
again felt convinced that that "gipsy" had not in
the least grasped the meaning of the letter. But
there was that jester Kupfer shouting: "A Rachel! A Viardot!" Then he went to his piano,
raised the cover in an abstracted sort of way, tried
to search out in his memory the melody of Tchaikóvsky's romance; but he immediately banged to
the piano-lid with vexation and went to his aunt,
in her own room, which was always kept very hot,
and was forever redolent of mint, sage, and other

medicinal herbs, and crowded with such a multitude of rugs, étagères, little benches, cushions and various articles of softly-stuffed furniture that it was difficult for an inexperienced person to turn round in it, and breathing was oppressive. Platonída Ivánovna was sitting by the window with her knitting-needles in her hand (she was knitting a scarf for Yáshenka—the thirty-eighth, by actual count, during the course of his existence!) —and was greatly surprised. Arátoff rarely entered her room, and if he needed anything he always shouted in a shrill voice from his study: "Aunt Platósha!"—But she made him sit down and, in anticipation of his first words, pricked up her ears, as she stared at him through her round spectacles with one eye, and above them with the other. She did not inquire after his health, and did not offer him tea, for she saw that he had not come for that. Arátoff hesitated for a while . . . . then began to talk . . . . to talk about his mother, about the way she had lived with his father, and how his father had made her acquaintance. He knew all this perfectly well . . . but he wanted to talk precisely about that. Unluckily for him, Platósha did not know how to converse in the least; she made very brief replies, as though she suspected that Yásha had not come for that purpose.

"Certainly!"—she kept repeating hurriedly, as she plied her knitting-needles almost in an angry way. "Every one knows that thy mother was a dove . . . . a regular dove. . . . And thy father loved her as a husband should love, faithfully and honourably, to the very grave; and he never loved any other woman,"—she added, elevating her voice and removing her spectacles.

"And was she of a timid disposition?" asked Arátoff, after a short pause.

"Certainly she was. As is fitting for the female sex. The bold ones are a recent invention."

"And were there no bold ones in your time?"

"There were such even in our day . . . . of course there were! But who were they? Some street-walker, or shameless hussy or other. She would drag her skirts about, and fling herself hither and thither at random. . . . What did she care? What anxiety had she? If a young fool came along, he fell into her hands. But steady-going people despised them. Dost thou remember ever to have beheld such in our house?"

Arátoff made no reply and returned to his study. Platonída Ivánovna gazed after him, shook her head and again donned her spectacles, again set to work on her scarf . . . . but more than once she fell into thought and dropped her knitting-needles on her knee.

And Arátoff until nightfall kept again and again beginning, with the same vexation, the same ire as before, to think about "the gipsy," the appointed tryst, to which he certainly would not go! During the night also she worried him. He kept constantly seeing her eyes, now narrowed, now widely opened, with their importunate gaze riveted directly on him, and those impassive features with their imperious expression.

On the following morning he again kept expecting Kupfer, for some reason or other; he came near writing him a letter . . . . however, he did nothing . . . . but spent most of his time pacing to and fro in his study. Not for one instant did he even admit to himself the thought that he would go to that stupid "rendezvous" . . . . and at half-past four, after having swallowed his dinner in haste, he suddenly donned his overcoat and pulling his cap down on his brows, he stole out of the house without letting his aunt see him and wended his way to the Tver boulevard.

VII

ARÁTOFF found few pedestrians on the boulevard. The weather was raw and quite cold. He strove not to think of what he was doing. He forced himself to turn his attention to all the objects he came across and pretended to assure himself that he had come out to walk precisely like the other people. . . . The letter of the day before was in his side-pocket, and he was uninterruptedly conscious of its presence. He walked the

length of the boulevard a couple of times, darting keen glances at every feminine form which
approached him, and his heart thumped, thumped
violently. . . . He began to feel tired, and sat
down on a bench. And suddenly the idea occurred to him: "Come now, what if that letter
was not written by her but by some one else, by
some other woman?" In point of fact, that
should have made no difference to him . . . . and
yet he was forced to admit to himself that he did
not wish this. "It would be very stupid," he
thought, "still more stupid than *that!*" A nervous restlessness began to take possession of him;
he began to feel chilly, not outwardly but inwardly. Several times he drew out his watch
from his waistcoat pocket, glanced at the face,
put it back again,—and every time forgot how
many minutes were lacking to five o'clock. It
seemed to him as though every one who passed
him stared at him in a peculiar manner, surveying
him with a certain sneering surprise and curiosity.
A wretched little dog ran up, sniffed at his legs
and began to wag its tail. He flourished his arms
angrily at it. He was most annoyed of all by a
small boy from a factory in a bed-ticking jacket,
who seated himself on the bench and first whis-
tled, then scratched his head, dangling his legs,
encased in huge, broken boots, the while, and
staring at him from time to time. "His employer
is certainly expecting him," thought Arátoff,

"and here he is, the lazy dog, wasting his time idling about. . . ."

But at that same moment it seemed to him as though some one had approached and taken up a stand close behind him . . . a warm current emanated thence. . . .

He glanced round. . . . It was she!

He recognised her immediately, although a thick, dark-blue veil concealed her features. He instantly sprang from the bench, and remained standing there, unable to utter a word. She also maintained silence. He felt greatly agitated . . . . but her agitation was as great as his: Arátoff could not help seeing even through the veil how deadly pale she grew. But she was the first to speak.

"Thank you," she began in a broken voice, "thank you for coming. I did not hope. . . ." She turned away slightly and walked along the boulevard. Arátoff followed her.

"Perhaps you condemn me," she went on, without turning her head.—"As a matter of fact, my action is very strange. . . . But I have heard a great deal about you . . . but no! I . . . . that was not the cause. . . . If you only knew. . . . I wanted to say so much to you, my God! . . . . But how am I to do it? . . . . How am I to do it!"

Arátoff walked by her side, but a little in the rear. He did not see her face; he saw only her hat and a part of her veil . . . . and her long, threadbare cloak. All his vexation against her and against himself suddenly returned to him; all the absurdity, all the awkwardness of this tryst, of these explanations between utter strangers, on a public boulevard, suddenly presented itself to him.

" I have come hither at your behest," he began in his turn, " I have come, my dear madame " (her shoulders quivered softly, she turned into a side path, and he followed her), "merely for the sake of having an explanation, of learning in consequence of what strange misunderstanding you were pleased to appeal to me, a stranger to you, who . . . . who only *guessed,* as you expressed it in your letter, that it was precisely you who had written to him . . . . because he guessed that you had tried, in the course of that literary morning to show him too much . . . . too much obvious attention."

Arátoff uttered the whole of this little speech in the same resonant but firm voice in which men who are still very young answer at examinations on questions for which they are well prepared. . . . He was indignant; he was angry. . . . And that wrath had loosed his tongue which was not very fluent on ordinary occasions.

She continued to advance along the path with somewhat lagging steps. . . . Arátoff followed her as before, and as before saw only her little old

mantilla and her small hat, which was not quite
new either. His vanity suffered at the thought
that she must now be thinking: "All I had to do
was to make a sign, and he immediately hastened
to me!"

Arátoff lapsed into silence . . . . he expected
that she would reply to him; but she did not utter
a word.

"I am ready to listen to you," he began again,
"and I shall even be very glad if I can be of service to you in any way . . . . although, I must
confess, nevertheless, that I find it astonishing
. . . that considering my isolated life . . . ."

But at his last words Clara suddenly turned to
him and he beheld the same startled, profoundly-
sorrowful visage, with the same large, bright
tears in its eyes, with the same woful expression
around the parted lips; and the visage was so fine
thus that he involuntarily broke off short and felt
within himself something akin to fright, and pity
and forbearance.

"Akh, why . . . . why are you like this? . . ."
she said with irresistibly sincere and upright
force—and what a touching ring there was to her
voice!—"Is it possible that my appeal to you can
have offended you? . . . Is it possible that you
have understood nothing? . . . Ah, yes! You
have not understood anything, you have not understood what I said to you. God knows what
you have imagined about me, you have not even

reflected what it cost me to write to you! . . .
You have been anxious only on your own account,
about your own dignity, your own peace! . . .
But did I . . . ." (she so tightly clenched her
hands which she had raised to her lips that her
fingers cracked audibly) . . . . "As though I had
made any demands upon you, as though explanations were requisite to begin with. . . . 'My dear
madame' . . . . 'I even find it astonishing' . . . .
'If I can be of service to you' . . . . Akh, how
foolish I have been!—I have been deceived in
you, in your face! . . . When I saw you for the
first time. . . . There . . . . There you stand.
. . . And not one word do you utter! Have you
really not a word to say?"

She had been imploring. . . . Her face suddenly flushed, and as suddenly assumed an evil
and audacious expression.—"O Lord! how stupid this is!"—she cried suddenly, with a harsh
laugh.—"How stupid our tryst is! How stupid
I am! . . . . and you, too! . . . . Fie!"

She made a disdainful gesture with her hand as
though sweeping him out of her path, and passing
around him she ran swiftly from the boulevard
and disappeared.

That gesture of the hand, that insulting laugh,
that final exclamation instantly restored Arátoff
to his former frame of mind and stifled in him the
feeling which had risen in his soul when she turned
to him with tears in her eyes. Again he waxed

wroth, and came near shouting after the retreating girl: "You may turn out a good actress, but why have you taken it into your head to play a comedy on me?"

With great strides he returned home, and although he continued to be indignant and to rage all the way thither, still, at the same time, athwart all these evil, hostile feelings there forced its way the memory of that wondrous face which he had beheld only for the twinkling of an eye. . . . He even put to himself the question: "Why did not I answer her when she demanded from me at least one word?"—"I did not have time," . . . . he thought. . . . "She did not give me a chance to utter that word . . . . And what would I have uttered?"

But he immediately shook his head and said, "An actress!"

And yet, at the same time, the vanity of the inexperienced, nervous youth, which had been wounded at first, now felt rather flattered at the passion which he had inspired. . . .

"But on the other hand," he pursued his reflections, "all that is at an end of course. . . . I must have appeared ridiculous to her." . . . .

This thought was disagreeable to him, and again he grew angry . . . . both at her . . . . and at himself. On reaching home he locked himself in his study. He did not wish to encounter Platósha. The kind old woman came to his door a couple of times, applied her ear to the key-hole, and merely sighed and whispered her prayer. . . .

" It has begun!" she thought. . . . "And he is only five-and-twenty. . . . . Akh, it is early, early!"

VIII

ARÁTOFF was very much out of sorts all the following day.

"What is the matter, Yásha?" Platonída Ivánovna said to him. " Thou seemest to be tousled to-day, somehow." . . . In the old woman's peculiar language this quite accurately defined Arátoff's moral condition. He could not work, but even he himself did not know what he wanted. Now he was expecting Kupfer again (he suspected that it was precisely from Kupfer that Clara had obtained his address . . . . and who else could have " talked a great deal" about him?) ; again he wondered whether his acquaintance with her was to end in that way? . . . . again he imagined that she would write him another letter; again he asked himself whether he ought not to write her a letter, in which he might explain everything to her,—as he did not wish to leave an unpleasant impression of himself. . . . But, in point of fact, *what* was he to explain?—Now he aroused in himself something very like disgust for her, for her persistence, her boldness; again

that indescribably touching face presented itself
to him and her irresistible voice made itself heard;
and yet again he recalled her singing, her recitation—and did not know whether he was right in
his wholesale condemnation.—In one word: he
was a tousled man! At last he became bored with
all this and decided, as the saying is, "to take it
upon himself" and erase all that affair, as it un-
doubtedly was interfering with his avocations
and disturbing his peace of mind.—He did not
find it so easy to put his resolution into effect. . . . More than a week elapsed before he
got back again into his ordinary rut. Fortu-
nately, Kupfer did not present himself at all,
any more than if he had not been in Moscow.
Not long before the "affair" Arátoff had begun
to busy himself with painting for photographic
ends; he devoted himself to this with redoubled
zeal.

Thus, imperceptibly, with a few "relapses" as
the doctors express it, consisting, for example in
the fact that he once came very near going to call
on the Princess, two weeks . . . . three weeks
passed . . . . and Arátoff became once more the
Arátoff of old. Only deep down, under the surface of his life, something heavy and dark secretly accompanied him in all his comings and
goings. Thus does a large fish which has just
been hooked, but has not yet been drawn out,
swim along the bottom of a deep river under the

very boat wherein sits the fisherman with his stout rod in hand.

And lo! one day as he was skimming over some not quite fresh numbers of the *Moscow News,* Arátoff hit upon the following correspondence:

"With great sorrow," wrote a certain local literary man from Kazán, "we insert in our theatrical chronicle the news of the sudden death of our gifted actress, Clara Mílitch, who had succeeded in the brief space of her engagement in becoming the favourite of our discriminating public. Our sorrow is all the greater because Miss Mílitch herself put an end to her young life, which held so much of promise, by means of poison. And this poisoning is all the more dreadful because the actress took the poison on the stage itself! They barely got her home, where, to universal regret, she died. Rumours are current in the town to the effect that unrequited love led her to that terrible deed."

Arátoff softly laid the newspaper on the table. To all appearances he remained perfectly composed . . . . but something smote him simultaneously in his breast and in his head, and then slowly diffused itself through all his members. He rose to his feet, stood for a while on one spot, and again seated himself, and again perused the letter. Then he rose once more, lay down on his bed and placing his hands under his head, he stared for a long time at the wall like one dazed.

Little by little that wall seemed to recede . . . .
to vanish . . . . and he beheld before him the
boulevard beneath grey skies and *her* in her black
mantilla . . . . then her again on the platform
. . . . he even beheld himself by her side.—That
which had smitten him so forcibly in the breast at
the first moment, now began to rise up . . . . to
rise up in his throat. . . . . He tried to cough, to
call some one, but his voice failed him, and to his
own amazement, tears which he could not restrain
gushed from his eyes. . . . What had evoked
those tears? Pity? Regret? Or was it simply
that his nerves had been unable to withstand the
sudden shock? Surely, she was nothing to him?
Was not that the fact?

"But perhaps that is not true," the thought
suddenly occurred to him. "I must find out!
But from whom? From the Princess?—No, from
Kupfer . . . . from Kupfer? But they say he
is not in Moscow.—Never mind! I must apply
to him first!"

With these ideas in his head Arátoff hastily
dressed himself, summoned a cab and dashed off
to Kupfer.

IX

HE had not hoped to find him . . . . but he did.
Kupfer actually had been absent from Moscow
for a time, but had returned about a week pre-

viously and was even preparing to call on Arátoff
again. He welcomed him with his customary cor-
diality, and began to explain something to him
. . . but Arátoff immediately interrupted him
with the impatient question:

" Hast thou read it?—Is it true? "

" Is what true? " replied the astounded Kupfer.

" About Clara Mílitch? "

Kupfer's face expressed compassion.—" Yes,
yes, brother, it is true; she has poisoned herself.
It is such a misfortune! "

Arátoff held his peace for a space.—" But
hast thou also read it in the newspaper? " he
asked:—" Or perhaps thou hast been to Kazán
thyself? "

" I have been to Kazán, in fact; the Princess
and I conducted her thither. She went on the
stage there, and had great success. Only I did
not remain there until the catastrophe. . . . I
was in Yaroslávl."

" In Yaroslávl? "

" Yes; I escorted the Princess thither. . . . She
has settled in Yaroslávl now."

" But hast thou trustworthy information? "

" The most trustworthy sort . . . . at first
hand! I made acquaintance in Kazán with her
family.—But stay, my dear fellow . . . . this
news seems to agitate thee greatly.—But I remember that Clara did not please thee that time!
Thou wert wrong! She was a splendid girl—

240

only her head! She had an ungovernable head!
I was greatly distressed about her!"

Arátoff did not utter a word, but dropped
down on a chair, and after waiting a while he
asked Kupfer to tell him . . . . he hesitated.

"What?" asked Kupfer.

"Why . . . . everything," replied Arátoff
slowly.—"About her family, for instance . . . .
and so forth. Everything thou knowest!"

"But does that interest thee?—Certainly!"

Kupfer, from whose face it was impossible to
discern that he had grieved so greatly over Clara,
began his tale.

From his words Arátoff learned that Clara Mílitch's real name had been Katerína Milovídoff;
that her father, now dead, had been an official
teacher of drawing in Kazán, had painted bad
portraits and official images, and moreover had
borne the reputation of being a drunkard and a
domestic tyrant . . . "and a *cultured* man into the
bargain!" . . . . (Here Kupfer laughed in a
self-satisfied manner, by way of hinting at the pun
he had made) ; [1]—that he had left at his death,
in the first place, a widow of the merchant class,
a thoroughly stupid female, straight out of one of
Ostróvsky's comedies; [2] and in the second place,

---

[1] An image, or holy picture, is *óbraz;* the adjective "cultured"
is derived from the same word in its sense of pattern, model—
obrazóvanny.—TRANSLATOR.

[2] Ostróvsky's comedies of life in the merchant class are irresistibly amusing, talented, and true to nature.—TRANSLATOR.

a daughter much older than Clara and bearing
no resemblance to her—a very clever girl and
"greatly developed, my dear fellow!" That the
two—widow and daughter—lived in easy circumstances, in a decent little house which had been
acquired by the sale of those wretched portraits
and holy pictures; that Clara . . . . or Kátya,
whichever you choose to call her, had astonished
every one ever since her childhood by her talent,
but was of an insubordinate, capricious disposition, and was constantly quarrelling with her father; that having an inborn passion for the theatre, she had run away from the parental house at
the age of sixteen with an actress. . . .

"With an actor?" interjected Arátoff.

"No, not with an actor, but an actress; to whom
she had become attached. . . . This actress had a
protector, it is true, a wealthy gentleman already
elderly, who only refrained from marrying her
because he was already married—while the actress, it appeared, was married also."

Further, Kupfer informed Arátoff that, prior
to her arrival in Moscow, Clara had acted and
sung in provincial theatres; that on losing her
friend the actress (the gentleman had died also, it
seems, or had made it up with his wife—precisely
which Kupfer did not quite remember . . . .),
she had made the acquaintance of the Princess,
"that woman of gold, whom thou, my friend Yákoff Andréitch," the narrator added with feeling,

" wert not able to appreciate at her true worth ";
that finally Clara had been offered an engagement in Kazán, and had accepted it, although she
had previously declared that she would never
leave Moscow!—But how the people of Kazán
had loved her—it was fairly amazing! At every
representation she received bouquets and gifts!
bouquets and gifts!—A flour merchant, the greatest bigwig in the government, had even presented
her with a golden inkstand!—Kupfer narrated
all this with great animation, but without, however, displaying any special sentimentality, and
interrupting his speech with the question:—
" Why dost thou want to know that? " . . . . or
" To what end is that? " when Arátoff, after listening to him with devouring attention, demanded more and still more details. Everything
was said at last, and Kupfer ceased speaking, re-
warding himself for his toil with a cigar.

" But why did she poison herself? " asked Arátoff. " The newspaper stated. . . ."

Kupfer waved his hands.—" Well. . . . That
I cannot say. . . . I don't know. But the newspaper lies. Clara behaved in an exemplary manner . . . . she had no love-affairs. . . . And
how could she, with her pride! She was as proud
as Satan himself, and inaccessible! An insubordinate head! Firm as a rock! If thou wilt believe me,—I knew her pretty intimately, seest
thou,—I never beheld a tear in her eyes!"

"But I did," thought Arátoff to himself.

"Only there is this to be said," went on Kupfer:—"I noticed a great change in her of late: she became so depressed, she would remain silent for hours at a time; you couldn't get a word out of her. I once asked her: 'Has any one offended you, Katerína Semyónovna?' Because I knew her disposition: she could not endure an insult. She held her peace, and that was the end of it! Even her success on the stage did not cheer her up; they would shower her with bouquets . . . and she would not smile! She gave one glance at the gold inkstand,—and put it aside!—She complained that no one would write her a genuine part, as she conceived it. And she gave up singing entirely. I am to blame, brother! . . . I repeated to her that thou didst not think she had any *school*. But nevertheless . . . . why she poisoned herself is incomprehensible! And the way she did it too. . . ."

"In what part did she have the greatest success?" . . . Arátoff wanted to find out what part she had played that last time, but for some reason or other he asked something else.

"In Ostróvsky's 'Grúnya'[1] I believe. But I repeat to thee: she had no love-affairs! Judge for thyself by one thing: she lived in her mother's house. . . . Thou knowest what some of those

[1] Turgénieff probably means Grúsha (another form for the diminutive of Agrippína, in Russian Agrafénya). The play is " Live as You Can."—TRANSLATOR.

merchants' houses are like; a glass case filled with
holy images in every corner and a shrine lamp in
front of the case; deadly, stifling heat; a sour
odour; in the drawing-room nothing but chairs
ranged along the wall, and geraniums in the windows;—and when a visitor arrives, the hostess begins to groan as though an enemy were approaching. What chance is there for love-making, and
amours in such a place? Sometimes it happened
that they would not even admit me. Their maid-
servant, a robust peasant-woman, in a Tur-
key red cotton sarafan,[1] and pendulous breasts,
would place herself across the path in the
anteroom and roar: 'Whither away?' No, I
positively cannot understand what made her
poison herself. She must have grown tired of
life," Kupfer philosophically wound up his
remarks.

Arátoff sat with drooping head.—" Canst thou
give me the address of that house in Kazán?" he
said at last.

"I can; but what dost thou want of it?—Dost
thou wish to send a letter thither?"

"Perhaps so."

"Well, as thou wilt. Only the old woman will
not answer thee. Her sister might . . . . . the
clever sister!—But again, brother, I marvel at
thee! Such indifference formerly . . . . and

[1] A full gown gathered into a narrow band just under the arm-
pits and suspended over the shoulders by straps of the same.—
TRANSLATOR.

now so much attention! All that comes of living
a solitary life, my dear fellow!"

Arátoff made no reply to this remark and went
away, after having procured the address in
Kazán.

Agitation, surprise, expectation had been depicted on his face when he went to Kupfer. . . .
Now he advanced with an even gait, downcast
eyes, and hat pulled low down over his brows; almost every one he met followed him with a
searching gaze . . . . but he paid no heed to the
passers-by . . . it was quite different from what
it had been on the boulevard! . . .

"Unhappy Clara! Foolish Clara!" resounded
in his soul.

X

NEVERTHELESS, Arátoff passed the following day
in a fairly tranquil manner. He was even able
to devote himself to his customary occupations.
There was only one thing: both during his busy
time and in his leisure moments he thought incessantly of Clara, of what Kupfer had told him the
day before. Truth to tell, his thoughts were
also of a decidedly pacific nature. It seemed to
him that that strange young girl interested him
from a psychological point of view, as something
in the nature of a puzzle, over whose solution it
was worth while to cudgel one's brains.—" She
ran away from home with a kept actress," he

thought, " she placed herself under the protection
of that Princess, in whose house she lived,—and
had no love-affairs? It is improbable! . . .
Kupfer says it was pride! But, in the first place,
we know " (Arátoff should have said: "we have
read in books") . . . . "that pride is compati-
ble with light-minded conduct; and in the second place, did not she, such a proud person, appoint a meeting with a man who might show her
scorn . . . . and appoint it in a public place,
into the bargain . . . . on the boulevard!"—At
this point there recurred to Arátoff's mind the
whole scene on the boulevard, and he asked himself: " Had he really shown scorn for Clara?"—
" No," he decided. . . . That was another feeling . . . . a feeling of perplexity . . . . of distrust, in short!"—"Unhappy Clara!" again
rang through his brain.—"Yes, she was unhappy," he decided again . . . . that was the
most fitting word.

"But if that is so, I was unjust. She spoke
truly when she said that I did not understand
her. 'Tis a pity!—It may be that a very remarkable being has passed so close to me . . . .
and I did not take advantage of the opportunity,
but repulsed her. . . . Well, never mind! My
life is still before me. I shall probably have
other encounters of a different sort!

"But what prompted her to pick out *me*, in
particular?"—He cast a glance at a mirror

which he was passing at the moment. "What is there peculiar about me? And what sort of a beauty am I?—My face is like everybody else's face. . . . However, she was not a beauty either.

"She was not a beauty . . . . but what an expressive face she had! Impassive . . . but expressive! I have never before seen such a face.— And she has talent . . . . that is to say, she had talent, undoubted talent. Wild, untrained, even coarse . . . . but undoubted.—And in that case also I was unjust to her."—Arátoff mentally transported himself to the musical morning . . . and noticed that he remembered with remarkable distinctness every word she had sung or recited, every intonation. . . . That would not have been the case had she been devoid of talent.

"And now all that is in the grave, where she has thrust herself. . . . But I have nothing to do with that. . . . I am not to blame! It would even be absurd to think that I am to blame."— Again it flashed into Arátoff's mind that even had she had "anything of that sort" about her, his conduct during the interview would indubitably have disenchanted her. That was why she had broken into such harsh laughter at parting. —And where was the proof that she had poisoned herself on account of an unhappy love? It is only newspaper correspondents who attribute every such death to unhappy love!—But life easily becomes repulsive to people with character, like Clara . . . . and tiresome. Yes, tiresome. Kupfer was right: living simply bored her.

"In spite of her success, of her ovations?"— Arátoff meditated.—The psychological analysis to which he surrendered himself was even agreeable to him. Unaccustomed as he had been, up to this time, to all contact with women, he did not suspect how significant for him was this tense examination of a woman's soul.

"Consequently," he pursued his meditations, "art did not satisfy her, did not fill the void of her life. Genuine artists exist only for art, for the theatre. . . . Everything else pales before that which they regard as their vocation. . . . She was a dilettante!"

Here Arátoff again became thoughtful.— No, the word "dilettante" did not consort with that face, with the expression of that face, of those eyes . . . .

And again there rose up before him the image of Clara with her tear-filled eyes riveted upon him, and her clenched hands raised to her lips. . . .

"Akh, I won't think of it, I won't think of it . . . ." he whispered. . . . "What is the use?"

In this manner the whole day passed. During dinner Arátoff chatted a great deal with Platósha, questioned her about old times, which, by the way, she recalled and transmitted badly, as she was not possessed of a very glib tongue, and

had noticed hardly anything in the course of her
life save her Yáshka. She merely rejoiced that
he was so good-natured and affectionate that day!
—Toward evening Arátoff quieted down to such
a degree that he played several games of trumps
with his aunt.

Thus passed the day . . . . but the night was
quite another matter!

XI

It began well; he promptly fell asleep, and when
his aunt entered his room on tiptoe for the purpose of making the sign of the cross over him
thrice as he slept—she did this every night—he
was lying and breathing as quietly as a child.—
But before daybreak he had a vision.

He dreamed that he was walking over the bare
steppes, sown with stones, beneath a low-hanging
sky. Between the stones wound a path; he was
advancing along it.

Suddenly there rose up in front of him something in the nature of a delicate cloud. He
looked intently at it; the little cloud turned into
a woman in a white gown, with a bright girdle
about her waist. She was hurrying away from
him. He did not see either her face or her hair
. . . . a long piece of tissue concealed them. But he
felt bound to overtake her and look into her eyes.
Only, no matter how much haste he made, she still
walked more quickly than he.

On the path lay a broad, flat stone, resembling a tomb-stone. It barred her way. The woman came to a halt. Arátoff ran up to her. She turned toward him—but still he could not see her eyes . . . . they were closed. Her face was white,—white as snow; her arms hung motionless. She resembled a statue.

Slowly, without bending a single limb, she leaned backward and sank down on that stone. . . . And now Arátoff was lying beside her, outstretched like a mortuary statue,—and his hands were folded like those of a corpse.

But at this point the woman suddenly rose to her feet and went away. Arátoff tried to rise also . . . . but he could not stir, he could not unclasp his hands, and could only gaze after her in despair.

Then the woman suddenly turned round, and he beheld bright, vivacious eyes in a living face, which was strange to him, however. She was laughing, beckoning to him with her hand . . . . and still he was unable to move.

She laughed yet once again, and swiftly retreated, merrily nodding her head, on which a garland of tiny roses gleamed crimson.

Arátoff strove to shout, strove to break that frightful nightmare. . . . Suddenly everything grew dark round about . . . . and the woman returned to him.

But she was no longer a statue whom he knew not . . . she was Clara. She halted in front of him, folded her arms, and gazed sternly and attentively at him. Her lips were tightly compressed, but it seemed to Arátoff that he heard the words:

"If thou wishest to know who I am, go thither!"

"Whither?" he asked.

"Thither!"—the moaning answer made itself audible.—"Thither!"

Arátoff awoke.

He sat up in bed, lighted a candle which stood on his night-stand, but did not rise, and sat there for a long time slowly gazing about him. It seemed to him that something had taken place within him since he went to bed; that something had taken root within him . . . . something had taken possession of him. "But can that be possible?" he whispered unconsciously. "Can it be that such a power exists?"

He could not remain in bed. He softly dressed himself and paced his chamber until daylight. And strange to say! He did not think about Clara for a single minute,—and he did not think about her because he had made up his mind to set off for Kazán that very day!

He thought only of that journey, of how it was to be made, and what he ought to take with him, —and how he would there ferret out and find out everything,—and regain his composure.

"If thou dost not go," he argued with himself,

"thou wilt surely lose thy reason!" He was afraid of that; he was afraid of his nerves. He was convinced that as soon as he should see all that with his own eyes, all obsessions would flee like a nocturnal nightmare.—"And the journey will occupy not more than a week in all," he thought. . . . "What is a week? And there is no other way of ridding myself of it."

The rising sun illuminated his room; but the light of day did not disperse the shades of night which weighed upon him, did not alter his decision.

Platósha came near having an apoplectic stroke when he communicated his decision to her. She even squatted down on her heels . . . . her legs gave way under her. "To Kazán? Why to Kazán?" she whispered, protruding her eyes which were already blind enough without that. She would not have been any more astounded had she learned that her Yásha was going to marry the neighbouring baker's daughter, or depart to America.—"And shalt thou stay long in Kazan?"

"I shall return at the end of a week," replied Arátoff, as he stood half-turned away from his aunt, who was still sitting on the floor.

Platósha tried to remonstrate again, but Arátoff shouted at her in an utterly unexpected and unusual manner:

"I am not a baby," he yelled, turning pale all over, while his lips quivered and his eyes flashed viciously.—"I am six-and-twenty years of age. I know what I am about,—I am free to do as I please!—I will not permit any one. . . . Give me money for the journey; prepare a trunk with linen and clothing . . . . and do not bother me! I shall return at the end of a week, Platósha," he added, in a softer tone.

Platósha rose to her feet, grunting, and, making no further opposition, wended her way to her chamber. Yásha had frightened her.—"I have not a head on my shoulders," she remarked to the cook, who was helping her to pack Yásha's things, —"not a head—but a bee-hive . . . . and what bees are buzzing there I do not know! He is going away to Kazán, my mother, to Ka-zá-án!"

The cook, who had noticed their yard-porter talking for a long time to the policeman about something, wanted to report this circumstance to her mistress, but she did not dare, and merely thought to herself: "To Kazán? If only it is n't some place further away!"—And Platonída Ivánovna was so distracted that she did not even utter her customary prayer.—In such a catastrophe as this even the Lord God could be of no assistance!

That same day Arátoff set off for Kazán.

XII

No sooner had he arrived in that town and engaged a room at the hotel, than he dashed off in search of the widow Milovídoff's house. During the whole course of his journey he had been in a sort of stupor, which, nevertheless, did not in the least prevent his taking all proper measures, —transferring himself at Nízhni Nóvgorod from the railway to the steamer, eating at the stations, and so forth. As before, he was convinced that everything would be cleared up *there,* and accordingly he banished from his thoughts all memories and speculations, contenting himself with one thing,—the mental preparation of the speech in which he was to set forth to Clara Mílitch's family the real reason of his trip.—And now, at last, he had attained to the goal of his yearning, and ordered the servant to announce him. He was admitted—with surprise and alarm—but he was admitted.

The widow Milovídoff's house proved to be in fact just as Kupfer had described it; and the widow herself really did resemble one of Ostróvsky's women of the merchant class, although she was of official rank; her husband had been a Collegiate Assessor.[1] Not without some difficulty

[1] The eighth from the top in the Table of Ranks won by service to the state, which Peter the Great instituted. A sufficiently high grade in that table confers hereditary nobility; the lower grades carry only personal nobility.—TRANSLATOR.

did Arátoff, after having preliminarily excused himself for his boldness, and the strangeness of his visit, make the speech which he had prepared, to the effect that he wished to collect all the necessary information concerning the gifted actress who had perished at such an early age; that he was actuated not by idle curiosity, but by a profound sympathy for her talent, of which he was a worshipper (he said exactly that—"a worshipper"); that, in conclusion, it would be a sin to leave the public in ignorance of the loss it had sustained,—and why its hopes had not been realized!

Madame Milovídoff did not interrupt Arátoff; it is hardly probable that she understood very clearly what this strange visitor was saying to her, and she merely swelled a little with pride, and opened her eyes widely at him on perceiving that he had a peaceable aspect, and was decently clad, and was not some sort of swindler . . . . and was not asking for any money.

"Are you saying that about Kátya?" she asked, as soon as Arátoff ceased speaking.

"Exactly so . . . . about your daughter."

"And you have come from Moscow for that purpose?"

"Yes, from Moscow."

"Merely for that?"

"Merely for that."

Madame Milovídoff suddenly took fright.—

" Why, you—are an author? Do you write in the newspapers?"

" No, I am not an author,—and up to the present time, I have never written for the newspapers."

The widow bent her head. She was perplexed.

"Consequently . . . . it is for your own pleasure?" she suddenly inquired. Arátoff did not immediately hit upon the proper answer.

"Out of sympathy, out of reverence for talent," he said at last.

The word "reverence" pleased Madame Milovídoff. "Very well!" she ejaculated with a sigh. . . . "Although I am her mother, and grieved very greatly over her. . . . It was such a catastrophe, you know! . . . . Still, I must say, that she was always a crazy sort of girl, and ended up in the same way! Such a disgrace. . . . Judge for yourself: what sort of a thing is that for a mother? We may be thankful that they even buried her in Christian fashion. . . . " Madame Milovídoff crossed herself.—"From the time she was a small child she submitted to no one,—she abandoned the paternal roof . . . . and finally, it is enough to say that she became an actress! Every one knows that I did not turn her out of the house; for I loved her! For I am her mother, all the same! She did not have to live with strangers,—and beg alms! . . . " Here the widow melted into tears.—"But if you, sir, " she began afresh, wiping her eyes with the ends of her kerchief, "really have that intention, and if you will not concoct anything dishonourable about us,—but if, on the contrary, you wish to show us a favour,—then you had better talk with my other daughter. She will tell you everything better than I can. . . . "Ánnotchka!" called Madame Milovídoff:—"Ánnotchka, come hither! There's some gentleman or other from Moscow who wants to talk about Kátya!"

There was a crash in the adjoining room, but no one appeared.—"Ánnotchka!" cried the widow again—"Anna Semyónovna! come hither, I tell thee!"

The door opened softly and on the threshold appeared a girl no longer young, of sickly aspect, and homely, but with very gentle and sorrowful eyes. Arátoff rose from his seat to greet her, and introduced himself, at the same time mentioning his friend Kupfer.—"Ah! Feódor Feódoritch!" ejaculated the girl softly, as she softly sank down on a chair.

"Come, now, talk with the gentleman," said Madame Milovídoff, rising ponderously from her seat: "He has taken the trouble to come expressly from Moscow,—he wishes to collect information about Kátya. But you must excuse me, sir," she added, turning to Arátoff. . . . "I shall go away, to attend to domestic affairs. You can have a good explanation with Ánnotchka—

she will tell you about the theatre . . . . and all
that sort of thing. She's my clever, well-edu-
cated girl: she speaks French and reads books
quite equal to her dead sister. And she educated
her sister, I may say. . . . She was the elder—
well, and so she taught her."

Madame Milovídoff withdrew. When Arátoff was left alone with Anna Semyónovna he repeated his speech; but from the first glance he
understood that he had to deal with a girl who
really was cultured, not with a merchant's daughter,—and so he enlarged somewhat, and em-
ployed different expressions;—and toward the
end he became agitated, flushed, and felt conscious that his heart was beating hard. Anna
Semyónovna listened to him in silence, with her
hands folded; the sad smile did not leave her face
. . . . bitter woe which had not ceased to cause
pain, was expressed in that smile.

"Did you know my sister?" she asked Arátoff.

"No; properly speaking, I did not know her,"
he replied. "I saw and heard your sister once
. . . . but all that was needed was to hear and
see your sister once, in order to . . . ."

"Do you mean to write her biography?" Anna
put another question.

Arátoff had not expected that word; nevertheless, he immediately answered "Why not?" But
the chief point was that he wished to acquaint the
public . . . .

Anna stopped him with a gesture of her hand.

"To what end? The public caused her much grief without that; and Kátya had only just begun to live. But if you yourself" (Anna looked at him and again smiled that same sad smile, only now it was more cordial . . . . apparently she was thinking: "Yes, thou dost inspire me with confidence") . . . . "if you yourself cherish such sympathy for her, then permit me to request that you come to us this evening . . . . after dinner. I cannot now . . . . so suddenly. . . . I will collect my forces. . . . I will make an effort. . . . . Akh, I loved her too greatly!"

Anna turned away; she was on the point of bursting into sobs.

Arátoff rose alertly from his chair, thanked her for her proposal, said that he would come without fail . . . . without fail! and went away, bearing in his soul an impression of a quiet voice, of gentle and sorrowful eyes—and burning with the languor of anticipation.

XIII

ARÁTOFF returned to the Milovídoffs' house that same day, and conversed for three whole hours with Anna Semyónovna. Madame Milovídoff went to bed immediately after dinner—at two o'clock—and "rested" until evening tea, at seven o'clock. Arátoff's conversation with Clara's sister was not, properly speaking, a conversation: she did almost the whole of the talking, at first with hesitation, with confusion, but afterward with uncontrollable fervour. She had, evidently, idolised her sister. The confidence wherewith Arátoff had inspired her waxed and strengthened; she was no longer embarrassed; she even fell to weeping softly, twice, in his presence. He seemed to her worthy of her frank revelations and effusions. Nothing of that sort had ever before come into her own dull life! . . . And he . . . . he drank in her every word.

This, then, is what he learned . . . . much of it, as a matter of course, from what she refrained from saying . . . . and much he filled out for himself.

In her youth Clara had been, without doubt, a disagreeable child; and as a young girl she had been only a little softer: self-willed, hot-tempered, vain, she had not got on particularly well with her father, whom she despised for his drunkenness and incapacity. He was conscious of this and did not pardon it in her. Her musical faculties showed themselves at an early age; her father repressed them, recognising painting as the sole art,—wherein he himself had had so little success, but which had nourished him and his family. Clara had loved her mother . . . in a careless way, as she would have loved a nurse; she worshipped her sister, although she squabbled with her, and bit her. . . . It is true that afterward

she had been wont to go down on her knees before
her and kiss the bitten places. She was all fire,
all passion, and all contradiction: vengeful and
kind-hearted, magnanimous and rancorous; " she
believed in Fate, and did not believe in God "
(these words Anna whispered with terror) ; she
loved everything that was beautiful, and dressed
herself at haphazard; she could not endure to
have young men pay court to her, but in books
she read only those pages where love was the
theme; she did not care to please, she did not
like petting and never forgot caresses as she never
forgot offences; she was afraid of death, and she
had killed herself! She had been wont to say
sometimes, " I do not meet the sort of man I want
—and the others I will not have! "—" Well, and
what if you should meet the right sort? " Anna
had asked her.—" If I do . . . . I shall take
him."—" But what if he will not give himself? "
—" Well, then . . . . I will make an end of
myself. It will mean that I am good for nothing."

Clara's father . . . . . (he sometimes asked
his wife when he was drunk: " Who was the father of that black-visaged little devil of thine?—I
was not! ")—Clara's father, in the endeavour to
get her off his hands as promptly as possible, undertook to betroth her to a wealthy young merchant, a very stupid fellow,—one of the " cultured " sort. Two weeks before the wedding (she

was only sixteen years of age), she walked up to her betrothed, folded her arms, and drumming with her fingers on her elbows (her favourite pose), she suddenly dealt him a blow, bang! on his rosy cheek with her big, strong hand! He sprang to his feet, and merely gasped,—it must be stated that he was dead in love with her. . . . He asked: "What is that for?" She laughed and left the room.—"I was present in the room," narrated Anna, "and was a witness. I ran after her and said to her: 'Good gracious, Kátya, why didst thou do that?'—But she answered me: 'If he were a real man he would have thrashed me, but as it is, he is a wet hen! And he asks what it is for, to boot. If he loved me and did not avenge himself, then let him bear it and not ask: "what is that for?" He 'll never get anything of me, unto ages of ages!' And so she did not marry him. Soon afterward she made the acquaintance of that actress, and left our house. My mother wept, but my father only said: 'Away with the refractory goat from the flock!' and would take no trouble, or try to hunt her up. Father did not understand Clara. On the eve of her flight," added Anna, "she almost strangled me in her embrace, and kept repeating: 'I cannot! I cannot do otherwise! . . . . My heart may break in two, but I cannot! our cage is too small . . . . it is not large enough for my wings! And one cannot escape his fate'" . . . .

" After that," remarked Anna, " we rarely saw each other. . . . When father died she came to us for a couple of days, took nothing from the inheritance, and again disappeared. She found it oppressive with us. . . . I saw that. Then she returned to Kazán as an actress."

Arátoff began to interrogate Anna concerning the theatre, the parts in which Clara had appeared, her success. . . . Anna answered in detail, but with the same sad, although animated enthusiasm. She even showed Arátoff a photographic portrait, which represented Clara in the costume of one of her parts. In the portrait she was looking to one side, as though turning away from the spectators; the ribbon intertwined with her thick hair fell like a serpent on her bare arm. Arátoff gazed long at that portrait, thought it a good likeness, inquired whether Clara had not taken part in public readings, and learned that she had not; that she required the excitement of the theatre, of the stage . . . . but another question was burning on his lips.

" Anna Semyónovna!" he exclaimed at last, not loudly, but with peculiar force, " tell me, I entreat you, why she . . . . why she made up her mind to that frightful step?"

Anna dropped her eyes.—" I do not know!" she said, after the lapse of several minutes.— " God is my witness, I do not know!" she continued impetuously, perceiving that Arátoff had flung his hands apart as though he did not believe her. . . . "From the very time she arrived here she seemed to be thoughtful, gloomy. Something must infallibly have happened to her in Moscow, which I was not able to divine! But, on the contrary, on that fatal day, she seemed . . . . if not more cheerful, at any rate more tranquil than usual. I did not even have any forebodings," added Anna with a bitter smile, as though reproaching herself for that.

"You see," she began again, "it seemed to have been written in Kátya's fate, that she should be unhappy. She was convinced of it herself from her early youth. She would prop her head on her hand, meditate, and say: 'I shall not live long!' She had forebodings. Just imagine, she even saw beforehand,—sometimes in a dream, sometimes in ordinary wise,—what was going to happen to her! 'I cannot live as I wish, so I will not live at all,' . . . . was her adage.— 'Our life is in our own hands, you know!' And she proved it."

Anna covered her face with her hands and ceased speaking.

"Anna Semyónovna," began Arátoff, after waiting a little: "perhaps you have heard to what the newspapers attributed . . . ."

"To unhappy love?" interrupted Anna, removing her hands from her face with a jerk. "That is a calumny, a calumny, a lie! . . . My

unsullied, unapproachable Kátya . . . . Kátya!
. . . . and an unhappy, rejected love? And
would not I have known about that? . . . Everybody, everybody fell in love with her . . . . but
she. . . . And whom could she have fallen in
love with here? Who, out of all these men, was
worthy of her? Who had attained to that ideal
of honour, uprightness, purity,—most of all,
purity,—which she constantly held before her, in
spite of all her defects? . . . . Reject her . . .
her . . . ."

Anna's voice broke. . . . Her fingers trembled slightly. Suddenly she flushed scarlet all
over . . . . flushed with indignation, and at that
moment—and only at that moment—did she resemble her sister.

Arátoff attempted to apologise.

"Listen," broke in Anna once more:—"I in-
sist upon it that you shall not believe that calumny yourself, and that you shall dissipate it, if
possible! Here, you wish to write an article about
her, or something of that sort:—here is an opportunity for you to defend her memory! That is
why I am talking so frankly with you. Listen:
Kátya left a diary. . . ."

Arátoff started.—"A diary," he whispered.

"Yes, a diary . . . . that is to say, a few
pages only.—Kátya was not fond of writing . . . .
for whole months together she did not write at all
. . . . and her letters were so short! But she

was always, always truthful, she never lied. . . .
Lie, forsooth, with her vanity! I . . . . I will
show you that diary! You shall see for yourself
whether it contains a single hint of any such unhappy love!"

Anna hastily drew from the table-drawer a thin
copy-book, about ten pages in length, no more,
and offered it to Arátoff. The latter grasped it
eagerly, recognised the irregular, bold handwriting,—the handwriting of that anonymous letter,
—opened it at random, and began at the following lines:

"Moscow—Tuesday . . . . June. I sang and recited at
a literary morning. To-day is a significant day for me.
It must decide my fate." (These words were doubly
underlined.) "Once more I have seen . . . ." Here followed several lines which had been carefully blotted out.
—And then: "No! no! no! . . . . I must return to my
former idea, if only . . . ."

Arátoff dropped the hand in which he held the
book, and his head sank quietly on his breast.

"Read!" cried Anna.—"Why don't you read?
Read from the beginning. . . . You can read the
whole of it in five minutes, though this diary ex-
tends over two whole years. In Kazán she wrote
nothing. . . ."

Arátoff slowly rose from his chair, and fairly
crashed down on his knees before Anna!

She was simply petrified with amazement and terror.

"Give . . . . give me this diary," said Arátoff in a fainting voice.—"Give it to me . . . . and the photograph . . . . you must certainly have another—but I will return the diary to you. . . . But I must, I must . . . . ."

In his entreaty, in the distorted features of his face there was something so despairing that it even resembled wrath, suffering. . . . And in reality he was suffering. It seemed as though he had not been able to foresee that such a calamity would descend upon him, and was excitedly begging to be spared, to be saved. . . .

"Give it to me," he repeated.

"But . . . . you . . . . you were not in love with my sister?" said Anna at last.

Arátoff continued to kneel.

"I saw her twice in all . . . . believe me! . . . and if I had not been impelled by causes which I myself cannot clearly either understand or explain . . . . if some power that is stronger than I were not upon me . . . . I would not have asked you. . . . I would not have come hither . . . I must . . . . I ought . . . . why, you said yourself, that I was bound to restore her image!"

"And you were not in love with my sister?" asked Anna for the second time.

Arátoff did not reply at once, and turned away slightly, as though with pain.

"Well, yes! I was! I was!—And I am in love with her now . . . . " he exclaimed with the same desperation as before.

Footsteps became audible in the adjoining room.

"Rise . . . . rise . . . . " said Anna hastily. "My mother is coming."

Arátoff rose.

"And take the diary and the picture. God be with you!—Poor, poor Kátya! . . . But you must return the diary to me," she added with animation.—"And if you write anything, you must be sure to send it to me. . . . Do you hear?"

The appearance of Madame Milovídoff released Arátoff from the necessity of replying.— He succeeded, nevertheless, in whispering:— "You are an angel! Thanks! I will send all that I write. . . . . "

Madame Milovídoff was too drowsy to divine anything. And so Arátoff left Kazán with the photographic portrait in the side-pocket of his coat. He had returned the copy-book to Anna, but without her having detected it, he had cut out the page on which stood the underlined words.

On his way back to Moscow he was again seized with a sort of stupor. Although he secretly rejoiced that he had got what he went for, yet he repelled all thoughts of Clara until he should

reach home again. He meditated a great deal
more about her sister Anna.—"Here now," he
said to himself, "is a wonderful, sympathetic
being! What a delicate comprehension of everything, what a loving heart, what absence of egoism! And how comes it that such girls bloom
with us, and in the provinces,—and in such sur-
roundings into the bargain! She is both sickly,
and ill-favoured, and not young,—but what a
capital wife she would make for an honest, well-
educated man! That is the person with whom one
ought to fall in love! . . ." Arátoff meditated
thus . . . . but on his arrival in Moscow the matter took quite another turn.

XIV

PLATONÍDA IVÁNOVNA was unspeakably delighted at the return of her nephew. She had
thought all sorts of things during his absence!—
"At the very least he has gone to Siberia!" she
whispered, as she sat motionless in her little chamber: "for a year at the very least!"—Moreover
the cook had frightened her by imparting the
most authentic news concerning the disappearance of first one, then another young man from
the neighbourhood. Yásha's complete innocence
and trustworthiness did not in the least serve to
calm the old woman.—"Because . . . . much
that signifies!—he busies himself with photog-

raphy . . . . well, and that is enough! Seize him!" And now here was her Yáshenka come back to her safe and sound! She did notice, it is true, that he appeared to have grown thin, and his face seemed to be sunken—that was comprehensible . . . . he had had no one to look after him. But she did not dare to question him concerning his trip. At dinner she inquired:

"And is Kazán a nice town?"

"Yes," replied Arátoff.

"Tatárs live there, I believe?"

"Not Tatárs only."

"And hast not thou brought a khalát [1] thence?"

"No, I have not."

And there the conversation ended.

But as soon as Arátoff found himself alone in his study he immediately felt as though something were embracing him round about, as though he were again in *the power,*—precisely that, in the power of another life, of another being. Although he had told Anna—in that outburst of sudden frenzy—that he was in love with Clara, that word now seemed to him devoid of sense and whimsical.—No, he was not in love; and how could he fall in love with a dead woman, whom, even during her lifetime he had not liked, whom he had almost forgotten?—No! But he was in the power of . . . . in *her* power . . . . he no

---

[1] The long Tatár coat, with large sleeves, and flaring, bias skirts.—TRANSLATOR.

longer belonged to himself. He had been *taken possession of*. Taken possession of to such a point that he was no longer trying to free himself either by ridiculing his own stupidity, or by arousing in himself if not confidence, at least hope that all this would pass over, that it was nothing but nerves,—or by seeking proofs of it,—or in any other way!—" If I meet him I shall take him " he recalled Clara's words reported by Anna . . . . and so now he had been taken.

But was not she dead? Yes; her body was dead . . . . but how about her soul?—Was not that immortal . . . . did it require bodily organs to manifest its power? Magnetism has demonstrated to us the influence of the living human soul upon another living human soul. . . . Why should not that influence be continued after death, if the soul remains alive?—But with what object? What might be the result of this?—But do we, in general, realise the object of everything which goes on around us?

These reflections occupied Arátoff to such a degree that at tea he suddenly asked Platósha whether she believed in the immortality of the soul. She did not understand at first what it was he had asked; but afterward she crossed herself and replied, " of course. How could the soul be otherwise than immortal?"

" But if that is so, can it act after death?" Arátoff put a second question.

CLARA MÍLITCH

The old woman replied that it could . . . . that is to say, it can pray for us; when it shall have passed through all sorts of tribulations, and is awaiting the Last Judgment. But during the first forty days it only hovers around the spot where its death occurred.

"During the first forty days?"

"Yes; and after that come its tribulations."[1]

Arátoff was surprised at his aunt's erudition, and went off to his own room.—And again he felt the same thing, that same power upon him. The power was manifested thus—that the image of Clara incessantly presented itself to him, in its most minute details,—details which he did not seem to have observed during her lifetime; he saw . . . he saw her fingers, her nails, the bands of hair on her cheeks below her temples, a small mole under the left eye; he saw the movement of her lips, her nostrils, her eyebrows . . . . and what sort of a gait she had, and how she held her head a little on the right side . . . . he saw everything!—He did not admire all this at all; he simply could not help thinking about it and seeing it.—Yet he did not dream about her during the first night after his return . . . . he was very weary and slept like one slain. On the other hand, no sooner did he awake than she again entered his room, and there she remained, as though she had been its owner; just as though she had

[1] See note on page 24.—TRANSLATOR.

273

purchased for herself that right by her voluntary death, without asking him or requiring his permission.

He took her photograph; he began to reproduce it, to enlarge it. Then it occurred to him to arrange it for the stereoscope. It cost him a great deal of trouble, but at last he succeeded. He fairly started when he beheld through the glass her figure which had acquired the semblance of bodily substance. But that figure was grey, as though covered with dust . . . . and moreover, the eyes . . . . the eyes still gazed aside, as though they were averting themselves. He began to gaze at them for a long, long time, as though expecting that they might, at any moment, turn themselves in his direction . . . . he even puckered up his eyes deliberately . . . . but the eyes remained motionless, and the whole figure assumed the aspect of a doll. He went away, threw himself into an arm-chair, got out the leaf which he had torn from her diary, with the underlined words, and thought: "They say that people in love kiss the lines which have been written by a beloved hand; but I have no desire to do that —and the chirography appears to me ugly into the bargain. But in that line lies my condemnation."—At this point there flashed into his mind the promise he had made to Anna about the article. He seated himself at his table, and set about writing it; but everything he wrote turned

out so rhetorical . . . . worst of all, so artificial
. . . . just as though he did not believe in what
he was writing, or in his own feelings . . . . and
Clara herself seemed to him unrecognisable, incomprehensible! She would not yield herself to
him.

"No," he thought, throwing aside his pen,
"either I have no talent for writing in general, or
I must wait a while yet!"

He began to call to mind his visit to the Milovídoffs, and all the narration of Anna, of that
kind, splendid Anna. . . . The word she had uttered: "unsullied!" suddenly struck him. It was
exactly as though something had scorched and illuminated him.

"Yes," he said aloud, "she was unsullied and I
am unsullied. . . . That is what has given her
this power!"

Thoughts concerning the immortality of the
soul, the life beyond the grave, again visited him.
"Is it not said in the Bible: 'O death, where is
thy sting?' And in Schiller: 'And the dead
also shall live!' (*Auch die Todten sollen leben!*) —
Or here again, in Mickiewicz, 'I shall love until
life ends . . . . and after life ends!'—While one
English writer has said: 'Love is stronger than
death!'"—The biblical sentence acted with peculiar force on Arátoff. He wanted to look up the
place where those words were to be found. . . .
He had no Bible; he went to borrow one from

Platósha. She was astonished; but she got out an old, old book in a warped leather binding with brass clasps, all spotted with wax, and handed it to Arátoff. He carried it off to his own room, but for a long time could not find that verse . . . . but on the other hand, he hit upon another:

"Greater love hath no man than this, that a man lay down his life for his friends" . . . . (the Gospel of John, Chap. XV, verse 13).

He thought: "That is not properly expressed. —It should read: 'Greater *power* hath no man!'" . . . .

"But what if she did not set her soul on me at all? What if she killed herself merely because life had become a burden to her?—What if she, in conclusion, did not come to that tryst with the object of obtaining declarations of love at all?"

But at that moment Clara before her parting on the boulevard rose up before him. . . . He recalled that sorrowful expression on her face, and those tears, and those words:—"Akh, you have understood nothing!"

No! He could not doubt for what object and for what person she had laid down her life. . .

Thus passed that day until nightfall.

XV

ARÁTOFF went early to bed, without feeling particularly sleepy; but he hoped to find rest in bed.

The strained condition of his nerves caused him a fatigue which was far more intolerable than the physical weariness of the journey and the road. But great as was his fatigue, he could not get to sleep. He tried to read .... but the lines got entangled before his eyes. He extinguished his candle, and darkness took possession of his chamber.—But he continued to lie there sleepless, with closed eyes. . . . And now it seemed to him that some one was whispering in his ear. . . . "It is the beating of my heart, the rippling of the blood," he thought. . . . But the whisper passed into coherent speech. Some one was talking Russian hurriedly, plaintively, and incomprehensibly. It was impossible to distinguish a single separate word. . . . But it was Clara's voice!

Arátoff opened his eyes, rose up in bed, propped himself on his elbows. . . . The voice grew fainter, but continued its plaintive, hurried, unintelligible speech as before. . . .

It was indubitably Clara's voice!

Some one's fingers ran over the keys of the piano in light arpeggios. . . . Then the voice began to speak again. More prolonged sounds made themselves audible . . . . like moans . . . . always the same. And then words began to detach themselves. . . .

"Roses . . . . roses . . . . roses." . . .

"Roses," repeated Arátoff in a whisper.—

"Akh, yes! The roses which I saw on the head of that woman in my dream. . . ."

"Roses," was audible again.

"Is it thou?" asked Arátoff, whispering as before.

The voice suddenly ceased.

Arátoff waited . . . . waited—and dropped his head on his pillow. "A hallucination of hearing," he thought. "Well, and what if . . . . what if she really is here, close to me? . . . What if I were to see her, would I be frightened? But why should I be frightened? Why should I rejoice? Possibly because it would be a proof that there is another world, that the soul is immortal. —But, however, even if I were to see anything, that also might be a hallucination of the sight". . . .

Nevertheless he lighted his candle, and shot a glance over the whole room not without some trepidation . . . . and descried nothing unusual in it. He rose, approached the stereoscope . . . . and there again was the same grey doll, with eyes which gazed to one side. The feeling of alarm in Arátoff was replaced by one of vexation. He had been, as it were, deceived in his expectations . . . . and those same expectations appeared to him absurd.—"Well, this is downright stupid!" he muttered as he got back into bed, and blew out his light. Again profound darkness reigned in the room.

Arátoff made up his mind to go to sleep this time. . . . But a new sensation had cropped up within him. It seemed to him as though some one were standing in the middle of the room, not far from him, and breathing in a barely perceptible manner. He hastily turned round, opened his eyes. . . . But what could be seen in that impenetrable darkness?—He began to fumble for a match on his night-stand . . . . and suddenly it seemed to him as though some soft, noiseless whirlwind dashed across the whole room, above him, through him—and the words: " 'T is I!" rang plainly in his ears. " 'T is I! 'T is I! . . ."

Several moments passed before he succeeded in lighting a match.

Again there was no one in the room, and he no longer heard anything except the violent beating of his own heart. He drank a glass of water, and remained motionless, with his head resting on his hand.

He said to himself: " I will wait. Either this is all nonsense . . . . or she is here. She will not play with me like a cat with a mouse!" He waited, waited a long time . . . so long that the hand on which he was propping his head became numb . . . . but not a single one of his previous sensations was repeated. A couple of times his eyes closed. . . . He immediately opened them . . . . at least, it seemed to him that he opened them. Gradually they became riveted on the

door and so remained. The candle burned out
and the room became dark once more . . . . but
the door gleamed like a long, white spot in the
midst of the gloom. And lo! that spot began to
move, it contracted, vanished . . . . and in its
place, on the threshold, a female form made its
appearance. Arátoff looked at it intently . . . .
it was Clara! And this time she was gazing
straight at him, she moved toward him. . . . On
her head was a wreath of red roses. . . . It kept
undulating, rising. . . .

Before him stood his aunt in her nightcap,
with a broad red ribbon, and in a white wrapper.

"Platósha!" he enunciated with difficulty.—
"Is it you?"

"It is I," replied Platonída Ivánovna. . . .
"It is I, Yashyónotchek, it is I."

"Why have you come?"

"Why, thou didst wake me. At first thou
seemedst to be moaning all the while . . . . and
then suddenly thou didst begin to shout: 'Save
me! Help me!'"

"I shouted?"

"Yes, thou didst shout, and so hoarsely: 'Save
me!'—I thought: 'O Lord! Can he be ill?' So
I entered. Art thou well?"

"Perfectly well."

"Come, that means that thou hast had a bad
dream. I will fumigate with incense if thou
wishest—shall I?"

Again Arátoff gazed intently at his aunt, and burst into a loud laugh. . . . The figure of the kind old woman in nightcap and wrapper, with her frightened, long-drawn face, really was extremely comical. All that mysterious something which had surrounded him, had stifled him, all those delusions dispersed on the instant.

"No, Platósha, my dear, it is not necessary," he said.—"Forgive me for having involuntarily alarmed you. May your rest be tranquil—and I will go to sleep also."

Platonída Ivánovna stood a little while longer on the spot where she was, pointed at the candle, grumbled: "Why dost thou not extinguish it? . . . . there will be a catastrophe before long!" —and as she retired, could not refrain from making the sign of the cross over him from afar.

Arátoff fell asleep immediately, and slept until morning. He rose in a fine frame of mind . . . . although he regretted something. . . . He felt light and free. "What romantic fancies one does devise," he said to himself with a smile. He did not once glance either at the stereoscope or the leaf which he had torn out. But immediately after breakfast he set off to see Kupfer.

What drew him thither . . . . he dimly recognised.

XVI

ARÁTOFF found his sanguine friend at home. He chatted a little with him, reproached him for having quite forgotten him and his aunt, listened to fresh laudations of the golden woman, the Princess, from whom Kupfer had just received, —from Yaroslávl,—a skull-cap embroidered with fish-scales . . . . and then suddenly sitting down in front of Kupfer, and looking him straight in the eye, he announced that he had been to Kazán.

"Thou hast been to Kazán? Why so?"

"Why, because I wished to collect information about that . . . . Clara Mílitch."

"The girl who poisoned herself?"

"Yes."

Kupfer shook his head.—"What a fellow thou art! And such a sly one! Thou hast travelled a thousand versts there and back . . . . and all for what? Hey? If there had only been some feminine interest there! Then I could understand everything! every sort of folly!"—Kupfer ruffled up his hair.—"But for the sake of collecting materials, as you learned men put it. . . . No, I thank you! That's what the committee of statistics exists for!—Well, and what about it—didst thou make acquaintance with the old woman and with her sister? She's a splendid girl, isn't she?"

CLARA MÍLITCH

"Splendid," assented Arátoff.—"She communicated to me many curious things."

"Did she tell thee precisely how Clara poisoned herself?"

"Thou meanest . . . . what dost thou mean?"

"Why, in what manner?"

"No . . . . She was still in such affliction. . . . I did not dare to question her too much. But was there anything peculiar about it?"

"Of course there was. Just imagine: she was to have acted that very day—and she did act. She took a phial of poison with her to the theatre, drank it before the first act, and in that condition played through the whole of that act. With the poison inside her! What dost thou think of that strength of will? What character, was n't it? And they say that she never sustained her rôle with so much feeling, with so much warmth! The audience suspected nothing, applauded, recalled her. . . . But as soon as the curtain fell she dropped down where she stood on the stage. She began to writhe . . . . and writhe . . . . and at the end of an hour her spirit fled! But is it possible I did not tell thee that? It was mentioned in the newspapers also."

Arátoff's hands suddenly turned cold and his chest began to heave. "No, thou didst not tell me that," he said at last.—"And dost thou not know what the piece was?"

Kupfer meditated.—"I was told the name of

283

the piece . . . . a young girl who has been be-
trayed appears in it. . . . It must be some drama
or other. Clara was born for dramatic parts.
Her very appearance. . . . But where art thou
going?" Kupfer interrupted himself, perceiving
that Arátoff was picking up his cap.

"I do not feel quite well," replied Arátoff.
"Good-bye. . . . I will drop in some other time."

Kupfer held him back and looked him in the
face.—"What a nervous fellow thou art, brother!
Just look at thyself. . . . . Thou hast turned as
white as clay."

"I do not feel well," repeated Arátoff, free-
ing himself from Kupfer's hands and going his
way. Only at that moment did it become clear to
him that he had gone to Kupfer with the sole object of talking about Clara. . . .

"About foolish, about unhappy Clara". . . .

But on reaching home he speedily recovered his
composure to a certain extent.

The circumstances which had attended Clara's
death at first exerted a shattering impression
upon him . . . . but later on that acting "with
the poison inside her," as Kupfer had expressed
it, seemed to him a monstrous phrase, a piece of
bravado, and he tried not to think of it, fearing
to arouse within himself a feeling akin to aversion. But at dinner, as he sat opposite Platósha,
he suddenly remembered her nocturnal appari-
tion, recalled that bob-tailed wrapper, that cap

with the tall ribbon (and why should there be a ribbon on a night-cap?), the whole of that ridiculous figure, at which all his visions had dispersed into dust, as though at the whistle of the machinist in a fantastic ballet! He even made Platósha repeat the tale of how she had heard him shout, had taken fright, had leaped out of bed, had not been able at once to find either her own door or his, and so forth. In the evening he played cards with her and went off to his own room in a somewhat sad but fairly tranquil state of mind.

Arátoff did not think about the coming night, and did not fear it; he was convinced that he should pass it in the best possible manner. The thought of Clara awoke in him from time to time; but he immediately remembered that she had killed herself in a "spectacular" manner, and turned away. That "outrageous" act prevented other memories from rising in him. Giving a cursory glance at the stereoscope it seemed to him that she was looking to one side because she felt ashamed. Directly over the stereoscope on the wall, hung the portrait of his mother. Arátoff removed it from its nail, kissed it, and carefully put it away in a drawer. Why did he do this? Because that portrait must not remain in the vicinity of that woman . . . . or for some other reason—Arátoff did not quite know. But his mother's portrait evoked in him memories of his father . . . . of that father whom he had seen dying in that same room, on that very bed. "What dost thou think about all this, father?" he mentally addressed him. "Thou didst understand all this; thou didst also believe in Schiller's world of spirits.—Give me counsel!"

"My father has given me counsel to drop all these follies," said Arátoff aloud, and took up a book. But he was not able to read long, and feeling a certain heaviness all through his body, he went to bed earlier than usual, in the firm conviction that he should fall asleep immediately.

And so it came about . . . . but his hopes for a peaceful night were not realised.

XVII

BEFORE the clock struck midnight he had a remarkable, a menacing dream.

It seemed to him that he was in a sumptuous country-house of which he was the owner. He had recently purchased the house, and all the estates attached to it. And he kept thinking: "It is well, now it is well, but disaster is coming!" Beside him was hovering a tiny little man, his manager; this man kept making obeisances, and trying to demonstrate to Arátoff how admirably everything about his house and estate was arranged.—"Please, please look," he kept reiterating, grinning at every word, "how everything

is flourishing about you! Here are horses . . . .
what magnificent horses!" And Arátoff saw a
row of huge horses. They were standing with
their backs to him, in stalls; they had wonderful
manes and tails . . . . but as soon as Arátoff
walked past them the horses turned their heads
toward him and viciously displayed their teeth.

"It is well," thought Arátoff, "but disaster is
coming!"

"Please, please," repeated his manager again;
"please come into the garden; see what splendid
apples we have!"

The apples really were splendid, red, and
round; but as soon as Arátoff looked at them,
they began to shrivel and fall. . . . "Disaster is
coming!" he thought.

"And here is the lake," murmurs the manager:
—"how blue and smooth it is! And here is a little golden boat! . . . . Would you like to have a
sail in it? . . . . It moves of itself."

"I will not get into it!" thought Arátoff; "a
disaster is coming!" and nevertheless he did seat
himself in the boat. On the bottom, writhing, lay
a little creature resembling an ape; in its paws it
was holding a phial filled with a dark liquid.

"Pray do not feel alarmed," shouted the manager from the shore. . . . "That is nothing!
That is death! A prosperous journey!"

The boat darted swiftly onward . . . . but
suddenly a hurricane arose, not like the one of

the day before, soft and noiseless—no; it is a black, terrible, howling hurricane!—Everything is in confusion round about;—and amid the swirling gloom Arátoff beholds Clara in theatrical costume: she is raising the phial to her lips, a distant "Bravo! bravo!" is audible, and a coarse voice shouts in Arátoff's ear:

"Ah! And didst thou think that all this would end in a comedy?—No! it is a tragedy! a tragedy!"

Arátoff awoke all in a tremble. It was not dark in the room. . . . A faint and melancholy light streamed from somewhere or other, impassively illuminating all objects. Arátoff did not try to account to himself for the light. . . . He felt but one thing: Clara was there in that room . . . . he felt her presence . . . . he was again and forever in her power!

A shriek burst from his lips: "Clara, art thou here?"

"Yes!" rang out clearly in the middle of the room illuminated with the motionless light.

Arátoff doubly repeated his question. . . .

"Yes!" was audible once more.

"Then I want to see thee!" he cried, springing out of bed.

For several moments he stood in one spot, treading the cold floor with his bare feet. His eyes roved: "But where? Where?" whispered his lips. . . .

Nothing was to be seen or heard.

He looked about him, and noticed that the faint light which filled the room proceeded from a night-light, screened by a sheet of paper, and placed in one corner, probably by Platósha while he was asleep. He even detected the odour of incense also, in all probability, the work of her hands.

He hastily dressed himself. Remaining in bed, sleeping, was not to be thought of.—Then he took up his stand in the centre of the room and folded his arms. The consciousness of Clara's presence was stronger than ever within him.

And now he began to speak, in a voice which was not loud, but with the solemn deliberation wherewith exorcisms are uttered:

"Clara,"—thus did he begin,—"if thou art really here, if thou seest me, if thou hearest me, reveal thyself!... If that power which I feel upon me is really thy power,—reveal thyself! If thou understandest how bitterly I repent of not having understood thee, of having repulsed thee,—reveal thyself!—If that which I have heard is really thy voice; if the feeling which has taken possession of me is love; if thou art now convinced that I love thee,—I who up to this time have not loved, and have not known a single woman;—if thou knowest that after thy death I fell passionately, irresistibly in love with thee, if thou dost not wish me to go mad—reveal thyself!"

No sooner had Arátoff uttered this last word than he suddenly felt some one swiftly approach him from behind, as on that occasion upon the boulevard—and lay a hand upon his shoulder. He wheeled round—and saw no one. But the consciousness of *her* presence became so distinct, so indubitable, that he cast another hasty glance behind him. . . .

What was that?! In his arm-chair, a couple of paces from him, sat a woman all in black. Her head was bent to one side, as in the stereoscope. . . . . It was she! It was Clara! But what a stern, what a mournful face!

Arátoff sank down gently upon his knees.— Yes, he was right, then; neither fear, nor joy was in him, nor even surprise. . . . His heart even began to beat more quietly.—The only thing in him was the feeling: "Ah! At last! At last!"

" Clara," he began in a faint but even tone, " why dost thou not look at me? I know it is thou . . . but I might, seest thou, think that my imagination had created an image like *that one*. . . ." (He pointed in the direction of the stereoscope.) . . . . " Prove to me that it is thou. . . . Turn toward me, look at me, Clara!"

Clara's hand rose slowly . . . . and fell again.

" Clara! Clara! Turn toward me!"

And Clara's head turned slowly, her drooping lids opened, and the dark pupils of her eyes were fixed on Arátoff.

He started back, and uttered a tremulous, long-drawn: " Ah! "

Clara gazed intently at him . . . . but her eyes, her features preserved their original thoughtfully-stern, almost displeased expression. With precisely that expression she had presented herself on the platform upon the day of the literary morning, before she had caught sight of Arátoff. And now, as on that occasion also, she suddenly flushed scarlet, her face grew animated, her glance flashed, and a joyful, triumphant smile parted her lips. . . .

"I am forgiven! "—cried Arátoff.—" Thou hast conquered. . . So take me! For I am thine, and thou art mine! "

He darted toward her, he tried to kiss those smiling, those triumphant lips,—and he did kiss them, he felt their burning touch, he felt even the moist chill of her teeth, and a rapturous cry rang through the half-dark room.

Platonída Ivánovna ran in and found him in a swoon. He was on his knees; his head was lying on the arm-chair; his arms, outstretched before him, hung powerless; his pale face breathed forth the intoxication of boundless happiness.

Platonída Ivánovna threw herself beside him, embraced him, stammered: " Yásha! Yáshenka!

Yashenyónotchek!!" [1] tried to lift him up with her bony arms . . . . he did not stir. Then Platonída Ivánovna set to screaming in an unrecognisable voice. The maid-servant ran in. Together they managed somehow to lift him up, seated him in a chair, and began to dash water on him—and water in which a holy image had been washed at that. . . .

He came to himself; but merely smiled in reply to his aunt's queries, and with such a blissful aspect that she became more perturbed than ever, and kept crossing first him and then herself. . . . . At last Arátoff pushed away her hand, and still with the same beatific expression on his countenance, he said:—

"What is the matter with you, Platósha?"

"What ails thee, Yáshenka?"

"Me?—I am happy . . . . happy, Platósha . . . . that is what ails me. But now I want to go to bed and sleep."

He tried to rise, but felt such a weakness in his legs and in all his body that he was not in a condition to undress and get into bed himself without the aid of his aunt and of the maid-servant. But he fell asleep very quickly, preserving on his face that same blissfully-rapturous expression. Only his face was extremely pale.

[1] Diminutives of Yákoff, implying great affection.—TRANSLATOR.

XVIII

WHEN Platonída Ivánovna entered his room on the following morning he was in the same condition . . . . but his weakness had not passed off, and he even preferred to remain in bed. Platonída Ivánovna did not like the pallor of his face in particular.

"What does it mean, O Lord!" she thought. "There is n't a drop of blood in his face, he refuses his beef-tea; he lies there and laughs, and keeps asserting that he is quite well!"

He refused breakfast also.—"Why dost thou do that, Yásha?" she asked him; "dost thou intend to lie like this all day?"

"And what if I do?" replied Arátoff, affectionately.

This very affection also did not please Platonída Ivánovna. Arátoff wore the aspect of a man who has learned a great secret, which is very agreeable to him, and is jealously clinging to it and reserving it for himself. He was waiting for night, not exactly with impatience but with curiosity.

"What comes next?" he asked himself;— "what will happen?" He had ceased to be surprised, to be perplexed; he cherished no doubt as to his having entered into communication with Clara; that they loved each other . . . . he did not doubt, either. Only . . . . what can come of such a love?—He recalled that kiss . . . . and a wondrous chill coursed swiftly and sweetly through all his limbs.—" Romeo and Juliet did not exchange such a kiss as that! " he thought. " But the next time I shall hold out better. . . . I shall possess her. . . . She will come with the garland of tiny roses in her black curls. . . . .

" But after that what? For we cannot live together, can we? Consequently I must die in order to be with her? Was not that what she came for,—and is it not in *that* way she wishes to take me?

" Well, and what of that? If I must die, I must. Death does not terrify me in the least now. For it cannot annihilate me, can it? On the contrary, only *thus* and *there* shall I be happy . . . . as I have never been happy in my life-time, as she has never been in hers. . . . For we are both unsullied!—Oh, that kiss! "

PLATONÍDA IVÁNOVNA kept entering Arátoff's room; she did not worry him with questions, she merely took a look at him, whispered, sighed, and went out again.—But now he refused his dinner also. . . . Things were getting quite too bad. The old woman went off to her friend, the medical man of the police-district, in whom she had faith simply because he did not drink and was married to a German woman. Arátoff was

astonished when she brought the man to him;
but Platónida Ivánovna began so insistently to
entreat her Yáshenka to permit Paramón Paramónitch (that was the medical man's name) to
examine him—come, now, just for her sake!—
that Arátoff consented. Paramón Paramónitch
felt his pulse, looked at his tongue, interrogated
him after a fashion, and finally announced
that it was indispensably necessary to "auscul-
tate" him. Arátoff was in such a submissive
frame of mind that he consented to this also.
The doctor delicately laid bare his breast,
delicately tapped it, listened, smiled, prescribed
some drops and a potion, but chief of all, advised him to be quiet, and refrain from violent
emotions.

"You don't say so!" thought Arátoff. . . .
"Well, brother, thou hast bethought thyself too
late!"

"What ails Yásha?" asked Platónida Ivánovna, as she handed Paramón Paramónitch a
three-ruble bank-note on the threshold. The dis-
trict doctor, who, like all contemporary doctors,
—especially those of them who wear a uniform,
—was fond of showing off his learned termin-
ology, informed her that her nephew had all the
dioptric symptoms of nervous cardialgia, and
that febris was present also.

"But speak more simply, dear little father,"
broke in Platónida Ivánovna; "don't scare me

with Latin; thou art not in an apothecary's shop!"

"His heart is out of order," explained the doctor;—"well, and he has fever also," . . . . and he repeated his advice with regard to repose and moderation.

"But surely there is no danger?" sternly inquired Platonída Ivánovna, as much as to say: "Look out and don't try your Latin on me again!"

"Not at present!"

The doctor went away, and Platonída Ivánovna took to grieving. . . . Nevertheless she sent to the apothecary for the medicine, which Aratóff would not take, despite her entreaties. He even refused herb-tea.

"What makes you worry so, dear?" he said to her. "I assure you I am now the most perfectly healthy and happy man in the whole world!"

Platonída Ivánovna merely shook her head. Toward evening he became slightly feverish; yet he still insisted upon it that she should not remain in his room, and should go away to her own to sleep. Platonída Ivánovna obeyed, but did not undress, and did not go to bed; she sat up in an arm-chair and kept listening and whispering her prayer.

She was beginning to fall into a doze, when suddenly a dreadful, piercing shriek awakened

her. She sprang to her feet, rushed into Arátoff's study, and found him lying on the floor,
as upon the night before.

But he did not come to himself as he had done
the night before, work over him as they would.
That night he was seized with a high fever, com-
plicated by inflammation of the heart.

A few days later he died.

A strange circumstance accompanied his second
swoon. When they lifted him up and put him
to bed, there proved to be a small lock of woman's
black hair clutched in his right hand. Where
had that hair come from? Anna Semyónovna
had such a lock, which she had kept after
Clara's death; but why should she have given
to Arátoff an object which was so precious
to her? Could she have laid it into the diary,
and not noticed the fact when she gave him the
book?

In the delirium which preceded his death Arátoff called himself Romeo . . . . after the poison; he talked about a marriage contracted, con-
summated;—said that now he knew the meaning
of delight. Especially dreadful for Platonída
Ivánovna was the moment when Arátoff, recov-
ering consciousness, and seeing her by his bedside,
said to her:

" Aunty, why art thou weeping? Is it because
I must die? But dost thou not know that love
is stronger than death? . . . . Death! O Death,

where is thy sting? Thou must not weep, but rejoice, even as I rejoice. . . ."

And again the face of the dying man beamed with that same blissful smile which had made the poor old woman shudder so.

POEMS IN PROSE

(1878–1882)

POEMS IN PROSE

From the Editor of the "European Messenger"

IN compliance with our request, Iván Sergyée-
vitch Turgénieff has given his consent to our
sharing now with the readers of our journal, without delay, those passing comments, thoughts, images which he had noted down, under one impression or another of current existence, during the
last five years,—those which belong to him personally, and those which pertain to society in general. They, like many others, have not found a
place in those finished productions of the past
which have already been presented to the world,
and have formed a complete collection in themselves. From among these the author has made
fifty selections.

In the letter accompanying the pages which we
are now about to print, I. S. Turgénieff says, in
conclusion:

" . . . . Let not your reader peruse these
'Poems in Prose' at one sitting; he will probably be bored, and the book will fall from his
hands. But let him read them separately,—to-
day one, to-morrow another,—and then perchance

some one of them may leave some trace behind in his soul. . . ."

The pages have no general title; the author has written on their wrapper: "Senilia—An Old Man's Jottings,"—but we have preferred the words carelessly dropped by the author in the end of his letter to us, quoted above,—"Poems in Prose"—and we print the pages under that general title. In our opinion, it fully expresses the source from which such comments might present themselves to the soul of an author well known for his sensitiveness to the various questions of life, as well as the impression which they may produce on the reader, "leaving behind in his soul" many things. They are, in reality, poems in spite of the fact that they are written in prose. We place them in chronological order, beginning with the year 1878.

M. S.[1]

October 28, 1882.

I

(1878)

THE VILLAGE

THE last day of July; for a thousand versts round about lies Russia, the fatherland.

The whole sky is suffused with an even azure;

[1] Mikhaíl Stasiulévitch.—TRANSLATOR.

there is only one little cloud in it, which is half floating, half melting. There is no wind, it is warm . . . . the air is like new milk!

Larks are carolling; large-cropped pigeons are cooing; the swallows dart past in silence; the horses neigh and munch, the dogs do not bark, but stand peaceably wagging their tails.

And there is an odour of smoke abroad, and of grass,—and a tiny whiff of tan,—and another of leather.—The hemp-patches, also, are in their glory, and emit their heavy but agreeable fragrance.

A deep but not long ravine. Along its sides, in several rows, grow bulky-headed willows, stripped bare at the bottom. Through the ravine runs a brook; on its bottom tiny pebbles seem to tremble athwart its pellucid ripples.—Far away, at the spot where the rims of earth and sky come together, is the bluish streak of a large river.

Along the ravine, on one side are neat little storehouses, and buildings with tightly-closed doors; on the other side are five or six pine-log cottages with board roofs. Over each roof rises a tall pole with a starling house; over each tiny porch is an openwork iron horse's head with a stiff mane.[1] The uneven window-panes sparkle with the hues of the rainbow. Jugs holding bouquets are painted on the shutters. In front

[1] The favourite decoration in rustic architecture.—TRANSLATOR.

of each cottage stands sedately a precise little bench; on the earthen banks around the foundations of the house cats lie curled in balls, with their transparent ears pricked up on the alert; behind the lofty thresholds the anterooms look dark and cool.

I am lying on the very brink of the ravine, on an outspread horse-cloth; round about are whole heaps of new-mown hay, which is fragrant to the point of inducing faintness. The sagacious householders have spread out the hay in front of their cottages: let it dry a little more in the hot sun, and then away with it to the barn! It will be a glorious place for a nap!

The curly heads of children project from each haycock; crested hens are searching in the hay for gnats and small beetles; a white-toothed puppy is sprawling among the tangled blades of grass.

Ruddy-curled youths in clean, low-girt shirts, and heavy boots with borders, are bandying lively remarks as they stand with their breasts resting on the unhitched carts, and display their teeth in a grin.

From a window a round-faced lass peeps out; she laughs, partly at their words, and partly at the pranks of the children in the heaped-up hay.

Another lass with her sturdy arms is drawing a huge, dripping bucket from the well. . . . The bucket trembles and rocks on the rope, scattering long, fiery drops.

In front of me stands an aged housewife in a new-checked petticoat of homespun and new peasant-shoes.

Large inflated beads in three rows encircle her thin, swarthy neck; her grey hair is bound about with a yellow kerchief with red dots; it droops low over her dimmed eyes.

But her aged eyes smile in cordial wise; her whole wrinkled face smiles. The old woman must be in her seventh decade . . . . and even now it can be seen that she was a beauty in her day!

With the sunburned fingers of her right hand widely spread apart, she holds a pot of cool, unskimmed milk, straight from the cellar; the sides of the pot are covered with dewdrops, like small pearl beads. On the palm of her left hand the old woman offers me a big slice of bread still warm from the oven. As much as to say: " Eat, and may health be thine, thou passing guest! "

A cock suddenly crows and busily flaps his wings; an imprisoned calf lows without haste, in reply.

" Hey, what fine oats! " the voice of my coachman makes itself heard. . . .

O Russian contentment, repose, plenty! O free village! O tranquillity and abundance!

And I thought to myself: " What care we for

the cross on the dome of Saint Sophia in Constantinople, and all the other things for which we strive, we people of the town?"

February, 1878.

A CONVERSATION

"Never yet has human foot trod either the
Jungfrau or the Finsteraarhorn."

THE summits of the Alps. . . . A whole chain of steep cliffs. . . . The very heart of the mountains.

Overhead a bright, mute, pale-green sky. A hard, cruel frost; firm, sparkling snow; from beneath the snow project grim blocks of ice-bound, wind-worn cliffs.

Two huge masses, two giants rise aloft, one on each side of the horizon: the Jungfrau and the Finsteraarhorn.

And the Jungfrau says to its neighbour: "What news hast thou to tell? Thou canst see better.—What is going on there below?"

Several thousand years pass by like one minute. And the Finsteraarhorn rumbles in reply: "Dense clouds veil the earth. . . . Wait!"

More thousands of years elapse, as it were one minute.

"Well, what now?" inquires the Jungfrau.

"Now I can see; down yonder, below, everything is still the same: party-coloured, tiny. The waters gleam blue; the forests are black; heaps of stones piled up shine grey. Around them small beetles are still bustling,—thou knowest, those two-legged beetles who have as yet been unable to defile either thou or me."

" Men? "

" Yes, men."

Thousands of years pass, as it were one minute.

" Well, and what now? " asks the Jungfrau.

" I seem to see fewer of the little beetles," thunders the Finsteraarhorn. " Things have become clearer down below; the waters have contracted; the forests have grown thinner."

More thousands of years pass, as it were one minute.

" What dost thou see? " says the Jungfrau.

" Things seem to have grown clearer round us, close at hand," replies the Finsteraarhorn; " well, and yonder, far away, in the valleys there is still a spot, and something is moving."

" And now? " inquires the Jungfrau, after other thousands of years, which are as one minute.

" Now it is well," replies the Finsteraarhorn; " it is clean everywhere, quite white, wherever one looks. . . . Everywhere is our snow, level snow and ice. Everything is congealed. It is well now, and calm."

"Good," said the Jungfrau.—"But thou and I have chattered enough, old fellow. It is time to sleep."

"It is time!"

The huge mountains slumber; the green, clear heaven slumbers over the earth which has grown dumb forever.

February, 1878.

THE OLD WOMAN

I was walking across a spacious field, alone.

And suddenly I thought I heard light, cautious footsteps behind my back. . . . Some one was following me.

I glanced round and beheld a tiny, bent old woman, all enveloped in grey rags. The old woman's face was visible from beneath them: a yellow, wrinkled, sharp-nosed, toothless face.

I stepped up to her. . . . She halted.

"Who art thou? What dost thou want? Art thou a beggar? Dost thou expect alms?"

The old woman made no answer. I bent down to her and perceived that both her eyes were veiled with a semi-transparent, whitish membrane or film, such as some birds have; therewith they protect their eyes from too brilliant a light.

But in the old woman's case that film did not move and reveal the pupils . . . . from which I inferred that she was blind.

308

"Dost thou want alms?" I repeated my question.—"Why art thou following me?"—But, as before, the old woman did not answer, and merely shrank back almost imperceptibly.

I turned from her and went my way.

And lo! again I hear behind me those same light, measured footsteps which seem to be creeping stealthily up.

"There's that woman again!" I said to myself.—"Why has she attached herself to me?" —But at this point I mentally added: "Probably, owing to her blindness, she has lost her way, and now she is guiding herself by the sound of my steps, in order to come out, in company with me, at some inhabited place. Yes, yes; that is it."

But a strange uneasiness gradually gained possession of my thoughts: it began to seem to me as though that old woman were not only following me, but were guiding me,—that she was thrusting me now to the right, now to the left, and that I was involuntarily obeying her.

Still I continue to walk on . . . . but now, in front of me, directly in my road, something looms up black and expands . . . . some sort of pit. . . . "The grave!" flashes through my mind.—"That is where she is driving me!"

I wheel abruptly round. Again the old woman is before me . . . . but she sees! She gazes at me with large, evil eyes which bode me ill . . . . the eyes of a bird of prey. . . . I bend down to her face, to her eyes. . . . Again there is the same film, the same blind, dull visage as before. . . .

" Akh! " I think . . . . " this old woman is my Fate—that Fate which no man can escape!

" I cannot get away! I cannot get away!— What madness. . . . I must make an effort." And I dart to one side, in a different direction.

I advance briskly. . . But the light footsteps, as before, rustle behind me, close, close behind me. . . . And in front of me again the pit yawns.

Again I turn in another direction. . . . And again there is the same rustling behind me, the same menacing spot in front of me.

And no matter in what direction I dart, like a hare pursued . . . . it is always the same, the same!

" Stay! " I think.—" I will cheat her! I will not go anywhere at all! "—and I instantaneously sit down on the ground.

The old woman stands behind me, two paces distant.—I do not hear her, but I feel that she is there.

And suddenly I behold that spot which had loomed black in the distance, gliding on, creeping up to me itself!

O God! I glance behind me. . . . The old woman is looking straight at me, and her toothless mouth is distorted in a grin. . . .

" Thou canst not escape! "

February, 1878.

POEMS IN PROSE

THE DOG

THERE are two of us in the room, my dog and I. . . . A frightful storm is raging out of doors.

The dog is sitting in front of me, and gazing straight into my eyes.

And I, also, am looking him straight in the eye.

He seems to be anxious to say something to me. He is dumb, he has no words, he does not understand himself—but I understand him.

I understand that, at this moment, both in him and in me there dwells one and the same feeling, that there is no difference whatever between us. We are exactly alike; in each of us there burns and glows the selfsame tremulous flame.

Death is swooping down upon us, it is waving its cold, broad wings. . . .

" And this is the end! "

Who shall decide afterward, precisely what sort of flame burned in each one of us?

No! it is not an animal and a man exchanging glances. . . .

It is two pairs of eyes exactly alike fixed on each other.

And in each of those pairs, in the animal and in the man, one and the same life is huddling up timorously to the other.

February, 1878.

THE RIVAL

I HAD a comrade-rival; not in our studies, not in the service or in love; but our views did not agree on any point, and every time we met, interminable arguments sprang up.

We argued about art, religion, science, about the life of earth and matters beyond the grave,— especially life beyond the grave.

He was a believer and an enthusiast. One day he said to me: " Thou laughest at everything; but if I die before thee, I will appear to thee from the other world. . . . We shall see whether thou wilt laugh then."

And, as a matter of fact, he did die before me, while he was still young in years; but years passed, and I had forgotten his promise,—his threat.

One night I was lying in bed, and could not get to sleep, neither did I wish to do so.

It was neither light nor dark in the room; I began to stare into the grey half-gloom.

And suddenly it seemed to me that my rival was standing between the two windows, and nodding his head gently and sadly downward from above.

I was not frightened, I was not even surprised . . . . but rising up slightly in bed, and propping myself on my elbow, I began to gaze with redoubled attention at the figure which had so unexpectedly presented itself.

The latter continued to nod its head.

"What is it?" I said at last.—"Art thou exulting? Or art thou pitying?—What is this—a warning or a reproach? . . . Or dost thou wish to give me to understand that thou wert in the wrong? That we were both in the wrong? What art thou experiencing? The pains of hell? The bliss of paradise? Speak at least one word!"

But my rival did not utter a single sound—and only went on nodding his head sadly and submissively, as before, downward from above.

I burst out laughing . . . . he vanished.

February, 1878.

THE BEGGAR MAN

I was passing along the street when a beggar, a decrepit old man, stopped me.

Swollen, tearful eyes, blue lips, bristling rags, unclean sores. . . . Oh, how horribly had poverty gnawed that unhappy being!

He stretched out to me a red, bloated, dirty hand. . . . He moaned, he bellowed for help.

I began to rummage in all my pockets. . . . Neither purse, nor watch, nor even handkerchief did I find. . . . I had taken nothing with me.

And the beggar still waited . . . . and extended his hand, which swayed and trembled feebly.

Bewildered, confused, I shook that dirty, tremulous hand heartily. . . .

" Blame me not, brother; I have nothing, brother."

The beggar man fixed his swollen eyes upon me; his blue lips smiled—and in his turn he pressed my cold fingers.

" Never mind, brother," he mumbled. " Thanks for this also, brother.—This also is an alms, brother."

I understood that I had received an alms from my brother.

February, 1878.

" THOU SHALT HEAR THE JUDG-MENT OF THE DULLARD . . . "

Púshkin

'" THOU shalt hear the judgment of the dullard . . . " Thou hast always spoken the truth, thou great writer of ours; thou hast spoken it this time, also.

" The judgment of the dullard and the laughter of the crowd." . . . Who is there that has not experienced both the one and the other?

All this can—and must be borne; and whosoever hath the strength,—let him despise it.

314

But there are blows which beat more painfully on the heart itself. . . . A man has done everything in his power; he has toiled arduously, lovingly, honestly. . . . And honest souls turn squeamishly away from him; honest faces flush with indignation at his name. "Depart! Begone!" honest young voices shout at him.—"We need neither thee nor thy work, thou art defiling our dwelling—thou dost not know us and dost not understand us. . . . Thou art our enemy!"

What is that man to do then? Continue to toil, make no effort to defend himself—and not even expect a more just estimate.

In former days tillers of the soil cursed the traveller who brought them potatoes in place of bread, the daily food of the poor man. . . . They snatched the precious gift from the hands outstretched to them, flung it in the mire, trod it under foot.

Now they subsist upon it—and do not even know the name of their benefactor.

So be it! What matters his name to them? He, although he be nameless, has saved them from hunger.

Let us strive only that what we offer may be equally useful food.

Bitter is unjust reproach in the mouths of people whom one loves. . . . But even that can be endured. . . .

POEMS IN PROSE

"Beat me—but hear me out!" said the Athenian chieftain to the Spartan chieftain.

"Beat me—but be healthy and full fed!" is what we ought to say.

February, 1878.

THE CONTENTED MAN

ALONG a street of the capital is skipping a man who is still young.—His movements are cheerful, alert; his eyes are beaming, his lips are smiling, his sensitive face is pleasantly rosy. . . . He is all contentment and joy.

What has happened to him? Has he come into an inheritance? Has he been elevated in rank? Is he hastening to a love tryst? Or, simply, has he breakfasted well, and is it a sensation of health, a sensation of full-fed strength which is leaping for joy in all his limbs? Or they may have hung on his neck thy handsome, eight-pointed cross, O Polish King Stanislaus!

No. He has concocted a calumny against an acquaintance, he has assiduously disseminated it, he has heard it—that same calumny—from the mouth of another acquaintance—and *has believed it himself.*

Oh, how contented, how good even at this moment is that nice, highly-promising young man.

February, 1878.

POEMS IN PROSE

THE RULE OF LIFE

" If you desire thoroughly to mortify and even
to injure an opponent," said an old swindler to
me, " reproach him with the very defect or vice
of which you feel conscious in yourself.—Fly
into a rage . . . . and reproach him!

" In the first place, that makes other people
think that you do not possess that vice.

" In the second place, your wrath may even be
sincere. . . . You may profit by the reproaches
of your own conscience.

" If, for example, you are a renegade, reproach
your adversary with having no convictions!

" If you yourself are a lackey in soul, say to him
with reproof that he is a lackey . . . . the lackey
of civilisation, of Europe, of socialism!"

" You may even say, the lackey of non-lackey-
ism!" I remarked.

" You may do that also," chimed in the old
rascal.

February, 1878.

THE END OF THE WORLD

A DREAM

It seems to me as though I am somewhere in
Russia, in the wilds, in a plain country house.

317

POEMS IN PROSE

The chamber is large, low-ceiled, with three windows; the walls are smeared with white paint; there is no furniture. In front of the house is a bare plain; gradually descending, it recedes into the distance; the grey, monotoned sky hangs over it like a canopy.

I am not alone; half a score of men are with me in the room. All plain folk, plainly clad; they are pacing up and down in silence, as though by stealth. They avoid one another, and yet they are incessantly exchanging uneasy glances.

Not one of them knows why he has got into this house, or who the men are with him. On all faces there is disquiet and melancholy . . . . all, in turn, approach the windows and gaze attentively about them, as though expecting something from without.

Then again they set to roaming up and down. Among us a lad of short stature is running about; from time to time he screams in a shrill, monotonous voice: " Daddy, I 'm afraid! "— This shrill cry makes me sick at heart—and I also begin to be afraid. . . . Of what? I myself do not know. Only I feel that a great, great calamity is on its way, and is drawing near.

And the little lad keeps screaming. Akh, if I could only get away from here! How stifling it is! How oppressive! . . . . But it is impossible to escape.

POEMS IN PROSE

That sky is like a shroud. And there is no wind. . . . Is the air dead?

Suddenly the boy ran to the window and began to scream with the same plaintive voice as usual: " Look! Look! The earth has fallen in! "

" What? Fallen in? "—In fact: there had been a plain in front of the house, but now the house is standing on the crest of a frightful mountain!—The horizon has fallen, has gone down, and from the very house itself a black, almost perpendicular declivity descends.

We have all thronged to the window. . . . Horror freezes our hearts.—" There it is . . . . there it is! " whispers my neighbour.

And lo! along the whole distant boundary of the earth something has begun to stir, some small, round hillocks have begun to rise and fall.

" It is the sea! " occurs to us all at one and the same moment.—" It will drown us all directly. . . . . Only, how can it wax and rise up? On that precipice? "

And nevertheless it does wax, and wax hugely. . . . . It is no longer separate hillocks which are tumbling in the distance. . . . A dense, monstrous wave engulfs the entire circle of the horizon.

It is flying, flying upon us!—Like an icy hurricane it sweeps on, swirling with the outer darkness. Everything round about has begun to quiver,—and yonder, in that oncoming mass,—

there are crashing and thunder, and a thousand-throated, iron barking. . . .

Ha! What a roaring and howling! It is the earth roaring with terror. . . .

It is the end of it! The end of all things!

The boy screamed once more. . . . I tried to seize hold of my comrades, but we, all of us, were already crushed, buried, drowned, swept away by that icy, rumbling flood, as black as ink.

Darkness . . . . eternal darkness!

Gasping for breath, I awoke.

March, 1878.

MASHA

WHEN I was living in Petersburg,—many years ago,—whenever I had occasion to hire a public cabman I entered into conversation with him.

I was specially fond of conversing with the night cabmen,—poor peasants of the suburbs, who have come to town with their ochre-tinted little sledges and miserable little nags in the hope of supporting themselves and collecting enough money to pay their quit-rent to their owners.

So, then, one day I hired such a cabman. . . . He was a youth of twenty years, tall, well-built, a fine, dashing young fellow; he had blue eyes and rosy cheeks; his red-gold hair curled in rings beneath a wretched little patched cap, which was pulled down over his very eyebrows. And how in the world was that tattered little coat ever got upon those shoulders of heroic mould!

But the cabman's handsome, beardless face seemed sad and lowering.

I entered into conversation with him. Sadness was discernible in his voice also.

"What is it, brother?" I asked him.—"Why art not thou cheerful? Hast thou any grief?"

The young fellow did not reply to me at once.

"I have, master, I have," he said at last.— "And such a grief that it would be better if I were not alive. My wife is dead."

"Didst thou love her . . . . thy wife?"

The young fellow turned toward me; only he bent his head a little.

"I did, master. This is the eighth month since . . . . but I cannot forget. It is eating away my heart . . . . so it is! And why must she die? She was young! Healthy! . . . . In one day the cholera settled her."

"And was she of a good disposition?"

"Akh, master!" sighed the poor fellow, heavily.—"And on what friendly terms she and I lived together! She died in my absence. When I heard here that they had already buried her, I hurried immediately to the village, home. It was already after midnight when I arrived. I entered my cottage, stopped short in the middle of it, and said so softly: 'Masha! hey, Masha!' Only a cricket shrilled.—Then I fell to weeping, and sat down on the cottage floor, and how I did beat my palm against the ground!—' Thy bowels are insatiable!' I said. . . . ' Thou hast devoured her . . . . devour me also!'—Akh, Masha!"

"Masha," he added in a suddenly lowered voice. And without letting his rope reins out of his hands, he squeezed a tear out of his eye with his mitten, shook it off, flung it to one side, shrugged his shoulders—and did not utter another word.

As I alighted from the sledge I gave him an extra fifteen kopéks. He made me a low obeisance, grasping his cap in both hands, and drove off at a foot-pace over the snowy expanse of empty street, flooded with the grey mist of the January frost.

April, 1878.

THE FOOL

ONCE upon a time a fool lived in the world.

For a long time he lived in clover; but gradually rumours began to reach him to the effect that he bore the reputation everywhere of a brainless ninny.

The fool was disconcerted and began to fret over the question how he was to put an end to those unpleasant rumours.

A sudden idea at last illumined his dark little

322

brain. . . . And without the slightest delay he put it into execution.

An acquaintance met him on the street and began to praise a well-known artist. . . . "Good gracious!" exclaimed the fool, "that artist was relegated to the archives long ago. . . . Don't you know that?—I did not expect that of you. . . . . You are behind the times."

The acquaintance was frightened, and immediately agreed with the fool.

"What a fine book I have read to-day!" said another acquaintance to him.

"Good gracious!" cried the fool.—"Are n't you ashamed of yourself? That book is good for nothing; everybody dropped it in disgust long ago.—Don't you know that?—You are behind the times."

And that acquaintance also was frightened and agreed with the fool.

"What a splendid man my friend N. N. is!" said a third acquaintance to the fool.—"There's a truly noble being for you!"

"Good gracious!"—exclaimed the fool,—"it is well known that N. N. is a scoundrel! He has robbed all his relatives. Who is there that does not know it? You are behind the times."

The third acquaintance also took fright and agreed with the fool, and renounced his friend. And whosoever or whatsoever was praised in the fool's presence, he had the same retort for all

He even sometimes added reproachfully:
" And do you still believe in the authorities? "

" A malicious person! A bilious man!" his
acquaintances began to say about the fool.—
" But what a head! "

" And what a tongue! " added others.

" Oh, yes; he is talented! "

It ended in the publisher of a newspaper pro-
posing to the fool that he should take charge of
his critical department.

And the fool began to criticise everything and
everybody, without making the slightest change
in his methods, or in his exclamations.

Now he, who formerly shrieked against authorities, is an authority himself,—and the young
men worship him and fear him.

But what are they to do, poor fellows? Although it is not proper—generally speaking—to
worship . . . . yet in this case, if one does not
do it, he will find himself classed among the men
who are behind the times!

There is a career for fools among cowards.

April, 1878.

AN ORIENTAL LEGEND

Who in Bagdad does not know the great Giaffar, the sun of the universe?

One day, many years ago, when he was still

a young man, Giaffar was strolling in the suburbs of Bagdad.

Suddenly there fell upon his ear a hoarse cry:
some one was calling desperately for help.

Giaffar was distinguished among the young
men of his own age for his good sense and pru-
dence; but he had a compassionate heart, and he
trusted to his strength.

He ran in the direction of the cry, and beheld
a decrepit old man pinned against the wall of the
city by two brigands who were robbing him.

Giaffar drew his sword and fell upon the malefactors. One he slew, the other he chased away.

The old man whom he had liberated fell at his
rescuer's feet, and kissing the hem of his garment, exclaimed: "Brave youth, thy magnanim-
ity shall not remain unrewarded. In appearance I am a beggar; but only in appearance. I
am not a common man.—Come to-morrow morning early to the chief bazaar; I will await thee
there at the fountain—and thou shalt convince
thyself as to the justice of my words."

Giaffar reflected: "In appearance this man
is a beggar, it is true; but all sorts of things happen. Why should not I try the experiment?"—
and he answered: "Good, my father, I will go."

The old man looked him in the eye and went
away.

On the following morning, just as day was
breaking, Giaffar set out for the bazaar. The

old man was already waiting for him, with his elbows leaning on the marble basin of the fountain.

Silently he took Giaffar by the hand and led him to a small garden, surrounded on all sides by high walls.

In the very centre of this garden, on a green lawn, grew a tree of extraordinary aspect.

It resembled a cypress; only its foliage was of azure hue.

Three fruits—three apples—hung on the slender up-curving branches. One of medium size was oblong in shape, of a milky-white hue; another was large, round, and bright red; the third was small, wrinkled and yellowish.

The whole tree was rustling faintly, although there was no wind. It tinkled delicately and plaintively, as though it were made of glass; it seemed to feel the approach of Giaffar.

" Youth! "—said the old man, " pluck whichever of these fruits thou wilt, and know that if thou shalt pluck and eat the white one, thou shalt become more wise than all men; if thou shalt pluck and eat the red one, thou shalt become as rich as the Hebrew Rothschild; if thou shalt pluck and eat the yellow one, thou shalt please old women. Decide! . . . . and delay not. In an hour the fruits will fade, and the tree itself will sink into the dumb depths of the earth! "

Giaffar bowed his head and thought.—" What am I to do?" he articulated in a low tone, as though arguing with himself.—" If one becomes too wise, he will not wish to live, probably; if he becomes richer than all men, all will hate him; I would do better to pluck and eat the third, the shrivelled apple!"

And so he did; and the old man laughed a toothless laugh and said: " Oh, most wise youth! Thou hast chosen the good part!—What use hast thou for the white apple? Thou art wiser than Solomon as thou art.—And neither dost thou need the red apple. . . . Even without it thou shalt be rich. Only no one will be envious of thy wealth."

" Inform me, old man," said Giaffar, with a start, " where the respected mother of our God-saved Caliph dwelleth?"

The old man bowed to the earth, and pointed out the road to the youth.

Who in Bagdad doth not know the sun of the universe, the great, the celebrated Giaffar?

April, 1878.

TWO FOUR-LINE STANZAS

THERE existed once a city whose inhabitants were so passionately fond of poetry that if several weeks passed and no beautiful new verses had

made their appearance they regarded that poet-
ical dearth as a public calamity.

At such times they donned their worst garments, sprinkled ashes on their heads, and gather-
ing in throngs on the public squares, they shed
tears, and murmured bitterly against the Muse
for having abandoned them.

On one such disastrous day the young poet
Junius, presented himself on the square, filled to
overflowing with the sorrowing populace.

With swift steps he ascended a specially-con-
structed tribune and made a sign that he wished
to recite a poem.

The lictors immediately brandished their
staves. " Silence! Attention!" they shouted in
stentorian tones.

"Friends! Comrades!" began Junius, in a
loud, but not altogether firm voice:

"Friends! Comrades! Ye lovers of verses!
Admirers of all that is graceful and fair!
Be not cast down by a moment of dark sadness!
The longed-for instant will come . . . . and light will
disperse the gloom!" [1]

Junius ceased speaking . . . . and in reply
to him, from all points of the square, clamour,
whistling, and laughter arose.

All the faces turned toward him flamed with

---

[1] These lines do not rhyme in the original.—TRANSLATOR.

indignation, all eyes flashed with wrath, all hands were uplifted, menaced, were clenched into fists.

"A pretty thing he has thought to surprise us with!" roared angry voices. "Away from the tribune with the talentless rhymster! Away with the fool! Hurl rotten apples, bad eggs, at the empty-pated idiot! Give us stones! Fetch stones!"

Junius tumbled headlong from the tribune . . . . but before he had succeeded in fleeing to his own house, outbursts of rapturous applause, cries of laudation and shouts reached his ear.

Filled with amazement, but striving not to be detected (for it is dangerous to irritate an enraged wild beast), Junius returned to the square.

And what did he behold?

High above the throng, above its shoulders, on a flat gold shield, stood his rival, the young poet Julius, clad in a purple mantle, with a laurel wreath on his waving curls. . . . And the populace round about was roaring: "Glory! Glory! Glory to the immortal Julius! He hath comforted us in our grief, in our great woe! He hath given us verses sweeter than honey, more melodious than the cymbals, more fragrant than the rose, more pure than heaven's azure! Bear him in triumph; surround his inspired head with a soft billow of incense; refresh his brow with the waving of palm branches; lavish at his feet all the spices of Arabia! Glory!"

Junius approached one of the glorifiers.—" Inform me, O my fellow-townsman! With what verses hath Julius made you happy?—Alas, I was not on the square when he recited them! Repeat them, if thou canst recall them, I pray thee! "

" Such verses—and not recall them? " briskly replied the man interrogated.—" For whom dost thou take me? Listen—and rejoice, rejoice together with us! "

" ' Ye lovers of verses! '—thus began the divine Julius . . . .

" ' Ye lovers of verses! Comrades! Friends!
Admirers of all that is graceful, melodious, tender!
Be not cast down by a moment of heavy grief!
The longed-for moment will come—and day will chase away the night! '

" What dost thou think of that? "

" Good gracious! " roared Junius. " Why, those are my lines!—Julius must have been in the crowd when I recited them; he heard and repeated them, barely altering—and that, of course, not for the better—a few expressions! "

" Aha! Now I recognise thee. . . . Thou art Junius," retorted the citizen whom he had accosted, knitting his brows.—" Thou art either envious or a fool! . . . Only consider just one thing, unhappy man! Julius says in such lofty style: ' And day will chase away the night! '

. . . But with thee it is some nonsense or other: 'And the light will disperse the gloom! ?'—What light? ! What darkness? !"

"But is it not all one and the same thing . . . . " Junius was beginning. . . .

" Add one word more," the citizen interrupted him, " and I will shout to the populace, and it will rend thee asunder."

Junius prudently held his peace, but a grey-haired old man, who had overheard his conversation with the citizen, stepped up to the poor poet, and laying his hand on his shoulder, said:

" Junius! Thou hast said thy say at the wrong time; but the other man said his at the right time. —Consequently, he is in the right, while for thee there remain the consolations of thine own conscience."

But while his conscience was consoling Junius to the best of its ability,—and in a decidedly-unsatisfactory way, if the truth must be told,— far away, amid the thunder and patter of jubilation, in the golden dust of the all-conquering sun, gleaming with purple, darkling with laurel athwart the undulating streams of abundant incense, with majestic leisureliness, like an emperor marching to his empire, the proudly-erect figure of Julius moved forward with easy grace . . . . and long branches of the palm-tree bent in turn before him, as though expressing by their quiet rising, their submissive obeisance, that incessantly-renewed adoration which filled to overflowing the hearts of his fellow-citizens whom he had enchanted!

April, 1878.

THE SPARROW

I HAD returned from the chase and was walking along one of the alleys in the garden. My hound was running on in front of me.

Suddenly he retarded his steps and began to crawl stealthily along as though he detected game ahead.

I glanced down the alley and beheld a young sparrow, with a yellow ring around its beak and down on its head. It had fallen from the nest (the wind was rocking the trees of the alley violently), and sat motionless, impotently expanding its barely-sprouted little wings.

My hound was approaching it slowly when, suddenly wrenching itself from a neighbouring birch, an old black-breasted sparrow fell like a stone in front of my dog's very muzzle—and, with plumage all ruffled, contorted, with a despairing and pitiful cry, gave a couple of hops in the direction of the yawning jaws studded with big teeth.

It had flung itself down to save, it was shielding, its offspring . . . . but the whole of its tiny body was throbbing with fear, its voice was wild and hoarse, it was swooning, it was sacrificing itself!

What a huge monster the dog must have appeared to it! And yet it could not have remained perched on its lofty, secure bough. . . . A force greater than its own will had hurled it thence.

My Trésor stopped short, retreated. . . . Evidently he recognised that force.

I hastened to call off the discomfited hound, and withdrew with reverence.

Yes; do not laugh. I felt reverential before that tiny, heroic bird, before its loving impulse.

Love, I thought, is stronger than death.—Only by it, only by love, does life support itself and move.

April, 1878.

THE SKULLS

A SUMPTUOUS, luxuriously illuminated ball-room; a multitude of cavaliers and ladies.

All faces are animated, all speeches are brisk. . . . . A rattling conversation is in progress about a well-known songstress. The people are lauding her as divine, immortal. . . . Oh, how finely she had executed her last trill that evening!

And suddenly—as though at the wave of a magic wand—from all the heads, from all the faces, a thin shell of skin flew off, and instantly there was revealed the whiteness of skulls, the naked gums and cheek-bones dimpled like bluish lead.

With horror did I watch those gums and cheek-bones moving and stirring,—those knobby, bony spheres turning this way and that, as they gleamed in the light of the lamps and candles, and smaller spheres—the spheres of the eyes bereft of sense—rolling in them.

I dared not touch my own face, I dared not look at myself in a mirror. But the skulls continued to turn this way and that, as before. . . . And with the same clatter as before, the brisk tongues, flashing like red rags from behind the grinning teeth, murmured on, how wonderfully, how incomparably the immortal . . . . yes, the immortal songstress had executed her last trill!

April, 1878.

THE TOILER AND THE LAZY MAN

A CONVERSATION

THE TOILER

WHY dost thou bother us? What dost thou want? Thou art not one of us. . . Go away!

THE LAZY MAN [1]

I am one of you, brethren!

[1] "The white-handed man" would be the literal translation.—TRANSLATOR.

POEMS IN PROSE

THE TOILER

Nothing of the sort; thou art not one of us! What an invention! Just look at my hands. Dost thou see how dirty they are? And they stink of dung, and tar,—while thy hands are white. And of what do they smell?

THE LAZY MAN—*offering his hands*

Smell.

THE TOILER—*smelling the hands*

What 's this? They seem to give off an odour of iron.

THE LAZY MAN

Iron it is. For the last six years I have worn fetters on them.

THE TOILER

And what was that for?

THE LAZY MAN

Because I was striving for your welfare, I wanted to liberate you, the coarse, uneducated people; I rebelled against your oppressors, I mutinied. . . . Well, and so they put me in prison.

THE TOILER

They put you in prison? It served you right for rebelling!

POEMS IN PROSE

Two Years Later

THE SAME TOILER TO ANOTHER TOILER

Hearken, Piótra! . . . Dost remember one of those white-handed lazy men was talking to thee the summer before last?

THE OTHER TOILER

I remember. . . . What of it?

FIRST TOILER

They 're going to hang him to-day, I hear; that 's the order which has been issued.

SECOND TOILER

Has he kept on rebelling?

FIRST TOILER

He has.

SECOND TOILER

Yes. . . . Well, see here, brother Mitry: can't we get hold of a bit of that rope with which they are going to hang him? Folks say that that brings the greatest good luck to a house.

FIRST TOILER

Thou 'rt right about that. We must try, brother Piótra.

April, 1878.

THE ROSE

THE last days of August. . . . Autumn had already come.

The sun had set. A sudden, violent rain, without thunder and without lightning, had just swooped down upon our broad plain.

The garden in front of the house burned and smoked, all flooded with the heat of sunset and the deluge of rain.

She was sitting at a table in the drawing-room and staring with stubborn thoughtfulness into the garden, through the half-open door.

I knew what was going on then in her soul. I knew that after a brief though anguished conflict, she would that same instant yield to the feeling which she could no longer control.

Suddenly she rose, walked out briskly into the garden and disappeared.

One hour struck . . . . then another; she did not return.

Then I rose, and emerging from the house, I bent my steps to the alley down which—I had no doubt as to that—she had gone.

Everything had grown dark round about; night had already descended. But on the damp sand of the path, gleaming scarlet amid the encircling gloom, a rounded object was visible.

I bent down. It was a young, barely-budded rose. Two hours before I had seen that same rose on her breast.

I carefully picked up the flower which had fallen in the mire, and returning to the drawing-room, I laid it on the table, in front of her arm-chair.

And now, at last, she returned, and traversing the whole length of the room with her light foot-steps, she seated herself at the table.

Her face had grown pale and animated; swiftly, with merry confusion, her lowered eyes, which seemed to have grown smaller, darted about in all directions.

She caught sight of the rose, seized it, glanced at its crumpled petals, glanced at me—and her eyes, coming to a sudden halt, glittered with tears.

"What are you weeping about?" I asked.

"Why, here, about this rose. Look what has happened to it."

At this point I took it into my head to display profundity of thought.

"Your tears will wash away the mire," I said with a significant expression.

"Tears do not wash, tears scorch," she replied, and, turning toward the fireplace, she tossed the flower into the expiring flame.

"The fire will scorch it still better than tears," she exclaimed, not without audacity,—and her beautiful eyes, still sparkling with tears, laughed boldly and happily.

I understood that she had been scorched also.

April, 1878.

IN MEMORY OF J. P. VRÉVSKY

In the mire, on damp, stinking straw, under the pent-house of an old carriage-house which had been hastily converted into a field military hospital in a ruined Bulgarian hamlet, she had been for more than a fortnight dying of typhus fever.

She was unconscious—and not a single physician had even glanced at her; the sick soldiers whom she had nursed as long as she could keep on her feet rose by turns from their infected lairs, in order to raise to her parched lips a few drops of water in a fragment of a broken jug.

She was young, handsome; high society knew her; even dignitaries inquired about her. The ladies envied her, the men courted her . . . . two or three men loved her secretly and profoundly. Life smiled upon her; but there are smiles which are worse than tears.

A tender, gentle heart . . . . and such strength, such a thirst for sacrifice! To help those who needed help . . . . she knew no other happiness . . . . she knew no other and she tasted no other. Every other happiness passed her by. But she had long since become reconciled to that, and all flaming with the fire of inextinguishable faith, she dedicated herself to the service of her fellow-men. What sacred treasures she held hidden there, in the depths of her soul, in her own secret recesses, no one ever knew—and now no one will ever know.

And to what end? The sacrifice has been made . . . . the deed is done.

But it is sorrowful to think that no one said "thank you" even to her corpse, although she herself was ashamed of and shunned all thanks.

May her dear shade be not offended by this tardy blossom, which I venture to lay upon her grave!

September, 1878.

THE LAST MEETING

WE were once close, intimate friends. . . . But there came an evil moment and we parted like enemies.

Many years passed. . . . And lo! on entering the town where he lived I learned that he was hopelessly ill, and wished to see me.

I went to him, I entered his chamber. . . . Our glances met.

I hardly recognised him. O God! How disease had changed him!

Yellow, shrivelled, with his head completely bald, and a narrow, grey beard, he was sitting in nothing but a shirt, cut out expressly. . . . He could not bear the pressure of the lightest garment. Abruptly he extended to me his frightfully-thin hand, which looked as though it had been gnawed away, with an effort whispered several incomprehensible words—whether of welcome or of reproach, who knows? His exhausted chest heaved; over the contracted pupils of his small, inflamed eyes two scanty tears of martyrdom flowed down.

My heart sank within me. . . . I sat down on a chair beside him, and involuntarily dropping my eyes in the presence of that horror and deformity, I also put out my hand.

But it seemed to me that it was not his hand which grasped mine.

It seemed to me as though there were sitting between us a tall, quiet, white woman. A long veil enveloped her from head to foot. Her deep, pale eyes gazed nowhere; her pale, stern lips uttered no sound. . . .

That woman joined our hands. . . . She reconciled us forever.

Yes. . . . It was Death who had reconciled us. . . .

April, 1878.

POEMS IN PROSE

THE VISIT

I WAS sitting at the open window . . . . in the morning, early in the morning, on the first of May.

The flush of dawn had not yet begun; but the dark, warm night was already paling, already growing chill.

No fog had risen, no breeze was straying, everything was of one hue and silent . . . . but one could scent the approach of the awakening, and in the rarefied air the scent of the dew's harsh dampness was abroad.

Suddenly, into my chamber, through the open window, flew a large bird, lightly tinkling and rustling.

I started, looked more intently. . . . It was not a bird: it was a tiny, winged woman, clad in a long, close-fitting robe which billowed out at the bottom.

She was all grey, the hue of mother-of-pearl; only the inner side of her wings glowed with a tender flush of scarlet, like a rose bursting into blossom; a garland of lilies-of-the-valley confined the scattered curls of her small, round head,—and two peacock feathers quivered amusingly, like the feelers of a butterfly, above the fair, rounded little forehead.

She floated past a couple of times close to the

ceiling: her tiny face was laughing; laughing
also were her huge, black, luminous eyes. The
merry playfulness of her capricious flight shivered their diamond rays.

She held in her hand a long frond of a steppe
flower—"Imperial sceptre"[1] the Russian folk
call it; and it does, indeed, resemble a sceptre.

As she flew rapidly above me she touched my
head with that flower.

I darted toward her. . . . But she had already
fluttered through the window, and away she flew
headlong. . . .

In the garden, in the wilderness of the lilac-
bushes, a turtle-dove greeted her with its first
cooing; and at the spot where she had vanished
the milky-white sky flushed a soft crimson.

I recognised thee, goddess of fancy! Thou
hast visited me by accident—thou hast flown in
to young poets.

O poetry! O youth! O virginal beauty of
woman! Only for an instant can ye gleam before
me,—in the early morning of the early spring!

May, 1878.

NECESSITAS—VIS—LIBERTAS

A BAS-RELIEF

A TALL, bony old woman with an iron face and a
dull, impassive gaze is walking along with great

[1] The pretty name for what we call mullein.—TRANSLATOR.

strides, and pushing before her, with her hand as harsh as a stick, another woman.

This woman, of vast size, powerful, corpulent, with the muscles of a Hercules, and a tiny head on a bull-like neck—and blind—is pushing on in her turn a small, thin young girl.

This girl alone has eyes which see; she resists, turns backward, elevates her thin red arms; her animated countenance expresses impatience and hardihood. . . . She does not wish to obey, she does not wish to advance in the direction whither she is being impelled . . . . and, nevertheless, she must obey and advance.

Necessitas—Vis—Libertas:

Whoever likes may interpret this.

May, 1878.

ALMS

In the vicinity of a great city, on the broad, much-travelled road, an aged, ailing man was walking.

He was staggering as he went; his emaciated legs, entangling themselves, trailing and stumbling, trod heavily and feebly, exactly as though they belonged to some one else; his clothing hung on him in rags; his bare head drooped upon his breast. . . . He was exhausted.

He squatted down on a stone by the side of the road, bent forward, propped his elbows on his knees, covered his face with both hands, and between his crooked fingers the tears dripped on the dry, grey dust.

He was remembering. . . .

He remembered how he had once been healthy and rich,—and how he had squandered his health, and distributed his wealth to others, friends and enemies. . . . And lo! now he had not a crust of bread, and every one had abandoned him, his friends even more promptly than his enemies. . . . Could he possibly humble himself to the point of asking alms? And he felt bitter and ashamed at heart.

And the tears still dripped and dripped, mottling the grey dust.

Suddenly he heard some one calling him by name. He raised his weary head and beheld in front of him a stranger: a face calm and dignified, but not stern; eyes not beaming, but bright; a gaze penetrating, but not evil.

"Thou hast given away all thy wealth," an even voice made itself heard. . . . "But surely thou art not regretting that thou hast done good?"

"I do not regret it," replied the old man, with a sigh, "only here am I dying now."

"And if there had been no beggars in the world to stretch out their hands to thee," pursued the stranger, "thou wouldst have had no one to whom to show thy beneficence; thou wouldst not have been able to exercise thyself therein?"

The old man made no reply, and fell into thought.

"Therefore, be not proud now, my poor man," spoke up the stranger again. "Go, stretch out thy hand, afford to other good people the possibility of proving by their actions that they are good."

The old man started, and raised his eyes . . . . but the stranger had already vanished,—but far away, on the road, a wayfarer made his appearance.

The old man approached him, and stretched out his hand.—The wayfarer turned away with a surly aspect and gave him nothing.

But behind him came another, and this one gave the old man a small alms.

And the old man bought bread for himself with the copper coins which had been given him, and sweet did the bit which he had begged seem to him, and there was no shame in his heart—but, on the contrary, a tranquil joy overshadowed him.

May, 1878.

THE INSECT

I DREAMED that a score of us were sitting in a large room with open windows.

Among us were women, children, old men. . . .

POEMS IN PROSE

We were all talking about some very unfamiliar subject—talking noisily and unintelligibly.

Suddenly, with a harsh clatter, a huge insect, about three inches and a half long, flew into the room . . . . flew in, circled about and alighted on the wall.

It resembled a fly or a wasp.—Its body was of a dirty hue; its flat, hard wings were of the same colour; it had extended, shaggy claws and a big, angular head, like that of a dragon-fly; and that head and the claws were bright red, as though bloody.

This strange insect kept incessantly turning its head downward, upward, to the right, to the left, and moving its claws about . . . . then suddenly it wrested itself from the wall, flew clattering through the room,—and again alighted, again began to move in terrifying and repulsive manner, without stirring from the spot. It evoked in all of us disgust, alarm, even terror. . . . None of us had ever seen anything of the sort; we all cried: "Expel that monster!" We all flourished our handkerchiefs at it from a distance . . . . for no one could bring himself to approach it . . . . and when the insect had flown in we had all involuntarily got out of the way.

Only one of our interlocutors, a pale-faced man who was still young, surveyed us all with surprise.—He shrugged his shoulders, he smiled, he positively could not understand what had happened to us and why we were so agitated. He had seen no insect, he had not heard the ominous clatter of its wings.

Suddenly the insect seemed to rivet its attention on him, soared into the air, and swooping down upon his head, stung him on the brow, a little above the eyes. . . . The young man emitted a faint cry and fell dead.

The dreadful fly immediately flew away. . . . Only then did we divine what sort of a visitor we had had.

May, 1878.

CABBAGE-SOUP

THE son of a widowed peasant-woman died—a young fellow aged twenty, the best labourer in the village.

The lady-proprietor of that village, on learning of the peasant-woman's affliction, went to call upon her on the very day of the funeral.

She found her at home.

Standing in the middle of her cottage, in front of the table, she was ladling out empty [1] cabbage-soup from the bottom of a smoke-begrimed pot, in a leisurely way, with her right hand (her left hung limply by her side), and swallowing spoonful after spoonful.

The woman's face had grown sunken and dark; her eyes were red and swollen . . . . but she car-

---

[1] That is, made without meat.—TRANSLATOR.

ried herself independently and uprightly, as in church.[1]

"O Lord!" thought the lady; "she can eat at such a moment . . . . but what coarse feelings they have!"

And then the lady-mistress recalled how, when she had lost her own little daughter, aged nine months, a few years before, she had refused, out of grief, to hire a very beautiful villa in the vicinity of Petersburg, and had passed the entire summer in town!—But the peasant-woman continued to sip her cabbage-soup.

At last the lady could endure it no longer.— "Tatyána!" said she. . . . "Good gracious!—I am amazed! Is it possible that thou didst not love thy son? How is it that thy appetite has not disappeared?—How canst thou eat that cabbage-soup?"

"My Vásya is dead," replied the woman softly, and tears of suffering again began to stream down her sunken cheeks,—"and, of course, my own end has come also: my head has been taken away from me while I am still alive. But the cabbage-soup must not go to waste; for it is salted."

The lady-mistress merely shrugged her shoulders and went away. She got salt cheaply.

May, 1878.

[1] The ideal bearing in church is described as standing "like a candle"; that is, very straight and motionless.—TRANSLATOR.

THE AZURE REALM

O AZURE realm! O realm of azure, light, youth, and happiness! I have beheld thee . . . . in my dreams.

There were several of us in a beautiful, decorated boat. Like the breast of a swan the white sail towered aloft beneath fluttering pennants.

I did not know who my companions were; but with all my being I felt that they were as young, as merry, as happy as I was!

And I paid no heed to them. All about me I beheld only the shoreless azure sea, all covered with a fine rippling of golden scales, and overhead an equally shoreless azure sea, and in it, triumphantly and, as it were, smilingly, rolled on the friendly sun.

And among us, from time to time, there arose laughter, ringing and joyous as the laughter of the gods!

Or suddenly, from some one's lips, flew forth words, verses replete with wondrous beauty and with inspired power . . . . so that it seemed as though the very sky resounded in reply to them, and round about the sea throbbed with sympathy. . . . And then blissful silence began again.

Diving lightly through the soft waves, our swift boat glided on. It was not propelled by the breeze; it was ruled by our own sportive hearts. Whithersoever we wished, thither did it move, obediently, as though it were gifted with life.

We encountered islands, magical, half-transparent islands with the hues of precious stones, jacinths and emeralds. Intoxicating perfumes were wafted from the surrounding shores; some of these islands pelted us with a rain of white roses and lilies-of-the-valley; from others there rose up suddenly long-winged birds, clothed in rainbow hues.

The birds circled over our heads, the lilies and roses melted in the pearly foam, which slipped along the smooth sides of our craft.

In company with the flowers and the birds, sweet, sweet sounds were wafted to our ears. . . . We seemed to hear women's voices in them. . . . And everything round about,—the sky, the sea, the bellying of the sail up aloft, the purling of the waves at the stern,—everything spoke of love, of blissful love.

And she whom each one of us loved—she was there . . . . invisibly and near at hand. Yet another moment and lo! her eyes would beam forth, her smile would blossom out. . . . Her hand would grasp thy hand, and draw thee after her into an unfading paradise!

O azure realm! I have beheld thee . . . . in my dream!

June, 1878.

POEMS IN PROSE

TWO RICH MEN

WHEN men in my presence extol Rothschild, who out of his vast revenues allots whole thousands for the education of children, the cure of the sick, the care of the aged, I laud and melt in admiration.

But while I laud and melt I cannot refrain from recalling a poverty-stricken peasant's family which received an orphaned niece into its wretched, tumble-down little hovel.

"If we take Kátka," said the peasant-woman; "we shall spend our last kopéks on her, and there will be nothing left wherewith to buy salt for our porridge."

"But we will take her . . . . and unsalted porridge," replied the peasant-man, her husband.

Rothschild is a long way behind that peasant-man!

July, 1878.

THE OLD MAN

THE dark, distressing days have come. . . .

One's own maladies, the ailments of those dear to him, cold and the gloom of old age. Everything which thou hast loved, to which thou hast surrendered thyself irrevocably, collapses and falls into ruins. The road has taken a turn down hill.

But what is to be done? Grieve? Lament? Thou wilt help neither thyself nor others in that way. . . .

On the withered, bent tree the foliage is smaller, more scanty—but the verdure is the same as ever.

Do thou also shrivel up, retire into thyself, into thy memories, and there, deep, very deep within, at the very bottom of thy concentrated soul, thy previous life, accessible to thee alone, will shine forth before thee with its fragrant, still fresh verdure, and the caress and strength of the spring-time!

But have a care . . . . do not look ahead, poor old man!

July, 1878.

THE CORRESPONDENT

Two friends are sitting at a table and drinking tea.

A sudden noise has arisen in the street. Plaintive moans, violent oaths, outbursts of malicious laughter have become audible.

"Some one is being beaten," remarked one of the friends, after having cast a glance out of the window.

"A criminal? A murderer?" inquired the other.—"See here, no matter who it is, such chas-

353

tisement without trial is not to be tolerated. Let us go and defend him."

"But it is not a murderer who is being beaten."

"Not a murderer? A thief, then? Never mind, let us go, let us rescue him from the mob."

"It is not a thief, either."

"Not a thief? Is it, then, a cashier, a railway employee, an army contractor, a Russian Mæcenas, a lawyer, a well-intentioned editor, a public philanthropist? . . . At any rate, let us go, let us aid him!"

"No . . . . they are thrashing a correspondent."

"A correspondent?—Well, see here now, let 's drink a glass of tea first."

July, 1878.

TWO BROTHERS

IT was a vision. . . .

Two angels presented themselves before me . . . . two spirits.

I say angels . . . . spirits, because neither of them had any garments on their naked bodies, and from the shoulders of both sprang long, powerful wings.

Both are youths. One is rather plump, smooth of skin, with black curls. He has languishing brown eyes with thick eyelashes; his gaze is ingratiating, cheerful, and eager. A charming, captivating countenance a trifle bold, a trifle malicious. His full red lips tremble slightly. The youth smiles like one who has authority,—confidently and lazily; a sumptuous garland of flowers rests lightly on his shining hair, almost touching his velvet eyebrows. The spotted skin of a leopard, pinned with a golden dart, hangs lightly from his plump shoulders down upon his curving hips. The feathers of his wings gleam with changeable tints of rose-colour; their tips are of a brilliant red, just as though they had been dipped in fresh, crimson blood. From time to time they palpitate swiftly, with a pleasant silvery sound, the sound of rain in springtime.

The other is gaunt and yellow of body. His ribs are faintly discernible at every breath. His hair is fair, thin, straight; his eyes are huge, round, pale grey in colour . . . . his gaze is uneasy and strangely bright. All his features are sharp-cut: his mouth is small, half open, with fish-like teeth; his nose is solid, aquiline; his chin projecting, covered with a whitish down. Those thin lips have never once smiled.

It is a regular, terrible, pitiless face! Moreover, the face of the first youth,—of the beauty,—although it is sweet and charming, does not express any compassion either. Around the head of the second are fastened a few empty, broken ears of grain intertwined with withered blades of grass. A coarse grey fabric encircles his loins; the wings at his back, of a dull, dark-blue colour, wave softly and menacingly.

Both youths appeared to be inseparable companions.

Each leaned on the other's shoulder. The soft little hand of the first rested like a cluster of grapes on the harsh collar-bone of the second; the slender, bony hand of the second, with its long, thin fingers, lay outspread, like a serpent, on the womanish breast of the first.

And I heard a voice. This is what it uttered:

" Before thee stand Love and Hunger—own brothers, the two fundamental bases of everything living.

" Everything which lives moves, for the purpose of obtaining food; and eats, for the purpose of reproducing itself.

" Love and Hunger have one and the same object; it is necessary that life should not cease, —one's own life and the life of others are the same thing, the universal life."

August, 1878.

THE EGOIST

HE possessed everything which was requisite to make him the scourge of his family.

He had been born healthy, he had been born rich—and during the whole course of his long life he had remained rich and healthy; he had never committed a single crime; he had never stumbled into any blunder; he had not made a single slip of the tongue or mistake.

He was irreproachably honest! . . . And proud in the consciousness of his honesty, he crushed every one with it: relatives, friends, and acquaintances.

His honesty was his capital . . . . and he exacted usurious interest from it.

Honesty gave him the right to be pitiless and not to do any good deed which was not prescribed; —and he was pitiless, and he did no good . . . . because good except by decree is not good.

He never troubled himself about any one, except his own very exemplary self, and he was genuinely indignant if others did not take equally assiduous care of it!

And, at the same time, he did not consider himself an egoist, and upbraided and persecuted egoists and egoism more than anything else!— Of course! Egoism in other people interfered with his own.

Not being conscious of a single failing, he did not understand, he did not permit, a weakness in any one else. Altogether, he did not understand anybody or anything, for he was completely surrounded by himself on all sides, above and below, behind and before.

He did not even understand the meaning of forgiveness. He never had had occasion to forgive himself. . . . Then how was he to forgive others?

Before the bar of his own conscience, before the face of his own God, he, that marvel, that monster of virtue, rolled up his eyes, and in a firm, clear voice uttered: "Yes; I am a worthy, a moral man!"

He repeated these words on his death-bed, and nothing quivered even then in his stony heart,—in that heart devoid of a fleck or a crack.

O monstrosity of self-satisfied, inflexible, cheaply-acquired virtue—thou art almost more repulsive than the undisguised monstrosity of vice!

December, 1878.

THE SUPREME BEING'S FEAST

ONE day the Supreme Being took it into his head to give a great feast in his azure palace.

He invited all the virtues as guests. Only the virtues . . . . he invited no men . . . . only ladies.

Very many of them assembled, great and small. The petty virtues were more agreeable and courteous than the great ones; but all seemed well pleased, and chatted politely among themselves, as befits near relatives and friends.

But lo! the Supreme Being noticed two very

beautiful ladies who, apparently, were entirely unacquainted with each other.

The host took one of these ladies by the hand and led her to the other.

" Beneficence! " said he, pointing to the first.

" Gratitude!" he added, pointing to the second.

The two virtues were unspeakably astonished; ever since the world has existed—and it has existed a long time—they had never met before.

December, 1878.

THE SPHINX

YELLOWISH-GREY, friable at the top, firm below, creaking sand . . . . sand without end, no matter in which direction one gazes!

And above this sand, above this sea of dead dust, the huge head of the Egyptian Sphinx rears itself aloft.

What is it that those vast, protruding lips, those impassively-dilated, up-turned nostrils, and those eyes, those long, half-sleepy, half-watchful eyes, beneath the double arch of the lofty brows, are trying to say?

For they are trying to say something! They even speak—but only Œdipus can solve the riddle and understand their mute speech.

Bah! Yes, I recognise those features . . . . there is nothing Egyptian about the low white forehead, the prominent cheek-bones, the short, straight nose, the fine mouth with its white teeth, the soft moustache and curling beard,—and those small eyes set far apart . . . . and on the head the cap of hair furrowed with a parting. . . . Why, it is thou, Karp, Sídor, Semyón, thou petty peasant of Yaroslávl, or of Ryazán, my fellow-countryman, the kernel of Russia! Is it long since thou didst become the Sphinx?

Or dost thou also wish to say something? Yes; and thou also art a Sphinx.

And thy eyes—those colourless but profound eyes—speak also. . . . And their speeches are equally dumb and enigmatic.

Only where is thine Œdipus?

Alas! 'T is not sufficient to don a cap to become thine Œdipus, O Sphinx of All the Russias!

December, 1878.

NYMPHS

I was standing in front of a chain of beautiful mountains spread out in a semi-circle; the young, verdant forest clothed them from summit to base. The southern sky hung transparently blue above us; on high the sun beamed radiantly; below, half hidden in the grass, nimble brooks were babbling.

And there recurred to my mind an ancient

legend about how, in the first century after the birth of Christ, a Grecian ship was sailing over the Ægean Sea.

It was midday. . . . The weather was calm. And suddenly, high up, over the head of the helmsman, some one uttered distinctly: " When thou shalt sail past the islands, cry in a loud voice, ' Great Pan is dead!' "

The helmsman was amazed . . . . and frightened. But when the ship ran past the islands he called out: " Great Pan is dead!"

And thereupon, immediately, in answer to his shout, along the whole length of the shore (for the island was uninhabited), there resounded loud sobbing groans, prolonged wailing cries: " He is dead! Great Pan is dead!"

This legend recurred to my mind . . . . and a strange thought flashed across my brain.— " What if I were to shout that call? "

But in view of the exultation which surrounded me I could not think of death, and with all the force at my command I shouted: " He is risen! Great Pan is risen!"

And instantly,—oh, marvel!—in reply to my exclamation, along the whole wide semi-circle of verdant mountains there rolled a vigorous laughter, there arose a joyous chattering and splashing. " He is risen! Pan is risen!" rustled youthful voices.—Everything there in front of me suddenly broke into laughter more brilliant than the

361

sun on high, more sportive than the brooks which were babbling beneath the grass. The hurried tramp of light footsteps became audible; athwart the green grove flitted the marble whiteness of waving tunics, the vivid scarlet of naked bodies. . . . . It was nymphs, nymphs, dryads, bacchantes, running down from the heights into the plain. . . .

They made their appearance simultaneously along all the borders of the forest. Curls fluttered on divine heads, graceful arms uplifted garlands and cymbals, and laughter, sparkling, Olympian laughter, rippled and rolled among them. . . .

In front floats a goddess. She is taller and handsomer than all the rest;—on her shoulders is a quiver; in her hands is a bow; upon her curls, caught high, is the silvery sickle of the moon. . . .

Diana, is it thou?

But suddenly the goddess halted . . . . and immediately, following her example, all the nymphs came to a halt also. The ringing laughter died away. I saw how the face of the goddess, suddenly rendered dumb, became covered with a deathly pallor; I saw how her feet grew petrified, how inexpressible terror parted her lips, strained wide her eyes, which were fixed on the remote distance. . . . What had she descried? Where was she gazing?

I turned in the direction in which she was gazing. . . .

At the very edge of the sky, beyond the low line of the fields, a golden cross was blazing like a spark of fire on the white belfry of a Christian church. . . . The goddess had caught sight of that cross.

I heard behind me a long, uneven sigh, like the throbbing of a broken harp-string,—and when I turned round again, no trace of the nymphs remained. . . . The broad forest gleamed green as before, and only in spots, athwart the close network of the branches, could tufts of something white be seen melting away. Whether these were the tunics of the nymphs, or a vapour was rising up from the bottom of the valley, I know not.

But how I regretted the vanished goddesses!

December, 1878.

ENEMY AND FRIEND

A CAPTIVE condemned to perpetual incarceration broke out of prison and started to run at a headlong pace. . . . After him, on his very heels, darted the pursuit.

He ran with all his might. . . . His pursuers began to fall behind.

But lo! in front of him was a river with steep

banks,—a narrow, but deep river. . . . And he did not know how to swim!

From one shore to the other a thin, rotten board had been thrown. The fugitive had already set foot upon it. . . . But it so happened that just at this point, beside the river, his best friend and his most cruel enemy were standing.

The enemy said nothing and merely folded his arms; on the other hand, the friend shouted at the top of his voice:—" Good heavens! What art thou doing? Come to thy senses, thou madman! Dost thou not see that the board is completely rotten?—It will break beneath thy weight, and thou wilt infallibly perish!"

" But there is no other way of crossing . . . . and hearest thou the pursuit?" groaned in desperation the unhappy wight, as he stepped upon the board.

" I will not permit it! . . . . No, I will not permit thee to perish!"—roared his zealous friend, snatching the plank from beneath the feet of the fugitive.—The latter instantly tumbled headlong into the tumultuous waters—and was drowned.

The enemy smiled with satisfaction, and went his way; but the friend sat down on the shore and began to weep bitterly over his poor . . . . poor friend!

" He would not heed me! He would not heed me!" he whispered dejectedly.

" However! " he said at last. " He would have been obliged to languish all his life in that frightful prison! At all events, he is not suffering now! Now he is better off! Evidently, so had his Fate decreed!

" And yet, it is a pity, from a human point of view! "

And the good soul continued to sob inconsolably over his unlucky friend.

December, 1878.

CHRIST

I SAW myself as a youth, almost a little boy, in a low-ceiled country church.—Slender wax tapers burned like red spots in front of the ancient holy pictures.

An aureole of rainbow hues encircled each tiny flame.—It was dark and dim in the church. . . . But a mass of people stood in front of me.

All reddish, peasant heads. From time to time they would begin to surge, to fall, to rise again, like ripe ears of grain when the summer breeze flits across them in a slow wave.

Suddenly some man or other stepped from behind and took up his stand alongside me.

I did not turn toward him, but I immediately felt that that man was—Christ.

Emotion, curiosity, awe took possession of me

simultaneously. I forced myself to look at my neighbour.

He had a face like that of everybody else,—a face similar to all human faces. His eyes gazed slightly upward, attentively and gently. His lips were closed, but not compressed; the upper lip seemed to rest upon the lower; his small beard was parted in the middle. His hands were clasped, and did not move. And his garments were like those of every one else.

" Christ, forsooth! " I thought to myself. " Such a simple, simple man! It cannot be! "

I turned away.—But before I had time to turn my eyes from that simple man it again seemed to me that it was Christ in person who was standing beside me.

Again I exerted an effort over myself. . . . And again I beheld the same face, resembling all human faces, the same ordinary, although unfamiliar, features.

And suddenly dread fell upon me, and I came to myself. Only then did I understand that precisely such a face—a face like all human faces—is the face of Christ.

December, 1878.

POEMS IN PROSE

II

1879–1882

THE STONE

HAVE you seen an old, old stone on the sea-shore, when the brisk waves are beating upon it from all sides, at high tide, on a sunny spring day —beating and sparkling and caressing it, and drenching its mossy head with crumbling pearls of glittering foam?

The stone remains the same stone, but brilliant colours start forth upon its surly exterior.

They bear witness to that distant time when the molten granite was only just beginning to harden and was all glowing with fiery hues.

Thus also did young feminine souls recently attack my old heart from all quarters,—and beneath their caressing touch it glowed once more with colours which faded long ago,—with traces of its pristine fire!

The waves have retreated . . . . but the colours have not yet grown dim, although a keen breeze is drying them.

May, 1879.

DOVES

I WAS standing on the crest of a sloping hill; in front of me lay outspread, and motley of hue, the ripe rye, now like a golden, again like a silvery sea.

But no surge was coursing across this sea; no sultry breeze was blowing; a great thunder-storm was brewing.

Round about me the sun was still shining hotly and dimly; but in the distance, beyond the rye, not too far away, a dark-blue thunder-cloud lay in a heavy mass over one half of the horizon.

Everything was holding its breath . . . . everything was languishing beneath the ominous gleam of the sun's last rays. Not a single bird was to be seen or heard; even the sparrows had hidden themselves. Only somewhere, close at hand, a solitary huge leaf of burdock was whispering and flapping.

How strongly the wormwood on the border-strips [1] smells! I glanced at the blue mass . . . . and confusion ensued in my soul. "Well, be quick, then, be quick!" I thought. "Flash out, ye golden serpent! Rumble, ye thunder! Move on, advance, discharge thy water, thou evil thunder-cloud; put an end to this painful torment!"

But the storm-cloud did not stir. As before, it continued to crush the dumb earth . . . . and seemed merely to wax larger and darker.

And lo! through its bluish monotony there flashed something smooth and even; precisely like a white handkerchief, or a snowball. It was a

---

[1] Strips of grass left as boundaries between the tilled fields allotted to different peasants.—TRANSLATOR.

white dove flying from the direction of the village.

It flew, and flew onward, always straight onward . . . . and vanished behind the forest.

Several moments passed—the same cruel silence still reigned. . . . But behold! Now *two* handkerchiefs are fluttering, *two* snowballs are floating back; it is *two* white doves wending their way homeward in even flight.

And now, at last, the storm has broken loose— and the fun begins!

I could hardly reach home.—The wind shrieked and darted about like a mad thing; low-hanging rusty-hued clouds swirled onward, as though rent in bits; everything whirled, got mixed up, lashed and rocked with the slanting columns of the furious downpour; the lightning flashes blinded with their fiery green hue; abrupt claps of thunder were discharged like cannon; there was a smell of sulphur. . . .

But under the eaves, on the very edge of a garret window, side by side sit the two white doves,—the one which flew after its companion, and the one which it brought and, perhaps, saved.

Both have ruffled up their plumage, and each feels with its wing the wing of its neighbour. . . .

It is well with them! And it is well with me as I gaze at them. . . Although I am alone . . . . alone, as always.

May, 1879.

TO-MORROW! TO-MORROW!

How empty, and insipid, and insignificant is almost every day which we have lived through! How few traces it leaves behind it! In what a thoughtlessly-stupid manner have those hours flown past, one after another!

And, nevertheless, man desires to exist; he prizes life, he hopes in it, in himself, in the future. . . . Oh, what blessings he expects from the future!

And why does he imagine that other future days will not resemble the one which has just passed?

But he does not imagine this. On the whole, he is not fond of thinking—and it is well that he does not.

" There, now, to-morrow, to-morrow! " he comforts himself—until that "to-morrow" overthrows him into the grave.

Well—and once in the grave,—one ceases, willy-nilly, to think.

May, 1879.

NATURE

I DREAMED that I had entered a vast subterranean chamber with a lofty, arched roof. It was completely filled by some sort of even light, also subterranean.

POEMS IN PROSE

In the very centre of the chamber sat a majestic woman in a flowing robe green in hue. With her head bowed on her hand, she seemed to be immersed in profound meditation.

I immediately understood that this woman was Nature itself,—and reverent awe pierced my soul with an instantaneous chill.

I approached the seated woman, and making a respectful obeisance, " O our common mother," I exclaimed, " what is the subject of thy meditation? Art thou pondering the future destinies of mankind? As to how it is to attain the utmost possible perfection and bliss?"

The woman slowly turned her dark, lowering eyes upon me. Her lips moved, and a stentorian voice, like unto the clanging of iron, rang out:

" I am thinking how I may impart more power to the muscles in the legs of a flea, so that it may more readily escape from its enemies. The equilibrium of attack and defence has been destroyed. . . . It must be restored."

" What! " I stammered, in reply.—" So that is what thou art thinking about? But are not we men thy favourite children?"

The woman knit her brows almost imperceptibly.—" All creatures are my children," she said, " and I look after all of them alike,—and I annihilate them in identically the same way."

" But good . . . . reason . . . . justice . . . ." I stammered again.

"Those are the words of men," rang out the iron voice. "I know neither good nor evil. . . . Reason is no law to me—and what is justice?—I have given thee life,—I take it away and give it to others; whether worms or men . . . . it makes no difference to me. . . . But in the meantime, do thou defend thyself, and hinder me not!"

I was about to answer . . . . but the earth round about me uttered a dull groan and trembled—and I awoke.

August, 1879.

"HANG HIM!"

"It happened in the year 1803," began my old friend, "not long before Austerlitz. The regiment of which I was an officer was quartered in Moravia.

"We were strictly forbidden to harry and oppress the inhabitants; and they looked askance on us as it was, although we were regarded as allies.

"I had an orderly, a former serf of my mother's, Egór by name. He was an honest and peaceable fellow; I had known him from his childhood and treated him like a friend.

"One day, in the house where I dwelt, abusive shrieks and howls arose: the housewife had been robbed of two hens, and she accused my orderly of the theft. He denied it, and called upon me to bear witness whether 'he, Egór Avtamónoff, would steal!' I assured the house-wife of Egór's honesty, but she would listen to nothing.

"Suddenly the energetic trampling of horses' hoofs resounded along the street: it was the Com-mander-in-Chief himself riding by with his staff. He was proceeding at a foot-pace,—a fat, pot-bellied man, with drooping head and epaulets dangling on his breast.

"The housewife caught sight of him, and fling-ing herself across his horse's path, she fell on her knees and, all distraught, with head uncovered, began loudly to complain of my orderly, pointing to him with her hand:

"'Sir General!' she shrieked. 'Your Ra-diance! Judge! Help! Save! This soldier has robbed me!'

"Egór was standing on the threshold of the house, drawn up in military salute, with his cap in his hand,—and had even protruded his breast and turned out his feet, like a sentry,—and not a word did he utter! Whether he was daunted by all that mass of generals halting there in the mid-dle of the street, or whether he was petrified in the presence of the calamity which had overtaken him,—at any rate, there stood my Egór blinking his eyes, and white as clay!

"The Commander-in-Chief cast an abstracted

and surly glance at him, bellowing wrathfully:
'Well, what hast thou to say?' . . . . Egór
stood like a statue and showed his teeth! If
looked at in profile, it was exactly as though the
man were laughing.

"Then the Commander-in-Chief said abruptly:
'Hang him!'—gave his horse a dig in the ribs
and rode on, first at a foot-pace, as before, then at
a brisk trot. The whole staff dashed after him;
only one adjutant, turning round in his saddle,
took a close look at Egór.

"It was impossible to disobey. . . . Egór was
instantly seized and led to execution.

"Thereupon he turned deadly pale, and only
exclaimed a couple of times, with difficulty,
'Good heavens! Good heavens!'—and then, in a
low voice—'God sees it was not I!'

"He wept bitterly, very bitterly, as he bade me
farewell. I was in despair.—'Egór! Egór!'
I cried, 'why didst thou say nothing to the general?'

"'God sees it was not I,' repeated the poor
fellow, sobbing.—The housewife herself was hor-
rified. She had not in the least expected such a
dreadful verdict, and fell to shrieking in her turn.
She began to entreat each and all to spare him,
she declared that her hens had been found, that
she was prepared to explain everything herself. . . .

"Of course, this was of no use whatsoever.

374

Military regulations, sir! Discipline!—The housewife sobbed more and more loudly.

"Egór, whom the priest had already confessed and communicated, turned to me:

"'Tell her, Your Well-Born, that she must not do herself an injury. . . . For I have already forgiven her.'"

As my friend repeated these last words of his servant, he whispered: "Egórushka[1] darling, just man!"—and the tears dripped down his aged cheeks.

August, 1879.

WHAT SHALL I THINK? . . . .

WHAT shall I think when I come to die,—if I am then in a condition to think?

Shall I think what a bad use I have made of my life, how I have dozed it through, how I have not known how to relish its gifts?

"What? Is this death already? So soon? Impossible! Why, I have not succeeded in accomplishing anything yet. . . . I have only been preparing to act!"

Shall I recall the past, pause over the thought of the few bright moments I have lived through, over beloved images and faces?

Will my evil deeds present themselves before

---

[1] The affectionate diminutive.—TRANSLATOR.

my memory, and will the corrosive grief of a be-
lated repentance descend upon my soul?

Shall I think of what awaits me beyond the
grave . . . . yes, and whether anything at all
awaits me there?

No . . . . it seems to me that I shall try not
to think, and shall compel my mind to busy itself
with some nonsense or other, if only to divert my
own attention from the menacing darkness which
looms up black ahead.

In my presence one dying person kept com-
plaining that they would not give him red-hot
nuts to gnaw . . . and only in the depths of his
dimming eyes was there throbbing and palpita-
ting something, like the wing of a bird wounded
unto death. . . .

August, 1879.

"HOW FAIR, HOW FRESH WERE THE ROSES"

SOMEWHERE, some time, long, long ago, I read a
poem. I speedily forgot it . . . . but its first
line lingered in my memory:

"How fair, how fresh were the roses. . . ."

It is winter now; the window-panes are coated
with ice; in the warm chamber a single candle is
burning. I am sitting curled up in one corner;
and in my brain there rings and rings:

POEMS IN PROSE

" How fair, how fresh were the roses. . . ."

And I behold myself in front of the low window of a Russian house in the suburbs. The summer evening is melting and merging into night, there is a scent of mignonette and linden-blossoms abroad in the warm air;—and in the window, propped on a stiffened arm, and with her head bent on her shoulder, sits a young girl, gazing mutely and intently at the sky, as though watching for the appearance of the first stars. How ingenuously inspired are the thoughtful eyes; how touchingly innocent are the parted, questioning lips; how evenly breathes her bosom, not yet fully developed and still unagitated by anything; how pure and tender are the lines of the young face! I do not dare to address her, but how dear she is to me, how violently my heart beats!

" How fair, how fresh were the roses. . . ."

And in the room everything grows darker and darker. . . . The candle which has burned low begins to flicker; white shadows waver across the low ceiling; the frost creaks and snarls beyond the wall—and I seem to hear a tedious, senile whisper:

" How fair, how fresh were the roses. . . ."

Other images rise up before me. . . . I hear the merry murmur of family, of country life. Two red-gold little heads, leaning against each other, gaze bravely at me with their bright eyes;

the red cheeks quiver with suppressed laughter; their hands are affectionately intertwined; their young, kind voices ring out, vying with each other; and a little further away, in the depths of a snug room, other hands, also young, are flying about, with fingers entangled, over the keys of a poor little old piano, and the Lanner waltz cannot drown the grumbling of the patriarchal samovár. . . .

" How fair, how fresh were the roses. . . ."

The candle flares up and dies out. . . . Who is that coughing yonder so hoarsely and dully? Curled up in a ring, my aged dog, my sole companion, is nestling and quivering at my feet. . . . I feel cold. . . . I am shivering . . . and they are all dead . . . . all dead. . . .

" How fair, how fresh were the roses."

September, 1879.

A SEA VOYAGE

I SAILED from Hamburg to London on a small steamer. There were two of us passengers: I and a tiny monkey, a female of the ouistiti breed, which a Hamburg merchant was sending as a gift to his English partner.

She was attached by a slender chain to one of the benches on the deck, and threw herself about and squeaked plaintively, like a bird.

Every time I walked past she stretched out to

me her black, cold little hand, and gazed at me with her mournful, almost human little eyes.—I took her hand, and she ceased to squeak and fling herself about.

There was a dead calm. The sea spread out around us in a motionless mirror of leaden hue. It seemed small; a dense fog lay over it, shrouding even the tips of the masts, and blinding and wearying the eyes with its soft gloom. The sun hung like a dim red spot in this gloom; but just before evening it became all aflame and glowed mysteriously and strangely scarlet.

Long, straight folds, like the folds of heavy silken fabrics, flowed away from the bow of the steamer, one after another, growing ever wider, wrinkling and broadening, becoming smoother at last, swaying and vanishing. The churned foam swirled under the monotonous beat of the paddle-wheels; gleaming white like milk, and hissing faintly, it was broken up into serpent-like ripples, and then flowed together at a distance, and vanished likewise, swallowed up in the gloom.

A small bell at the stern jingled as incessantly and plaintively as the squeaking cry of the monkey.

Now and then a seal came to the surface, and turning an abrupt somersault, darted off beneath the barely-disturbed surface.

And the captain, a taciturn man with a surly,

sunburned face, smoked a short pipe and spat angrily into the sea, congealed in impassivity.

To all my questions he replied with an abrupt growl. I was compelled, willy-nilly, to have recourse to my solitary fellow-traveller—the monkey.

I sat down beside her; she ceased to whine, and again stretched out her hand to me.

The motionless fog enveloped us both with a soporific humidity; and equally immersed in one unconscious thought, we remained there side by side, like blood-relatives.

I smile now . . . . but then another feeling reigned in me.

We are all children of one mother—and it pleased me that the poor little beastie should quiet down so confidingly and nestle up to me, as though to a relative.

November, 1879.

N. N.

GRACEFULLY and quietly dost thou walk along the path of life, without tears and without smiles, barely animated by an indifferent attention.

Thou art kind and clever . . . . and everything is alien to thee—and no one is necessary to thee.

Thou art very beautiful—and no one can tell whether thou prizest thy beauty or not.—Thou art devoid of sympathy thyself and demandest no sympathy.

Thy gaze is profound, and not thoughtful; emptiness lies in that bright depth.

Thus do the stately shades pass by without grief and without joy in the Elysian Fields, to the dignified sounds of Gluck's melodies.

November, 1879.

STAY!

STAY! As I now behold thee remain thou evermore in my memory!

From thy lips the last inspired sound hath burst forth—thine eyes do not gleam and flash, they are dusky, weighted with happiness, with the blissful consciousness of that beauty to which thou hast succeeded in giving expression,—of that beauty in quest of which thou stretchest forth, as it were, thy triumphant, thine exhausted hands!

What light, more delicate and pure than the sunlight, hath been diffused over all thy limbs, over the tiniest folds of thy garments?

What god, with his caressing inflatus, hath tossed back thy dishevelled curls?

His kiss burneth on thy brow, grown pale as marble!

Here it is—the open secret, the secret of poetry, of life, of love! Here it is, here it is—immortality! There is no other immortality—and no other is needed.—At this moment thou art deathless.

I will pass,—and again thou art a pinch of dust, a woman, a child. . . . But what is that to thee!—At this moment thou hast become loftier than all transitory, temporal things, thou hast stepped out of their sphere.—This *thy* moment will never end.

Stay! And let me be the sharer of thy immortality, drop into my soul the reflection of thine eternity!

November, 1879.

THE MONK

I USED to know a monk, a hermit, a saint. He lived on the sweetness of prayer alone,—and as he quaffed it, he knelt so long on the cold floor of the church that his legs below the knee swelled and became like posts. He had no sensation in them, he knelt—and prayed.

I understood him—and, perhaps, I envied him; but let him also understand me and not condemn me—me, to whom his joys are inaccessible.

He strove to annihilate himself, his hated *ego;* but the fact that I do not pray does not arise from self-conceit.

My ego is, perchance, even more burdensome and repulsive to me than his is to him.

He found a means of forgetting himself . . . . and I find a means to do the same, but not so constantly.

He does not lie . . . . and neither do I lie.

November, 1879.

WE SHALL STILL FIGHT ON!

WHAT an insignificant trifle can sometimes put the whole man back in tune!

Full of thought, I was walking one day along the highway.

Heavy forebodings oppressed my breast; melancholy seized hold upon me.

I raised my head. . . . Before me, between two rows of lofty poplars, the road stretched out into the distance.

Across it, across that same road, a whole little family of sparrows was hopping, hopping boldly, amusingly, confidently!

One of them in particular fairly set his wings akimbo, thrusting out his crop, and twittering audaciously, as though the very devil was no match for him! A conqueror—and that is all there is to be said.

But in the meantime, high up in the sky, was soaring a hawk who, possibly, was fated to devour precisely that same conqueror.

I looked, laughed, shook myself—and the melancholy thoughts instantly fled. I felt daring, courage, a desire for life.

And let *my* hawk soar over *me* if he will. . . .
"We will still fight on, devil take it!"

November, 1879.

PRAYER

No matter what a man may pray for he is praying for a miracle.—Every prayer amounts to the following: "Great God, cause that two and two may not make four."

Only such a prayer is a genuine prayer from a person to a person. To pray to the Universal Spirit, to the Supreme Being of Kant, of Hegel —to a purified, amorphous God, is impossible and unthinkable.

But can even a personal, living God with a form cause that two and two shall not make four?

Every believer is bound to reply, "He can," and is bound to convince himself of this.

But what if his reason revolts against such an absurdity?

In that case Shakspeare will come to his assistance: "There are many things in the world, friend Horatio . . . ." and so forth.

And if people retort in the name of truth,—all he has to do is to repeat the famous question: "What is truth?"

POEMS IN PROSE

And therefore, let us drink and be merry—and pray.

July, 1881.

THE RUSSIAN LANGUAGE

In days of doubt, in days of painful meditations concerning the destinies of my fatherland, thou alone art my prop and my support, O great, mighty, just and free Russian language!—Were it not for thee, how could one fail to fall into despair at the sight of all that goes on at home?—But it is impossible to believe that such a language was not bestowed upon a great people!

June, 1882.